DOUBLE SALUTE

MARK TOTILO

This book is a work of fiction. Names, characters, places, and incidents are the product of the author's imagination or are used fictitiously. Any resemblance to actual events, locales or persons, living or dead, is coincidental.

DOUBLE SALUTE

Cover photo: Photographer's Mate 2nd Class Chad McNeeley, United States Navy
Cover photo: USS O'Bannon DD-987 Photo – Paul Farley
Back Cover Photo: Firefighting at Recruit Training Command - PHC(NAO) Chris Desmond, United States Navy

Author photo: Rebecca Park Totilo

Printed in the United States of America.

Published by Rebecca At The Well Foundation, PO Box 60044, St. Petersburg, FL 33784.

http://RebeccaAtTheWell.org

ISBN: 978-0-9889583-9-5 (Printed)
ISBN: 978-0-9898280-0-0 (Electronic)

Contents

DEDICATION

I would like to dedicate this book to Becca my beloved bride who filled my ink well with love and devotion. She encouraged me to write this story and kept me going when I had no gas left in the tank.

PREFACE

The projected power of the United States' as a blue-water Navy allows this country to maintain control over the shipping lanes across the globe. Over these deep waters, vigilant American men and women serve aboard armed flotillas to safeguard the torch of freedom. These guardians are poised to strike anywhere in the world at any time those who would attempt to snuff out the light of liberty.

One such guardian, the *USS Ingersoll DD-990* patrolled the mouth of the Persian Gulf in the North Arabian Sea. *Ingersoll* named for Admiral Royal *Ingersoll*, commissioned on April 12 1980 is the 28th of its class, built by *Ingalls Shipbuilding* of Pascagoula, MS. The Spruance Class Destroyer, an innovative modular designed ship, devised to allow easier and quicker modernization was the blueprint all new Navy ships would follow.

This being her second Western Pacific deployment as a member of Battle Group Charlie which would be the first task force to test the new operational procedures from lessons learned during the Libyan Crisis of 1982. *Ingersoll* maintained a northern 300 mile Naval Tactical Data System (NTDS) picket station from the aircraft carrier *USS Carl Vinson CVN-70* in the North Arabian Sea.

The American Navy distinguished itself by being able to operate on the high seas and replenish themselves by noncommissioned replenishment ships which are a true and strong sign of a blue-water navy. *Ingersoll* made ready to do just that and go along side the floating gas station *USNS Kiska AE-35*.

CHAPTER 1: HIGH SEAS

Sweet it is, when on the high seas the winds are lashing the waters, to gaze from the land on another's struggles. - Lucretius

A tear rolled off the cheek of a chambray clad seaman into the phosphorescent blue waters of the Indian Ocean. Mingled together with the saline sea, a tear now captured in the bottle of the cavernous deep, inscribed on the parchment of eternity. The gentle sea breeze answered his anguished mind with one word, *Peace* as a gust of wind softened his wary brow and tortured heart. With a deep breath, he inhaled the fresh air and watched the darkness envelope the calm lifeless sea.

Boatswains Mate Second Class Ben Mattingly took one final moment to ponder the course that lie ahead. Approaching voices coaxed him back to the task at hand as he worked the pelican hook release back and forth one more time.

The warm calm winds of spring energized the gentle salt spray misting the port bridge wing of the *Ingersoll* on patrol in the Indian Ocean. A lookout scanned the horizon for contacts silhouetted on the backdrop of a blazing ball of fire melting into the horizon. The glorious pinks and oranges yielded to the purples and grays. He peered to the deck below as preparations continued for this evening's underway replenishment, then to the glassy sea. He swept the sea and sky one more time for signs of other vessels or aircraft. The crewman lowered his binoculars and keyed the microphone of his sound powered phone set, "Port bridge wing lookout, reporting. All clear except for *USNS Kiska.*"

Darkness fully enveloped the destroyer; blood red lights bathed the bridge of *Ingersoll* in an eerie crimson glow. Shadowy figures slid in and out of patches of ruby-colored light which illuminated the weathered face of Commander Tyler Austin, Commanding Officer.

The tall pocked faced officer rolled thoughts over in his mind like a rotisserie as he peered out the starboard bridge wing window. The scheduled 107 days underway were wearing on him, his men and the equipment. His voice cracked when he spoke, "Conning Officer, distance to *Kiska*?"

The conning officer lowered his binoculars and turned toward the captain's chair. "Four hundred and fifty yards astern, we are at six degrees to the left of Romeo Corpen. All engines are ahead standard, indicating revolutions for thirteen knots, steering course zero, zero, five, sir."

"Excellent ship handling Mr. Steiner. Has *Kiska* closed up Romeo?"

"No sir, she has not, Romeo is still dipped. She's not completed her preparations to receive us alongside."

Deep within the bowels of *Ingersoll* men pined the remaining hours of the day in berthing areas. These compartments were for enlisted men to sleep, shower and stow personal gear. There are three forward and another three aft, with about 50 men each. Beds or racks as they are better known are three high, with storage underneath each and a standup locker for hanging uniforms.

"C'mon Alex. I'm growing a beard over here," said a young black sailor sitting around a circular table squirreled in the back of the compartment.

Alex Sievers, a sandy blonde, wore a crisp bleached white t-shirt with sleeves rolled up to his shoulders. He studied his playing cards and rubbed his square chin.

"We don't have all night, Sievers," said Rod Peach, a lanky second class who stretched his long arm over the table and flicked Alex's forehead. "Hello. Is anyone home?"

Alex grabbed his hand and glared deep into Rod's dark brown eyes.

"Am I bothering you, Alex?" Rod said and then looked at his hand. "If you'd really like to hold my hand, maybe we can find another place more private." Rod batted his eyelashes at him.

The two other poker players chuckled.

Jerk. Alex released his hand in embarrassment and refocused on his cards. He picked up a chip and tossed it into the pot. "I'll see you and," Alex said and paused for a moment, picked up the rest of his chips and shoved them in the kitty. "Raise you, whatever I got here."

Rod raised an eyebrow then thought for a moment as he rubbed his jet black hair and then pushed the rest of his chips into the pot. "Call."

The sailor to Rod's right whistled and laid his cards down. "Too rich for my blood, I'm out."

"Me too," the Seaman Apprentice to Rod's left said.

Rod took a puff of his cigar and blew a grey-blue haze of smoke in Alex's face. Alex coughed as he laid his cards down. "Full House."

Rod's half smile drooped as Alex wrapped his arms around the pile of chips. "Not so fast, transceivers," Rod said through cigar clenched teeth. He snapped his cards on the table and grinned. "Royal Flush. Read 'em and weep sucker." He smiled, stood and pulled the chips away from Alex. "Nice playing with you loser."

When he leaned over, two playing cards in his open pocket caught Alex's eye. "Hold your peaches." Alex yanked the cards out so everyone around could see them. "You're a blasted cheat."

Rod shoved the table into Alex, pinning him into his seat. Adrenaline shot through his body, tightened his senses and with catlike quickness, he knocked the table over and pounced on Rod.

Poker chips skittered across the polished deck. Alex lunged like a linebacker; he caught Rod in the mid section, wrapped his arms around him and threw him to the deck. Rod rabbit punched the back of Alex's head as Alex pummeled him with body blows to the midsection. Several crewmen yanked Alex off while others jerked Rod to his feet. Rod straightened his blue chambray shirt and said, "I'm ok." When the men released him he grabbed for Alex's throat, but could not breach the blockade.

"I'll destroy you, if it's the last thing I do," Rod said puffing through gritted-teeth. The vein in his neck pulsated with each word. "Next time, you won't have anybody to save your behind."

Alex tried to wrench free from his captors and shouted back at him red faced, "Let's go man. How about we go down to the weight room right now and finish this?"

The 1MC crackled. A boatswain's pipe twittered a long blast. "All hands, man your underway replenishment stations. All hands, man your unrep station. Smoking Lamp is out through out the ship."

Rod yanked free from the sailors, glared and snorted at Alex, then stormed out of the room banging up the ladder to the main deck.

The underway refueling is conducted in radio silence and is orchestrated via the use of signal flags hoisted to the yard arms in the lofty masts. The receiving ship takes station behind the oiler and orders the course to sail on.

"Are we ready to go alongside Lieutenant?" Commander Austin barked.

"All refueling stations indicate manned and ready. *Kiska* still has romeo dipped."

The signal flag, red field with a yellow cross is used for the 'R' in phonetic language and is communicated as Romeo. The flag is hoisted on either the port are starboard yard arm by the oiler to indicate which side to approach and be refueled.

A signalman sang out, "Romeo closed up."

"Belay that sir, *Kiska* has closed up Romeo and is ready to receive us," Lieutenant Steiner said. "Request permission to go alongside?"

"Permission granted."

"All engines ahead full," barked Lieutenant Steiner. "Indicate revolutions for eighteen knots."

The lee helmsman repeated the order back to the conning officer. The quartermaster taking bearings shouted out, "Four hundred yards to

Kiska."

Electronics Technician Second Class Alex Sievers, peered into the thick impenetrable darkness. He closed his eyes and let the salty, humid wind invigorate him and chase away the remnants of confrontation. Sea billows lapped the hull in a hypnotic tempo and relaxed his cavitating mind. He inhaled the warm night air, and allowed his thoughts to drift beyond the sea, back to his beloved Cathreen. A conundrum of passions juxtaposed his two loves and begged a paradoxical question in his mind that always went unanswered. *Why when at sea I long for my wife, but when in port I long for my mistress the sea?*

The sea was Alex's first love; he adored the whole shipboard life, the thrill and energy that came with underway replenishment. It exhilarated him; the high speed approach, getting the lines across, the breakaway and the smell of the JP5 jet fuel. Other sailors hated these menial tasks. Not Alex, he volunteered for everything he could: underway replenishment, vertical replenishment, flight quarters and even painting the ship. He did it because that's what fleet sailor do. They sail, fix and run ships.

His passion for the sea began as a small boy when his Daddy would tell him tales of journeys on the ocean blue. Embers were fanned into full blown holocausts of zeal as he read stories of dashing young officers, gallant battles and exotic ports of call. When his fantasy became reality he wanted to enjoy every minute of it.

He loved his job and did it well. The Navy provided equal opportunity for all, but rewards those who pursue excellence. His superiors took notice of this and it reflected in great evaluations which allowed him to ascend the ranks quicker than others.

Ben Mattingly clomped his big hand down on Alex's broad shoulder interrupting his daydream. "Petty Officer Sievers, what's up?"

"Mattingly! What's going on? Thought you were afraid of the dark."

"The guy I usually have be rig captain has the flu and has a rack pass. Doc says he needs to rest for 24 hours."

Alex leaned up against the lifeline. "Why don't you get another one of your deck apes to do it?"

"Lots of new guys and nobody's trained to do it yet and you know how the old man likes everything to be perfect. So I volunteered. Besides, I needed some fresh air. It was getting a little stale in the compartment. They had beans for chow tonight."

"I know what you mean," Alex said.

"I've been meaning to ask you if you believed in God?"

"I'm pretty busy and I'm sure running the universe keeps him pretty busy too. So I don't give him much thought and he probably doesn't give me much thought either. Why?"

"The way you're leaning on that life line. I thought for sure you were a man of faith. I'm a Christian and I wouldn't lean on a life line like that," Mattingly said. "If that thing snaps, we might find you and-" He paused and shrugged his shoulders. "Then again we might not. Oh well. What do you think is going to happen when you die?"

Alex jumped off the life line like he'd been bitten by a snake and nervously chuckled. "Never gave it much thought; besides I got my whole life ahead of me to think about it."

"I wouldn't be too sure about that. Anything could happen-"

"Is holy Joe preaching at you Petty Officer Sievers?" The Safety Officer interjected from about 10 feet away.

"Yeah I guess so," Alex said.

"Well, tell him to leave you alone and come over here. We're going alongside, get your men ready."

Lieutenant Latham, Outboard Officer, donned a white vest with the words SAFETY OFFICER, stenciled on the back. Regulations required either a commissioned officer or a Chief Petty Officer to be present to insure safety precautions are followed during any hazardous evolution.

The Lieutenant corralled Alex and lowered his voice. "Hey Alex, I heard about what happened in the berthing compartment. If you know what's good for you, stay away from Peach. Him I don't mind busting, but I'd rather not see you get in any trouble. You're on the skipper's short list for Command Advancement. Keep your nose clean." He winked and walked away.

"Yes sir," Alex said and smiled. "Thank you sir." He paused for a moment and stared in disbelief at the officer's back. Alex mouthed the word "yes" and pumped his fist in jubilation. He grinned and said out of the corner of his mouth, "Line up they've closed up Romeo we're going alongside." Seaman stirred who'd been hiding in the shadows.

"Don't forget what I said Alex," Mattingly said, as he walked away.

Ooh, that Mattingly. He had to go and start talking about God, he thought to himself.

Gas turbine engines roared to life and belched clouds of gas and smoke into the air. Jet engines spun the massive variable pitch propellers and thrashed the water. The ship shook and lurched forward. The props boiled the sea water into a caldron of frothing foaming, while the entire perimeter hissed into a shroud of bubbles by the Prairie Masking System. This agitation created an acoustic impedance mismatch around the hull and disguised the low frequency noise emanating from within the vessel. This process rendered the ship's noise signature anonymous.

The Spruance Class Destroyer knifed through the placid dark ocean water toward the tanker for what should be a routine refueling.

USNS Kiska, awash with red lights buzzed with men scurrying about the deck making last minute preparations for the refueling. About eight seconds after *Ingersoll's* bow crossed the stern of the ammunition ship it slowed to a matching speed and glided into parallel course. Alex watched the main deck pitching and rolling. The refueling towers flanked the port and starboard sides, one forward and one aft, which would shuttle the refueling apparatus and deliver the JP5 fuel to the thirsty destroyer.

Ingersoll pitched and rolled with each wave and glided alongside the seagoing gas station in to Romeo Corpen position (parallel course). One hundred and forty seven feet separated the oiler/ammunition ship and the surface combatant. One blast from a whistle blown on the *Kiska* communicated to *Ingersoll* to be ready to standby to receive the shot line.

Alex shouted, ""Take Cover. Stand by for shot lines both fore and aft."

A whistle blew twice, indicating that the shot line was about to be fired.

The Romeo signal flag is hauled down men scrambled to the opposite side of the ship. *Crack. Thud.* A Gunners Mate fired a rubber projectile from a modified M14 rifle, which hit the superstructure of *Ingersoll*. This star line (nylon line) was pulled over by the refueling teams on the Destroyer, and then a rope attached to a steel span cable which is attached to the pelican hook on the receiver station.

Mattingly reached for the steel cable fastened it to the pelican hook, closed it and secured it with a cotter pin. He checked it then rigged the easing out line. "Tension cable."

The sound powered phone talker keyed the microphone, "Tension Cable."

A few seconds passed and the cable stiffened. Mattingly watched the cable tighten. "Ok."

"She's tight," the seaman said into the sound powered phones.

"Alright guys, lets get that bad boy seated. I want it on the first shot." Alex stood in front of the line crew and watched the refueling hose coming down the cable. "Heave around hand over hand," Alex shouted.

When the hose was about 8 feet away, Alex yelled, "Run with it, Run with it." The team turned, ran aft with the rope, while the refueling hose barreled down the steel cable and slammed into the receiver on the port side of the ship. "Man I love that part."

After the hose seated, Mattingly, inspected the hose for a proper seal. He gave the thumbs up to phone talker and he passed on the information, "We've got a good seal, filler up."

Alex watched with anticipation as Mattingly gave the thumbs up and threw his arms in the air in a victory sign. "Good job guys. I'm still perfect." Men high-fived each other and applauded. "I'll stay tonight. Who wants to stay with me?"

"I'll stay," a voice said from the back of the group. Seaman Odom stepped from behind the crowd. The rest of the group scattered like a bunch of ants to salvage what was left of the evening.

Alex walked over to the refueling hose to chat with Mattingly, when the phone talker ripped the headset, leaned over the lifeline and emptied the contents of his stomach.

"You alright?" Mattingly said.

"No. Don't feel so good."

Mattingly turned to Alex, "Can you man the phones for me?"

"Yeah man."

Commander Austin jumped down from his chair and swaggered over to the Conning Officer. He turned so no one could hear the conversation. "Be ready to make an emergency breakaway. The Intel report says Iraqi jets have been out sight-seeing. This is my last cruise before being promoted, so I don't need one of those terrorists blowing a hole in my boat."

"Aye, aye sir. I'll get us out of here, if one of those birds so much as spits in this direction." The junior officer studied the line-etched face of the old salt standing before him. He eyed the captain's granite jaw jutting out and his deep-set eyes glowing in the crimson light, it made him look like a demon. He swallowed and shook off the shiver up his spine.

The skipper rubbed his chin and furrowed his brow. He wondered, *when did the salt start to rust my steel will?* Commanding the lead ship in the Destroyer Squadron 31 (DESRON) didn't turn out to be the walk in the park he expected. Constantly under the DESRON Commander's scrutiny, he wondered if he would be recommended for promotion to a full bird captain.

He convinced the Commodore to fly his flag on *Ingersoll* by passing the readiness examination with flying colors. For months, he'd worked his crew hard preparing the ship for this Western Pacific deployment. But, he earned their respect, when he got down on his hands and knees to help make the engine room *sparkle* for the annual Operational Propulsion Plant Examination (OPPE). Commander Austin learned long ago to motivate by example. He spent countless hours with each department head insuring success and proudly stood on the bridge wing when the Engineering 'E' was painted on the side of the ship.

A flawless performance is all he needed, to have the inside track to being promoted to captain and eventually flag rank. For two years he'd worked and trained his crew and so far the cruise had gone off without a hitch. With five months behind him, the pressure mounted. He could see the finish line. Would he make it? He could feel a cold, twinge of the possibility of failure ebbing at his confidence. He kept telling himself *stay vigilant; don't let your guard down.* "Conning Officer, how long until we run up the prep flag?"

The prep flag is a green and yellow trapizodial shaped flag ran up the yard arm by the receiving ship and dipped below the yard arm to indicate 15 minutes until completion of refueling and breakaway.

The startled junior officer groped in the darkness for words. "Uh . . . ah . . . I don't know sir."

"Well, find out or I will relieve you of your duties," Commander Austin barked.

"Uh . . . Aye sir." The Conning officer yanked the phone on the conning station and cranked the handle on the box. The phone made a *whir-whir* sound, when he cranked it. "How long before we are 100 percent?" He nodded his head a few times. "Ok, thanks." He jammed the phone back in the cradle and approached the captain.

The junior officer cleared his throat hoping to get the captain's attention. "What is it Mr. Steiner?"

"Captain, they just dipped the prep flag."

He reached his high water mark and fired back, "That's not good enough. We need to get out of here now!"

The bustle on the bridge quieted. "Sir, they can't go any faster. It'll be just a few more..."

"Mr. Steiner, I don't think you understand where we are," Commander Austin said and took a step toward the frightened lieutenant. "This is a war zone. There are planes flying around up there." The captain pointed to the overhead and twirled his index finger. "Planes with missiles that can sink this ship. Do you remember the *HMS Sheffield*, Mr. Steiner?"

"No sir," the young officer said, cursing himself for not remembering.

"The British ship, *Sheffield*, took an Exocet missile at the waterline amidships and almost sank her." He took another step closer and lowered his voice, "Do you want to be responsible for that happening to my boat?"

Unable to defend himself, he eked out the only two words Commander Austin would tolerate, "No sir."

"Then get it done. Now!"

"Aye sir." He backed away, he kept his head up and remembered, *I am an officer and I must be an example to the sailors around me.* He took a deep breath and composed himself.

"Tell the TAO to call me," Commander Austin called to his back.

The Tactical Action Officer (TAO) manned the radar console in the Combat Information Center (CIC) and stood ready to make immediate tactical decisions to insure the safety of the ship against any attack.

"Yes sir."

The phone mounted on the bulkhead by the captain's chair rang. "This is the Captain."

"Captain, this is the TAO."

"Notify me immediately if any targets come into our air space."

"Aye sir."

"Bring up the Phalanx and have it on stand by. Do not put it online without my permission. I've got a boat to protect, but I don't want to start an international incident either."

Phalanx or Close in Weapons System (CIWS) is a 20mm Gatling gun, the block one is able to shoot up to 3000 armor piercing tungsten penetrator rounds of depleted Uranium235 per minute with a magazine holding 1550 rounds. It houses two RADARS in a white case making it look like R2-D2, one to track the target and the other for fire control. The high speed machine gun renders the airframe of an approaching missile un-aerodynamic keeping the exploding shrapnel to a minimum.

"Yes sir, I'll do it now."

Commander Austin hung up the phone, jumped back up into his chair and blankly stared into the darkness.

Ingersoll would fight a war from its Combat Information Center

(CIC), the tactical nerve center of a combatant ship. It looked like a *Star Wars* movie with the blinking lights and displays.

Men sat behind different consoles watching for any hint of hostility. Operation Specialists peered into a SPS-40 air search RADAR scope for planes and surface targets. Sonar Technicians scoured the deep for submarines with SONAR. In another part of the room, Fire Control Technicians waited for orders to fire weapons like Antisubmarine Rockets (ASROC), NATO Sea Sparrow, Harpoon ship to ship missile, the 5" gun and the last line of defense Phalanx.

The TAO hung up the phone. "Ensign Hodge, what's the status?"

He approached another officer crouching over the large Naval Tactical Data System (NTDS) radar screen. The display, a large cathode ray tube with pin pricks of light depicting positions of ships and air contacts. Along side each blip an Identification Friend or Foe (IFF) transponder code. The entire battle group's RADAR data on display for all to observe. "Skies are clear, no bogies in the air."

"Good. The old man will be glad to hear that." The TAO wiped a bead of sweat from his forehead. "He is wound way too tight. I'll be glad when this cruise is over."

"This has got to be the worst deployment I've ever been on," Hodge said.

The TAO punched him in the arm and said, "This is only your first cruise you Bozo."

"It's still the worst cruise I've ever been on," Hodge said and grinned.

"I'll watch the screen for a minute. Go tell the EW's to watch the RF spectrum for any Iraqi RADAR emissions and make sure the chaff launchers are on line."

"Aye sir."

Commander Austin rubbed his hands together as he wore a track into the non-skid deck coating of the port side bridge wing trying to calm him self. He leaned over and watched the refueling hoses swaying and dipping towards the water as the two ships rolled in and out.

"Mr. Steiner, is everything-"

"Bridge, CIC. We have inbound bogies," an intercom box squawked from the dark ceiling over the conning station.

The captain yelled in the direction of the Boatswains Mate of the watch, "Sound General Quarters and breakaway, now."

The officer of the deck yanked the ships whistle five times.

"Aye, aye sir." The Boatswains mate grabbed the 1MC intercom microphone. "Emergency breakaway, emergency breakaway. Cut all lines." A brief pause then the bonging of the General Quarters alarm. "This is not a drill, this is not a drill. General Quarters, general quarters. All hands man your battle stations. Set condition Zebra throughout the ship. On the double." *Bong, bong, bong.*

The fueling probe sprayed JP5 as it was retracted back to the *Kiska*. The sudden release of pressure allowed fuel to flood from the intake line on the deck. The others manning the station scattered. The tensioned span wire released when the cotter pin was pulled on the pelican hook. The easing out line twisted and wouldn't release. Mattingly and Alex were soaked in the spray of fuel.

Alex yelled at Mattingly, "What's taking so long?"

"It won't break loose," He shouted back. "Get me an ax."

Alex keyed the phones, "Cable won't come loose." A shadow on the flight deck above the refueling station distracted him for a split second but he was jerked back to the moment by the screaming on the other end of the phones.

"Captain, they can't break the aft span wire free," the seaman on the other end of the sound powered phones said.

Commander Austin stormed across the bridge and held his hand out to the seaman. "Give me those phones!" The harness would not release and the seaman couldn't get them off. "Forget it. Boats give me the 1MC." Boats handed the captain the microphone. "This is the Captain."

"Cut that cable now," Commander Austin's voice boomed in Mattingly's ears from the speaker close by as he wrestled to free the cable.

"I'm trying. Give me the ax." Mattingly grabbed the ax from Alex and whacked the ease out rope. "Ahhhhh, Break you stupid thing," he yelled at the rope. He whacked it with all his might and the rope broke. When it released, the ship rolled to the starboard side Alex fell into the refueling pit. The misting fuel sparked and ignited with a blinding flash. A fervent heat washed over the deck. Alex raised his arms to his face, to shield himself against the heat. The pit he fell into protected him from the flames. Fire engulfed Mattingly. He let out a blood curdling yowl of pain when his clothes melted into his skin.

Alex ran through the flames and dragged Mattingly out of the fire. The sleeves of Alex's uniform ignited, he ignored the nerves sending pain signals to his brain. He grabbed a nearby tarp, smothered the flames on himself and Mattingly, then dragged him inside the ship. He collapsed in exhaustion and pain. He struggled to maintain consciousness and checked to see if his injured comrade was breathing. He leaned over and heard labored breaths escaping from his lungs. "He's still alive," Alex said. He could hear voices coming toward them. "Hang in there buddy. Cavalries coming." Turning toward the empty passageway, Alex weakly yelled to the approaching voices, "Over here. Please help."

Mattingly grabbed Alex's shirt. "Alex, no greater love," Mattingly rasped then swallowed hard and bit his lip so hard from the anguish, blood spurted out. He shrieked and convulsed. When the pain subsided, he started to speak again. "No greater love, than a man has then to lay down his life for a friend," Mattingly squeezed his eyes tight and gasped for his last breath. His face relaxed and his grip loosened on his shirt. He exhaled his last breath and his head rolled away.

Alex tried to touch him with his burned hands, but winced in agony. Shocked, he stared at the lifeless body. *Look at how peaceful he is*, Alex thought to himself.

"Come on man. Breathe." He tried to bring his mouth down on Mattingly's lips to breathe life into his lungs.

A Hospital Corpsman rushed around the corner and quickly accessed the situation. He put his ear to Mattingly's chest. "He's in cardiac arrest. Set up the defibrillator." The corpsman started pushing on the chest of the lifeless body, while the assistant unpacked the machine. The assistant handed the paddles to the corpsman. "Clear" he said. He fired the paddles and Mattingly's body convulsed from the shock. He put his ear to his chest to listen for a heart beat. None. He reset the defibrillator to give him another blast. "Clear." *Wallop*, another shot of electricity. Again he put his ear to his chest, but still no heart beat.

"Come on, man. Don't give up." He puts his mouth to his mouth and blew air into his lungs. He did it once and then pushed on his chest five times. Sweat dripped from his brow as he worked with ferocious passion to save Mattingly.

Others arrived and watched in horror. Finally, the corpsman leaned back against the wall in frustration. Tears and sweat streamed down his face and he shook his head, *what more could I have done.*

Alex watched through a haze of semi-consciousness, "It's all my fault. If I had just gotten the cable free faster." He fought for consciousness but a heavy fog rolled in to his mind and voices faded in to echoes then silence.

Rod Peach stood in the doorway. He watched and listened unmoved by the situation. If anyone had been paying attention, they would've seen the corner of his mouth raise a crooked smile and the glee in his eyes.

One of the men, who stood by, knelt in front of the corpsman and said, "Doc."

The corpsman sat and looked right through the man in front of him.

"Doc," he said again. This time he shook him.

"What?" The Doc said detached.

"Sievers is still alive and is badly burned. He's passed out. You need to help him."

"Yeah," the Corpsman said. "Cover him," as he pointed to Mattingly. "Get a stretcher from the repair locker and take him to sick bay. Notify the bridge, tell them we have to air lift Petty Officer Sievers to the carrier immediately." He looked back as they covered the body, "Tell them about Petty Officer Mattingly."

"Sir, Repair 3 is reporting fire is out and two casualties."

The captain turned in somberness to the report. "How bad?"

"It's not good, sir. One dead. The other badly burned. He's going to have to be airlifted to the carrier."

"Notify *Vinson* and have them send a chopper. Tell them to get two Tomcats here to get those fighters off my back."

"Aye sir," said the Conning Officer.

The captain grabbed the phone by his chair. "TAO, if they break 50 miles turn the Phalanx on them."

"Aye sir."

The captain slammed the phone down and cursed. "I didn't need this."

CHAPTER 2: BRIEFING

Battle is the most magnificent competition in which a human being can indulge. It brings out all that is best; it removes all that is base. All men are afraid in battle. The coward is the one who lets his fear overcome his sense of duty. Duty is the essence of manhood. - George S. Patton

A bird farm is the nick name fleet sailors attach to an air craft carrier and the *USS Carl Vinson CVN-70* is a big bird farm. The floating fortress measures three football fields in length and its primary mission is to project United States air power worldwide. Nicknamed the Golden Eagle, it is the third of the Nimitz Class built by *Newport News Shipbuilding*. The super carrier is powered by two Westinghouse A4W nuclear powered reactors, which drive 4 steam plants turning the four shafts propelling it in excess of 30 knots.

Vinson sported four different types of radar: air search, target acquisition, air traffic control and air craft landing aid. Weapons system include: MK57 Mod 3 NATO Sea Sparrow, RIM 116 Rolling Air Frame Missiles and Phalanx.

The ships company is around 3200 souls and swelled to over 6000 when the air wing, Commander Carrier Group three, Cruiser Destroyer Group five and Destroyer Squadron 31 came aboard.

The 24 story sovereign American airfield sped through the waters at 35 knots maintaining 25mph winds across the deck for the non stop flight operations.

"Sir," A lanky Lieutenant Junior Grade, approached the two-star

Rear Admiral Starger, who watched the flight operations from the flag bridge wing.

"Just a second." The Admiral held a bony finger in the air and smiled a child like grin. "Watch this bird coming in. I think he's going to trap the number three."

The junior officer turned and watched an F-14 Tomcat fighter, glide over the stern of the huge flight deck. The powerful Pratt and Whitney F401-400 engines whistled and whined. The fuselage wrenched in the cross winds over the pitching and rolling angled deck of the *Vinson*. The pilot slammed the plane on the deck and throttled up to full military power igniting the afterburners for a possible bolter. The tail hook snagged the number three wire, forward momentum stopped and the pilot cut the engines. The Tomcat turned toward a yellow shirted crewmen with glowing orange flashlights, the place where he would park his aircraft.

"Alright," The Admiral shouted. "Way to go Tomcat. Give the guy an underlined OK." He pumped his fist and slapped the junior officer on the back.

"Sir, what is an underline OK?"

The admiral looked at the JG for a bewildered moment, "How long have you been an officer?"

"Two years, sir."

The admiral cleared his throat. "Uh huh. And how did you get on my staff?"

"Well . . ."

"Never mind," the admiral raised his hand in the air, went back inside the flag bridge to get out of the wind. He jumped up in the padded chair where all the flight deck operations could be observed. "I wish I had the time to get back in the cockpit," he said.

The young officer raised an eyebrow at the elder Carrier Group Commander. "Sir, not to be disrespectful, but you haven't flown in over 15 years."

"Yeah, I guess you're right. Wishful thinking. Only thing I'll be flying is my desk." The admiral cleared his throat and dropped the smile. "What do you need Lieutenant?"

"Rear Admiral, *Ingersoll* is sending casualties over and we need your authorization to suspend flight operations to recover the helo."

"Permission granted. What happened and how bad?"

"One dead and one severely burned. Accident during refueling."

"That's too bad."

Muffled voices filled Alex's pounding head as he slipped in and out of consciousness. Restless and choked by the odor of jet fuel and burnt flesh a fog of horror, hideous faces and stabbing words crashed into his mind with an unholy vengeance. The searing pain jolted him back to reality, with screams of anguish and torment escaping his throat.

He could hear himself moaning and forced his eyes open. Alex awoke in time to see the corpsman kneel over him with a syringe. His eyes widened and cried out, "No." Before the protest registered with the corpsman, he plunged the needle of morphine into Alex's arm. The pain subsided and consciousness slipped away and he never felt the bump of the helicopter landing on the deck of the *Vinson*.

Two Months Later

San Diego has long been a partner with the United States Navy. The city donated the land which was Balboa Park in 1919 for what would be the 85 acre sprawling complex known at the *Naval Medical Center San Diego*. It is affectionately called, Balboa Hospital.

"Hello. Petty Officer Sievers," a familiar female voice said entering the plain cinder blocked walls. The brilliant bouquet of flowers sitting atop an adjacent night stand provided the only color in the sterile white room.

The pursed lips relaxed into a soft smile on Alex's stern face, "Hello to you to Petty Officer Sievers."

A petite blond with a bright smile bent to kiss his toothy grin and hug his neck. "You seem to be better today." She unbuttoned a blue coat with an eagle, a crossed manual with a quill and one chevron on her left arm. Personnelman Third Class Cathreen Sievers removed her combination cap, placing it over the top of her coat.

Alex watched her make herself more comfortable. "Have the advancement results come in yet? I'm curious to see if-"

"You made first class."

"No," He said. "To see if you made second class."

"Look. I'll let you know as soon as the results come in. They'll be here in a few days," she said. "Take it easy. Did you get some rest?"

"I slept better last night. Pain wasn't as intense. But it still hurts a lot."

Cathreen Sievers gently patted the bandaged arms of her husband and sat down next to him. "How long before the bandages come off?"

"Soon I hope, Doc says he's got to be really sure about those skin grafts he did. He doesn't want them falling off."

"Oh I see."

"There's something else bothering me."

With a concerned look, Cathreen, bolted upright, "What do you mean? Are there some complications they didn't tell you about?"

"No. It's not physical. I want to feel you in my arms again," he said. "All during the deployment that was all I could think about. Now look at me, I'm a mess and I can't even hug my wife."

"Aw honey, that's sweet and I appreciate it. It won't be long and you can do all the hugging you want."

"You don't think I'm grotesque like this. You're still going to love me and all. You know, there's still are going to be scars."

Cathreen took Alex's face in her hands and said, "I didn't marry your arms, I married you honey and that means nothing to me. I'm just glad you're ok. You could've died and then I wouldn't have you or your grotesque arms."

"Don't remind me, I think about it all the time. I should've been able to save that kid. That was my job and I didn't do it."

"Look Alex, you're in this hospital bed because you tried to save him.

You wouldn't have been able to live with yourself if you hadn't tried to save him. That should count for something, don't beat yourself up with it. Ok?" Cathreen said. She flashed a smile, patted his leg, sighed and rubbed her tired eyes.

"What's wrong Cat?" Alex asked.

"Tired. Haven't been able to sleep."

"That's too bad. How's thing's going at the office?"

"A battle group is getting ready to deploy in two weeks and some of the ships have not completed their inspections. You know what that means?"

"Lot's of paperwork," they said in unison.

"Yup and guess who gets to make sure everything is in order?" She pointed to herself. "So that doesn't leave much time for sleeping. If I make second class they're going to load me up with even more work. I'll probably take over as section leader."

"I'm sorry, honey and you coming over here to visit me every night," Alex said. He huffed. "You go home and get some rest and don't come tomorrow."

"Now Alex J. Sievers, don't be trying to get rid of me like that. I'll come when I want to and go home when I want to. You know, there are some times you burn me up with the way you treat me."

"Cat, I'm sorry."

"I wish you would . . . Oh, never mind." She scrunched her lips and wheeled around to look out the window.

"Never mind." Alex said with an attitude. "Never Mind! What is that suppose to mean? You got something to say, say it." *I wish I hadn't said that.* Words jumped out of his mouth like one of those coiled up snake tricks in a can with out giving any thought to how it would affect someone.

"Every night I come in here, you've got this major pity party going on. It's wearing me out. You are so self absorbed. Let somebody else into that kidney bean heart of yours for a change," she said.

"You weren't there and you aren't the one laying in this bed with the french-fried arms."

She snapped an about face and shot her words like a missile at him. "Let it go, Alex. You're not bringing that kid back, so stop trying to."

"Yeah, you're right. I'm sorry. I'm just a little worried about the report. It's coming in today and that stuff always bothers me. Even the word 'inquiry' bugs me. It sounds like 'inquisition' or something like that," Alex said. "Sheesh!"

"What are you afraid of? They might put you on a rack and stretch you?" She paused and her face softened as she visualized her husband on a rack being stretched. "That's not a bad idea. I wouldn't mind it if you were a little taller. Do you think they could add three or four more inches?" She giggled.

"Cut it out Cat. I'm serious. I have no clue what's in that report."

A young sailor, in a crisp dress blue uniform knocked and entered the room. "Petty Officer Sievers?"

"Yes that's me."

The sailor put an envelope on the table in front of him and lifted up a clip board for a signature and awkwardly paused when he saw both of his hands and arms bandaged. Red faced, he looked at Cathreen for help. She took the clipboard and scrawled her name.

"Thank you," She said to the sailor and he turned to leave. "You want me to open it for you or would you like to do it yourself?" She flashed a mischievous smile at him. "Hmh?"

"Cute Cat, please open it and help me with it."

Cathreen unsealed the envelope and propped it up on Alex's chest so he could read. She looked over his shoulder and read with him. "What!" He exclaimed and threw his head back. "That's not true. I never said that. I can't read any more."

Cathreen took the report and read on. She gasped and put her hand to her mouth.

"What?" He said and stared at her face. When she didn't answer, he chided her, "Cat. Tell me what does it say?"

"They are saying you are fully responsible for the incident."

Alex stared at her in shock and disbelief.

"It goes on to say, after your recovery you will be transferred to another duty station."

Alex shook his head, "Where?"

Two Years Later

Alex Sievers emerged from the ink black darkness of the tunnel connecting *Recruit Training Command* (RTC) with *Camp Moffett*. The tunnel ran under a main street outside the fences of the base. He walked oblivious to the sign above him that read, 'All companies must sing *Anchors Away* when entering this tunnel.' Off in the distance a company of recruits could be heard. The Recruit Chief Petty Officer (RCPO), better known as 'Rpock' to the recruits, barked, "Your left. Your left. Your left, right, left."

He admired and watched as the achievement flags whipped and snapped in the brisk wind. When the company turned the corner to cross the street, he spotted the Color Company Flag. The gold fringed, white flag emblazoned with the words, 'Color Company, Recruit Training,' marked this company as the company who achieved the highest score in four areas of training for a graduating class. The flag depicted four blue boxes in a diamond formation, one with a star for compartment readiness, another of a crossed rifles for drill, an 'A' for physical fitness and an 'S' for scholastics.

Alex swept the tight formation for any breaks in their stride. He deduced by their synchronized step they were ready for graduation. The Rpock snapped a crisp salute; Alex returned the salute with a nod of approval. The company marched down the ramp and disappeared into the blackness of the tunnel. The melody of 75 male voices singing *Anchor's Away* wafted back to him. He watched until the last row of the formation disappeared into the darkness and the voices faded.

A red aiguillette hung from the shoulder of his dark blue uniform which distinguished him as an RTC company commander. Aiguillette's found their origin as the lace to fasten the plates of armor by French knights. Short loops on one side would act as a hinge, while longer braided; more ornate cords tied the armor. When the cumbersome armor passed into antiquity the cords continued as part of the uniform worn by soldiers and the complexity of the aiguillette signified which division or regiment one may belong to.

Petty Officer First Class Alex Sievers slipped on a pair of aviator sunglasses and flipped open his worn leather bound notebook. The notes in his folder fluttered in the cold spring wind. He slapped the notebook in time to keep them from being scattered in the gust.

"Alex, Alex. Wait up," said Boatswains Mate Second Class John McCarthy. "Whew. I didn't know if I was going to catch up to you."

"I thought only the recruits had to double-time-it around here," Alex said and laughed at his panting over weight assistant company commander.

"Don't get smart their transceivers or I'll twist you into a pretzel."

Alex smiled and started toward the Division 12 barracks.

John tucked his shirt in around his oversized pot belly and in a futile effort tried to straighten his gig line. As he struggled to get the buttons on his shirt in line with his belt buckle he snorted. "You know Alex, I really hate this monkey suit."

"Maybe if you cut back on the cheese burgers, it would fit you better."

"I wouldn't go there if I were you. They've already threatened me with the fat boy program if I don't shed a few bricks."

Alex smiled and bit his lip to keep from laughing.

"Go ahead and laugh. We'll see how well you do without me."

"I'm not laughing," Alex said and tried not to laugh.

John pulled back his fist and punched Alex in the shoulder.

"Ow, that hurt." He grabbed his shoulder and rubbed out the pain.

"Good I'm glad and if you keep laughing I'm going to knock you into next week. You skinny little twerps ought to try being fat. See how you like it."

"I keep in shape and try to eat right. You want to go work out with me tonight. Maybe we can put the gloves on and spar a few rounds."

John thought for a moment. "You're on. Then I can really beat the tar out of you for laughing at me."

"We'll just see about that."

John paused, grimaced and snapped his fingers. "I got to take Mary Lou to church tonight, but how does tomorrow sound?"

"Church?" Alex said. "Do you go to Sunday School too?" Alex laughed and slapped his husky 6' 4" assistant on the back.

"Yes, What's it to you? By the way after what you went through I'm surprised you don't go too."

"I don't talk about religion or politics. So let's not go there. Ok?"

"Alright, but don't blame me if you don't get your fire insurance paid up."

He stopped walking and fired back at him. "Look John, I'm not against God, but I am not for him either so don't try to cram your religious garbage down my throat. And while we are on the subject I got one question, where was God when that kid was dying?" Alex said disgusted. "Aw, never mind." He waved his hand at John and started walking again.

John backed off. "Did you get a look at the list of new recruits?"

"Yep," Alex said flatly.

"Slim pickings again?"

"We got a couple that might help, but other than that not much else to speak of." Alex said. The thought of not having a very good class silenced both of them. "Let's stay positive. If we work them hard, who knows what can happen?"

"That last class was a mess. How did we even finish fifth I'll never know?"

"Don't worry John. I think I've figured this thing out. I compared all the classes we pushed and I've been talking to some other commanders. I don't think it's about high ASVAB scores and muscles. It's about helping them catch the Navy vision and embrace it. I think I am starting to finally understand what we are trying to accomplish here. We light the fire and let it burn. We can do this John."

"Wow, when did you turn motivational speaker?"

Company commander's Lounge Division 12 teemed with activity as commanders waited for the division officer to arrive for the new graduation class briefing. Every week a new group of recruits arrived and is assigned to companies for an eight week training cycle. There are ten companies in each graduation class, with a company commander responsible to school the recruits in basic naval traditions, duties and prepare recruits to serve in the fleet. Each company commander is provided with an assistant to help conduct the training.

Voices buzzed from the lounge engaged in coking and joking; a fine naval tradition. It is reserved for times when engaged in another fine tradition of hurry up and wait. To participate in the ritual one must grab a Coke, shoot the breeze and try to catch up on the latest scuttle butt going around. A familiar voice pierced the cacophony of voices, "Alex." The voice was accompanied by a hand and a big toothy grin.

"Hatch," Alex said, when he grasped the outstretched hand. "How the heck are ya? First company?"

"I'm fine. Yeah. Thought I would push boots to get my career out of the dog house."

"Theresa and the kids?" Alex pumped his hand again and let go.

"They're taking some time to get settled. The kids weren't too happy moving from sunny San Diego to the Windy City. It's quite a change from beaches and 75 degrees all the time to -35 degrees wind chill."

"How hard was that?"

"They still haven't talked to me since they found out we were coming here," Hatch said.

"They'll thaw out. Give it time. Look at you, you still look like the Notre Dame mascot."

"Why do you think I moved here? The golden dome is only 100 miles from here. Maybe we can do a little; Cheer, Cheer for old Notre Dame."

"Wake up the Echo's cheering her name," Alex sang the next line to the University of Notre Dame fight song.

Then the rest of the company commanders jumped in, "Send a volley cheer on high, shake down the thunder from the sky. What through the odds be great or small, Notre Dame will win after all. While her loyal sons are marching onward to victory." When finished, they all let out a big cheer.

When the cheering died down, Alex said to Hatch, "I'd like that. Only if they're playing Kansas, that's my team. But I'd have to check with-"

The door to the lounge banged open, plunging the room into a startled silence. Rod Peach emerged from a cloud of blue cigar smoke. He swaggered around the room checking out the competition. "Don't we sound like a bunch of canaries? I personally like the Miami Hurricanes," Rod sneered, turned to Hatch and extended his hand, "Hatch Harris, how the heck are ya?"

Hatch took his hand out of courtesy and pumped it once then let go. "Rod."

"Been a long time. Last time I saw you, you were going to Captain's Mast for welding the old man's escape hatch shut."

Hatch smiled and said, "Don't remind me, but it was one of my crowning achievements."

Rod took the cigar from his gritted teeth and flicked ashes on Alex's shoe.

"Do you mind?" Alex said and shook the ashes from his shoe.

"I'm sorry transceivers," Rod said with a note of sarcasm. "I didn't see you standing there."

Alex glared back at Rod and started to respond when a company commander announced, "Attention on deck." Each commander snapped to attention.

"As you were gentlemen," Lieutenant Commander Chris Hendrick said. He stepped to the podium and put a leather folder on it and rubbed his eye. "Peach, put the cigar out."

"Yes sir," Rod said and shoved it into an ash tray next to Alex, but didn't fully snuff it out.

His eyes started to water from the smoldering cigar, so he shoved it into the sand to snuff it out. He flashed Rod the evil eye. Rod put his hand up to his face and made like he was crying.

I'm going to get that guy. If it's the last freaking thing, I do, Alex thought to himself.

LCDR Hendrick shuffled his papers and did a quick visual inspection. "Ok gents. The new captain has made some changes to the training schedule and it's not good. Inspections will start one week earlier."

The men murmured and chattered amongst themselves. A commander sitting by the door raised his voice above the din. "We barely have enough time with two weeks to get them ready. How are we going to do it with only one week, sir?"

All the other company commanders agreed and pelted LCDR Hendrick with questions.

"Hold it down! I know, I know. I said the same thing myself. But the new CO wants to spend less time on folding clothes and making a rack."

"I got enough trouble just trying to teach these yahoos how to march in a week, let alone trying to get them to swing an M1 Carbide through the sixteen count manual," another commander said.

LCDR Hendrick stood like a statue behind the podium and let his commanders vent their frustration.

"What are we going to do with the extra week? Or are they just going to 86 another week off the schedule and save some money," Alex probed.

The question gave LCDR Hendrick the segue he needed to drop the real bomb on them. "Captain Calaghan, spent the last two years out in the fleet and found some serious discrepancies in the firefighting training." No one made a sound. "The extra week will be dedicated to firefighting."

Alex swallowed hard and grabbed his right arm when it twitched.

A crooked smile crossed Rod's face as he took in Alex's reaction.

"The . . . the school has been severely understaffed for months. How will they handle the extra load?" Alex blurted out.

"That's a good question Petty Officer Sievers," LCDR Hendrick said. "The company commanders will conduct most of the training and the school staff will provide limited assistance." Commander Hendrick trailed off and then gathered his notes. "You guys will have to brush up on your firefighting skills."

The commanders whispered amongst themselves.

"Are there anymore questions?" LCDR Hendrick looked around the room. "If not, then you're dismissed."

The men started to leave. "Hold on a second. I almost forgot there is one more thing," LCDR Hendrick said above the mounting ruckus. "Sit for one more minute. I do have some good news."

"Whew, that's a relief," Hatch said.

"There will no longer be a 'Color Company.' Instead the captain will be reinstating the *Double Salute* at the graduation ceremony. Many of you are too young to remember it. It used to be a very prestigious award, until it was ended during the Vietnam War." He paused for a moment and cleared his throat. "During Nam moral was so bad, some of the traditions got lost. Many became apathetic and did only enough to scoot by. Captain Callaghan, is a throw back to the days when high value was attached to Naval tradition. He wants to change that and this is part of that push."

"What exactly is the *Double Salute*, commander?" Hatch said.

"The company that most displays military bearing, excellence throughout the training and rises above the other companies in the grad class will be eligible for the *Double Salute*. However here's the twist. It carries a mystique about it, because no one ever knows for sure who will get it until the reviewing officer saluted one company on graduation day twice. It was the ultimate honor because it put you on your toes right until the passing in review."

"What's in it for us?" Rod said.

"You will receive a letter of commendation and it will be the highest honor here at *Recruit Training Command*."

"Wow," the commanders said. They started to talk again amongst themselves.

"There are other changes in the works. Your graduation class will be implementing many of these. With all the changes there's going to be a lot more work to be done. I'll be calling on each of you for input and a lot of overtime. Good luck gentlemen," LCDR Hendrick said.

John leaned into Alex and said, "What do you think? Think we got a shot?"

"Well I-" Alex said

"You might as well forget about it right now," Rod sneered. He strutted over to where Alex sat, leaned into him and almost touched his nose with his own. "You haven't even been close to finishing first in any other class. What makes you think you got any shot? The *Double Salute* will be the pen that will write my ticket."

"What? A ticket on Mr. Toad's wild ride?"

The other company commanders snickered. Rod stood up straight and took an unwrapped cigar out of his shirt pocket and then a silver Zippo lighter out of his pant pocket. They all stared at him until he lit the lighter and thrust it into Alex's face.

Alex jerked to avoid the lunge.

"Afraid of a little fire scarecrow?"

Alex stood and glared. The two stood nose to nose. Rod looked down at Alex's shoes then met his glare again. "Maybe that's why you're still a loser who can't win anything. That crow on your shoulder is only from kissing a long line of butts."

John slapped Alex on the back and pushed him toward the door, "Come on Alex, this chump is not worth it."

Rod lit his cigar, "Don't forget *Ingersoll* scarecrow," he said and laughed.

To break up the tension LCDR Hendrick asked, "Alex, I just wanted to let you know your application has been completed and submitted for review for the Limited Duty Officer program."

With a mock laugh Rod whirled around, "Ha. That'll be the day. Your chances of being an officer are as good as you winning the *Double Salute*."

Alex moved toward Rod, when John grabbed him from behind, spun him around and pushed him out the door. "Ooooo, that guy burns me up."

Hatch came up from behind and gave Alex the thumbs up. "He's a jerk. Always has been and always will be."

"You're right. I let him get under my skin."

"I've got to run. I'll catch up with you later," Hatch said.

Alex nodded to Hatch. "This is our chance, John. I know how to beat him."

"What about the firefighting?" John asked.

"We'll find a way around it. I'll figure something out."

"I didn't know you applied to the Limited Duty Officer program." John slapped him on the back. "Congratulations. That's great," he said, then wagged his finger in Alex's face. "But I'm not going to salute you even if you become an officer. No way, not going to do it."

"If we win the *Double Salute*, that Letter of Commendation could be enough to get me in the door. It's my dream John. I decided on LDO first and then after meeting the requirements I can convert to being a regular line officer," Alex said excitedly. "Meet me at the NCO club for lunch and we'll talk about it. I got some things I got to do."

Alex stood in the foyer and allowed his eyes to adjust to the low light. The pungent smell of alcohol prickled his olfactory nerve conjuring up memories of a less stressful time in exotic ports of call with his beloved shipmates. The pleasant thought settled his reeling mind.

"Little early for a drink Petty Officer," an unseen voice said in the inky blackness.

"No sir, looking for Rat."

"Looking for a rat, did you say?"

"No sir, Robert Torcellini. We call him Rat because of his initials."

The older gentlemen turned on his bar stool and chuckled. "Oh you mean Torch. He's not here, said something about having to run over to Supply. He'll be back in about 20 minutes."

"Dang," Alex said. "I guess I'll come back then."

"Why don't you wait for him," the older gentlemen said as he pulled out a bar stool.

"Alright," Alex said as he welcomed the thought of resting his tired legs.

Alex's eyes adjusted to the light and could see the officer uniform of the man bidding him to sit. "Good afternoon sir," Alex said as he sat down in awe of the four gold bars on the old man's shoulders.

The old man raised his glass to acknowledge the more formal greeting. "You know Petty Officer?"

"Sievers, Alex Sievers."

"You know Petty Officer Sievers, Alex Sievers. I've met a lot of Petty Officers like you through out my career who have shown me the same kind of respect and only now at the end of my career do I understand the value of each and every one of them."

"Sir, I don't follow you."

"That rope on your shoulder commands the respect with out question by the men in your company as do these bars on my shoulders your respect with out question. These bars didn't come with out a price; they weren't just given to me. I had to earn them."

"When you say 'earn,' what exactly do you mean?"

"You're a Petty Officer First Class, right?"

"Yes sir," Alex responded.

"Then be the best First Class then become a Chief. Then be a great Chief and become a Senior Chief. Then be a great Senior Chief and so on, and so on up through the ranks."

"Ok?"

"Be the best where you are at and the advancement will come." He leaned over to Alex and lowered his voice. "But the key to advancement is not kissing the butt of the guy over you." He leaned back and swirled his glass around in his left hand. "Well maybe, just a little. The key is to respect the guys under you." He pointed with his right index finger to the floor. "That's where us big cheeses lose it. We think we are prima donnas and forget about you boys down in the bilges covered in God knows what." He took a long pull on his drink and then stared at Alex. "Then maybe some day you'll be sitting on this bar stool telling some wide eyed Petty Officer the same thing."

"Thank you sir, I appreciate that. Sir what's your name?"

"Captain Orr. Retired."

Alex stifled the smile.

The old man waved his hand at Alex. "Don't bother trying to hold it in. I've gotten used to it I get it all the time."

"Retired Sir?"

"Yep. Putting me out to pasture after 34 years. This is my retirement party. I'm just a little early. Doesn't start for another four hours."

"Wow. That is phenomenal. Congratulations."

"Thank you," Captain Orr said flatly. "What about you son, what are your plans? I see you're pushing boots so that means you're career minded."

"Well sir, I'm being considered for Chief, but I really want to be an officer. I've applied to the LDO program."

"Limited Duty Officer, why not a regular Line Officer and pursue command."

"I'm working on my degree now, but I just feel I've got to make the jump as soon as possible and I love the job I'm in so I thought I could combine both worlds. Once I get my degree I'll try to convert to a Line Officer."

"Good for you. If you ever need any advice, let me know. I'll be around. Just can't up and leave the old girl after all these years."

CHAPTER 3: OH-DARK-THIRTY

It follows then as certain as that night succeeds the day, that without a decisive naval force we can do nothing definitive, and with it, everything honorable and glorious. – President George Washington

Rows of bunk beds stood like silent sentries casting disjointed shadows on the wall from the moonlight spilling in from the un-shaded windows. Steady, rhythmic breathing and the musty odor of an aging building filled the receiving barracks.

At the end of the row of beds, a frosted glass door allowed light to diffract into the room and illuminate one of the sleeping recruits. The door knob turned and protested with an annoying squeak as it opened. Two silhouettes slid into the room and split up. The taller figure disappeared into the shadows, while the other stood fast by the door. From the shadows a rustle of plastic is heard, then a whisper, "Ok."

With a crash and a bang, a steel garbage can skittered down the center of the columns of beds. In the same instant, harsh fluorescent lights snapped on to stab the eyes of the sleeping beauties.

The two black uniformed figures paraded and yelled in front of the recruits jolted from their slumbers.

"Oh four hundred, time to rise and shine my little pretties. Get out of those racks, on the double," Alex yelled. "It's time to start your Navy careers."

A concert of groans greeted him from the startled recruits. It was all part of the Navy training; tear them down and build them up. Mold them and shape them into sailors. The second nightmarish day began in earnest, shocked out of the comfortable and into the harshness of willful submission to every command.

"Stand at attention at the end of your bunk," John yelled.

The company commanders continued the diatribe, but stopped when Alex noticed a body unfazed by the verbal assault. He motioned to John to join him. Alex sat on the edge of the bunk next to the unresponsive recruit. He put his finger to his lips when John approached and then shook the young, fair-haired recruit awake. "Excuse me son, I'm your new company commander, it's time to get up now," Alex said sweetly. "Would you mind joining the rest of us, we're all waiting for you?"

"If you all don't mind I'd like to sleep a little longer," the young recruit said. "Is that ok with you?"

Alex looked at John and shook his head, then moved in closer to the recruit in the rack. "No, it's not ok with me." Alex shouted and grabbed the mattress and dumped the recruit out of the rack onto the floor. "Now get your butt up and put your toes on the line."

A roar of laughter went up, after the young man hit the deck. Alex whirled around, "Shut up. Do you think this is funny? I don't. You're in my Navy now." Alex marched back and forth from recruit to recruit with a scowl on his face. "For the next eight weeks I'm your Mama and your Daddy. It's my job to turn you into sailors fit for duty in the United States Navy. Which I might add is the greatest Navy in the history of the world and we are second to none. I am going to push you harder than you've ever been pushed-"

"And I am going to pull you harder than you've ever been pulled," John resounded from the other end of the room where he prowled the ranks.

"We are going to break you down and find out what kind of men you are. Another thing, there is no 'I' in TEAM. We do not work as individuals we work as a team. When one person succeeds, we all succeed. When one person fails, we all fail. We're going to make you stronger-"

"Tougher-" John shouted on cue.

"And ready to protect-"

"And defend-" John shouted.

"The Constitution of the United States against all enemies foreign and domestic," Alex said. He paused for a moment and let the thought hang in the air. "Do you understand?"

"Yes," the recruits said.

"You will also refer to me and Petty Officer McCarthy as sir," Alex said. "Is that clear?"

"Yes sir," the recruits said with no emotion.

"Is that clear?" Alex said with his pitch rising.

"Yes sir," the recruits said with a little more spirit.

"I can't hear you. Is that clear?" Alex shouted.

The recruits echoed back a resounding, "Yes sir."

"That's better. I want to hear that all the time," Alex said. "Make up your mind right now to be the best you can be and not just gold brick for the next four years. If you don't pull your weight someone else will have to. If you reach down inside and yank out the very best you have to offer you will be successful. Learn the best way to do your job and then learn how to do your bosses job."

Alex paced and stalked the ranks of his new recruits looking them over.

"Duty is not just a word to be thrown around; it is a code to live by. There's an old saying 'Wooden ships with men of steel will defeat steel ships manned by wooden men.' It is your duty to follow orders and to show respect to those placed in authority over you and follow the chain of command. To fight a successful battle the officers placed over us require discipline, training and the knowledge orders will be followed immediately and accurately. To delay or question such orders could cost lives, the loss a ship and ultimately the freedom we hold dear. "

Alex paused for a moment.

"Dereliction of duty of any kind jeopardizes the mission and goals of the US Navy and benefits our enemies. It will not be tolerated. If you are found to neglect your duties you will be disciplined for your actions. It is our duty as United States Sailors to remain vigilant and trustworthy in the performance of the tasks assigned to us. You don't do your duty because you 'have to' or because you will get in trouble 'if you don't.' You do it, because it is an honor and a privilege to do so."

He paused for a long moment and paced the ranks and glared at each man he walked by. "Do I make myself clear?" he shouted.

The recruits responded with a spirited, "Yes sir."

Alex waved to Petty Officer McCarthy to take the floor.

"Thank you Petty Officer Sievers," The big gruff man said. "Is there anyone here who is prior military?" John looked around the room for anyone lifting their hand.

"I do sir," a voice called from behind John.

John twirled around and walked to a tall black man. "Step forward." The man took one step out of ranks. "What's your name?"

"Scott, David Scott, sir."

Alex walked up behind John as the man announced his name and looked him over. Once satisfied he gave John a nod of approval.

"You will be the Recruit Chief Petty Officer, also known as the Rpock. You will be in charge of the company when a company commander is not present," John said and handed him two anchor pins which had USN emblazoned on them. "Put these on your collar when you get your uniform." John held out his big paw and the new Rpock shook it. "Congratulations."

"Thank you sir."

Alex turned away from the new Rpock and paced back and forth in front of the men. "You will salute all officers and any petty officer wearing a red rope on their uniforms. Is that clear?"

"Yes sir," the recruits yelled back at him.

"Rpock," Alex said. "Fall them out on the grinder. Line them up tallest to shortest."

"Yes sir." He turned to the rest of the recruits and yelled, "Company 197, fall out."

Recruits hustled past Alex and John. The room cleared quickly, leaving the two company commanders.

"They don't look too promising," Alex said.

"I don't think your ugly mug would look to promising if you only had 45 minutes of sleep either."

Rod Peach stood tall at the front of the room, flanked by his assistant Paul Santello who stood at parade rest.

"We will be the best company *Recruit Training Command* has ever seen. You will not only be training to be sailors in the US Navy, but will be competing to be the best company in the graduating class. I am already convinced you are the best."

When he finished his speech, he turned to his assistant, "Petty Officer Santello fall them out."

Paul yelled, "Fall out."

The recruits hustled past Peach and he smiled as each recruit jogged by. "What to you think Paul?"

"I guess you've got another winner."

"It's not hard when you can hand pick them and make sure the others get the rejects."

"How'd you do that?"

Rod smiled a crooked smile. "You just got to know what other people need."

"Rod, you are one smooth customer."

"I know."

Five Philipino barbers stood behind five barber chairs. Ten recruits filed into the room in two groups of five. The barbers shot playful looks at each other as they looked at the mops trying to pass as hair dos.

Alex stepped in front of the barbers. "Alright gents take your seats."

Seaman Recruit Cade Keller thumped his big body down in the barber's chair. He smiled at the barber and said in a heavy southern accented voice, "If you don't mind sir, I'd appreciate it if you would take just a little bit off the top. My Mama told me to keep my head warm, because she says it gets down right cold here."

The barber looked at Alex and smiled. Alex leaned into Keller,

"Oooh! I'm sure he'll take a little off the top for you."

"Much obliged sir." Keller smiled and nodded to the recruit sitting next to him.

Alex pointed at Keller's head and pulled his finger across his throat. The barber laughed and switched on his razor. He made a big swipe down the center of his head barely leaving a trace of hair. A clump of the hair fell into Keller's hand which turned his wide smile into a look of horror. Alex, the barbers and the other recruits roared in laughter.

The Navy is most known for her majestic ships, but many are lured to explore the seven seas by the rhythmic song of the tides. They beckon the young men to come and sail the crystal blue waters, to see what lies on a distant shore and unlock mysteries entombed in the deep. But the romance with sea ends when cruel reality hits with disastrous results. Many have watched their man-made leviathans sink beneath the tide as a result of storms, collisions and war.

Survival on the high seas requires common sense, determination and the ability to float. The Aquatic Center at RTC provided the proper proving ground to meet this requirement. Each boot must pass a third class swim qualification: which meant jumping off a ten-foot tower, swim 50 meters, float on a pair of dungaree for five-minutes and then hoist them selves from the pool. All the while instructors in scuba gear prowled the pool floor making sure feet don't touch bottom.

The tower rose above the teal colored water of the survival training tank. Suspended from a semicircle ceiling above the pool is a rubber life raft for advanced training. On the facing wall the recruits are reminded of days gone by with a tall ship painting and a modern day counterpart destroyer on the other side of a pair of doors, each with a dolphin painted on it.

Members of Company 197 filed into the pool area. "Take a seat along the wall."

Alex walked over to the Water Survival Instructor who smiled when he saw Alex. "What's up home slice?" Bob Chambers, a sun tanned faced instructor with an athletic build thrust his hand to him.

"Not too much homie," Alex shot back at him and slapped his hand. "Gang's all here waiting for a dunking."

"How do you stay so tanned when it's freezing around here all the time?"

"Hey man I'm from Calli anybody who's anybody always has a good tan. I try to get in the sun as much I can."

"You're crazy man. That's got to be a site to see."

"I heard about all the changes. Think you got a shot?"

"I don't know." Alex looked over his shoulder at his company. "They're a motley crew. Did you do Peach's company?"

"Monster's. He's got some big dude's. I'm surprised they ain't playing starting offensive line for the Nebraska Cornhuskers."

"Please. I don't do Huskers. I'm a J-Hawk through and through. I bleed Jayhawk purple," Alex said. "How does he manage to get these giants every time?"

"You know, it's funny you mention that." Bob shook his head. "I was at personnel the other day and I saw Peach there with a pile of service records. I asked the Personnelman (PN) what the deal was. He told me he was doing some research for the CO."

"Why would the Commanding Officer ask a boot pusher to do some research for him?"

"Can't help you," Bob said, "But what I can help you with is a little water survival training." He blew his whistle and shouted, "Let's get started."

"I'll talk to you later," Alex said and walked toward the exit mulling over the information Bob shared with him.

The company stood to attention.

"We are a blue water Navy which means we can go any where in the world on our ships. And from time to time a ship might stop floating." He paused a moment. "If that happens, what are you going to do to survive?"

One of the recruits spoke out, "Use a lifeline."

"That's a good idea. What kind of lifeline?"

Another recruit shouted out, "Phone a friend."

All the recruits laughed. Bob smiled and shook his head. "That's cute, but I think you're going to need a little more help than that. If your ship goes down, you can be out there for hours, days or even weeks before you're rescued." He walked over to the tower and leaned against it. "You may have to save a buddy who's been injured and can't swim. Today, I'm going to show you how to survive in the water, even if you forget your life jacket. But first I got to know if you can swim."

Seaman Recruit Thompson, a tall muscular black man, turned to Seaman Recruit Keller and whispered to him. "Hey man, I'm from New York City and never even been in a pool. Let alone learn to swim."

"Really," Keller said.

"Yeah, the only water we ever saw outside of home was when somebody cracked open a fire hydrant on a really hot day."

"Does anybody want to volunteer to be the first," Bob said? "I see we've got a couple of gabbers over there. Hey you two."

Keller didn't notice Bob talking to him and continued to whisper to Thompson.

"I know what you mean, that lower-" Keller whispered.

"Hey you two," Bob yelled, finally getting Keller's attention.

Keller looked around to see who Bob was yelling at. Then looked back to see him staring at him. "Me," Keller squeaked out.

"Yeah you big boy. Up the ladder you're our first pair off the tower."

"But I . . . I"

"Up the ladder," Bob said. "Once on the platform cross your arms and legs. It's imperative you do this or else you'll be hurtin' for certain."

"Why's that Petty Officer Chambers?" Thompson asked.

"That force will hit you right in your privates and you'll be in a lot of pain. Y'all got it?"

"Yes sir," The Company said.

"Ok, you two up the ladder."

Keller and Thompson made a slow climb up the ladder and then baby stepped out to the edge of the platform. They shot each other scared looks.

"Once in the pool, you'll swim the perimeter and finish where you start. Then pull yourself out of the pool and you pass. Don't put your feet down or you get to do it all over again. Do you understand?"

"Yes sir," Company 197 said.

"Alright you two munchkins have at it," Bob said.

Neither one of them jumped.

"Let's go."

They still wouldn't jump.

"Now!" Bob shouted at the top of his lungs, which frightened the two recruits off the platform. They came to the surface arms flailing and gasping for air. "There's always one or two in every class." After a few moments the instructor signaled a rescue diver to go after the two and haul them out.

The diver jumped into the water, collared Keller, brought him to the side of the pool and pointed up the ladder. Then went back and did the same for Thompson. The two climbed out of the pool, where Chambers waited for them. "You two mermaids will be seeing me for some water ballet. Three times a week for the next six weeks," Bob said.

Keller and Thompson walked over to the wall and sat with their heads down.

"Don't worry guys, it'll be fun. Who knows maybe you'll like it so much you'll want to become Navy Seals."

Condensation dripped down the side of Alex's water glass and soaked the paper napkin it rested on. He twirled the ice cubes with his finger as his thoughts drifted back to the fleet. He longed for his mistress, the sea, with her soothing swish of waves slapping against the hull and the gentle rock that lulled him to sleep each night. He felt safe in her arms by keeping himself immersed in his duties and drowned his sorrows in the day to day routine.

The harshness of Great Lakes, Illinois offered no relief from the throbbing deep in his soul. The detailer who cut his orders to RTC told him, "This would look good on your record and will help your career goals." The idea of pushing boots appealed to him. He saw it as another gold coin to toss in his pot so when the time was right he could cash in on his dream. It did not occur to him to count the cost and what it would entail to be successful all he could see was the pot of gold at the end of his rainbow.

The accident, the results of the inquiry and not getting the command advancement to first class on *Ingersoll* forced him to take this unplanned detour to Great Mistakes. Becoming a first class sooner could've accelerated his plan to enroll in the Limited Duty Officer program a year sooner.

If I had to push boots, why couldn't I've done it in San Diego? Why come here to the middle-of-no-where to do it? Then to have to compete with Peach every graduation class. What were the odds? Alex thought to himself.

"Alex are you listening to me?" John bellowed. "Hello, Earth to Oz. You asked me here to talk and you ain't doing much talking. What gives?"

"Hmh. What did you say?"

"Are you Ok?" John got up and put his hand on Alex's head to check for a fever.

Alex rocked back in his chair to get away from John. "I was just trying to figure what the odds are Peach would be here and in the same Grad Class as me. I shouldn't even be here."

"What you've told me about him? I wouldn't put it past him if he is here just to torture you."

"That's an interesting point," Alex said and slammed his chair down and leaned into John. "But Peach only does what serves Peach's best interest. But I might agree with you that he wouldn't mind taking a few shots at me in the process."

"Hey Petty Officer Sievers take it easy on my chair there. Tax payers can't afford to be replacing them."

Alex's face brightened and extended his hand to greet his new friend. "Hey Captain Orr, what are you doing here playing bartender. Shouldn't you be at some congressional hearing or something like that?"

John stood in respect when he heard the word 'captain.'

"Nope. When I hung up the uniform that was it for me. I thought it would be fun just to get to know people in a less obtrusive environment. Everybody is the same; no senior, no junior. My wife wants to travel some, so I thought a part time job would be fun. Torch needed some help managing the place."

"Sir, this is my assistant Petty Officer McCarthy."

John extended his hand and shook Captain Orr's hand. "Pleasure to meet you sir."

"Look guys. I know about all the formalities of rank and all, but do you think we can all forget about that when we're in here. I know it is unconventional and not the norm, but I'm retired now and I get to make my own rules now."

"All righty then, what should we call you then?"

"All my friends call me Buddy, so why don't you guys too."

"All right sir, I mean Buddy."

"Alright then. What's all the commotion about over here anyway?"

John jumped in. "We've got this knuckle head we're competing against and well," John turned toward Alex. "What gives with him, anyway? What burr did you shove up his butt to make him so mad at you?"

Buddy grabbed a chair and sat at the table with the two men. "This sounds good. What did you do?"

"Aw man." Alex rubbed his head. "It goes way back I can't even tell you how long this has been going on with him. It is the strangest thing. Where ever I go he seems to just show up. I just can't seem to get rid of him," he said and let out a long sigh. "We sort of grew up together. You know we were even friends at one time."

"Yick, you and Peach friends?"

"Peach? Is that the guy's name? What is he a fruit?" Buddy joked. "What's his assistants name Nectarine?"

John laughed.

Alex chuckled and continued. "No. He sort of warped. He's not a bad guy. When he was younger he was great to hang out with, but he changed in High School. He did whatever it took to be popular. He'd lie, cheat and steal if he had to. If he got caught he always found a way to wiggle his way out of it some how. He was Teflon man, nothing stuck to him."

"You'll be surprised at how small this Navy is and how everybody's got their Peaches to deal with. There are a lot of ambitious and self serving pukes with varying agendas. You've got to learn how to use them to your advantage and realize your own goals," Buddy said. "Have a plan to reach your goal, keep your cool when attacked. Pare the attack, counter attack with your original plan. Stick to the plan, if your adversary keeps you from accomplishing your plan, he wins. When guys lie and cheat to get what they want it can't stand up to . . . what's that old saying, Wooden ships with men of steel . . ."

"Will defeat steel ships manned by wooden men," Alex finished and laughed. "I just said that this morning when we greeted the new recruits."

"So what we going to do to beat him," John asked.

"I'm not sure yet, I'm more concerned about the fire fighting. I thought not being in the fleet would keep me from having to face fire again. I heard-"

"Heard what?" Cathreen said, as she came up from behind Alex and tickled his ribs.

Alex stood to greet his wife as did the other two men sitting at the table. "Oh nothing. Just some changes in the training schedule," Alex said. He kissed his wife of four years. He pulled out a chair for her and then scooted it in when she sat down. "Cat this Captain, I mean Buddy Orr. He's the new assistant manager and bartender here. Buddy this is my wife Cathreen."

Cat extended her hand to Buddy and he took it and kissed it. "Such a beautiful thing and a Petty Officer too. Alex she's lovely."

Cat's face glowed, "Thank you," she said, breathy and astonished. "Captain?"

"Captain Bernard Orr, retired at your service," Buddy said as he sat down. "My friends call me Buddy."

"Maybe we should call you Casanova," Alex interjected.

"Thank you, Buddy," Cat said as she too sat down. "Hi John,"

"Hey Cat. How's it going in the real Navy?"

"Fine," she said. Cat looked at Alex's somber and expressionless face. She pursed her lips and touched his hand. "What's wrong honey?"

"The old man is changing the training schedule," Alex said and looked over at Buddy. "Sorry sir."

"I understand. I know what you young bucks call us old goats."

Alex continued, "They want us to do twice as much work in half the time."

"What's the matter with that? Extra work never bothered you before." Both men would not look her in the eye and stared at the table. "That's not all. Alright what is it?"

"Answer the lady. Besides I want to know too," Buddy piped up.

John looked at Alex and saw he wasn't going to say it so he decided to spill the beans. "Firefighting has been extended to a week and company commanders are required to do the training. They are also-" Alex punched John in the arm. "Ow."

"They're making the mass conflagration drill the final test for all companies. If we don't pass, the entire company is set back a week and will be ineligible for the *Double Salute*," Alex said.

Cat stood to her feet and the chair banged to the floor. "My gosh Alex, can you do it?" She said horrified.

"I guess I'll have to. What else am I going to do? If I don't, I could forget about ever being an officer." He muttered and then looked down at the table in disgust.

"Hey chin up there Alex," Buddy said. "What happened to my man of steel."

John and Cat filled Buddy in with an occasional point of correction by Alex about the accident aboard the *Ingersoll*.

"Alex I'm no shrink, but I've seen some heroic action by men under my command and the aftermath of their action. Many of them recovered because they made a choice to not let it derail them or there plans."

Alex looked up from the floor at the wiry captain laying his wisdom on him. "Thank you sir. I appreciate that very much."

John slapped him on the back. "Cheer up old buddy. Maybe we can win the Cheerio flag, but I-"

Alex sat straight up and his eyes widened. "What did you say?"

"I said maybe we can win the Cheerio flag."

"What's the Cheerio flag?" Cat interjected.

"Captain's Cup. It's an athletic competition. Whoever wins gets the Olympic flag-" Alex said.

"And 500 points toward your cumulative score," John said.

"Why didn't I think of this before? But how are we going to win the Iron Man competition. We never have any really gifted athletes. That's the one we've got to win in order to have a shot at the rag."

"How 'bout that goofy kid with the southern drawl hanging from his lip? What's his name?"

"Keller. You notice he's built like an M1 Abrams tank," Alex said.

"He is a little dingy. I'm not sure he's got all his oars in the water. You think he's smart enough to pull this off. The other thing too, he's not doing real good in any of the other training. He might not make it. We might have to ASMO him back a couple of weeks if he doesn't shape up."

"He's perfect," Alex said. "He could be the key to beating Peach."

"Peach!" Cat said. "What the heck is he doing still pushing boots? I thought he went to MTD."

"I told you he was being groomed for MTD. I never said he-" Alex said and then paused. The wheels turned in his head while he thought.

"What?" Cat said.

Alex put a finger in the air. "Something is not stirring the Kool-aid here. I'm not sure but I think we're being-"

"What," Cat asked again.

Alex shook his head. "I need to think about it a little more and then I'll let you know." He cleared his throat. "This is the last class for Peach, he's being considered for chief and if he gets it he is off to MTD."

"Knowing our luck he probably would be our inspector every event," John interjected.

"If he hadn't gotten away with that garbage on *Ingersoll*, you'd be moving over to MTD instead of him. He is such a pain in my-"

"Cat!" Alex exclaimed. "You were getting ready to cuss like a sailor."

She lifted her hand to smack Alex. He put up his arms to playfully cower from her aggression. "I am a sailor, you ninny. Buddy will you talk some sense into these two lunk heads."

"These boys are doing just fine," Buddy said. He rocked back in his chair and rubbed his chin and relished the banter between the two young petty officers.

Alex and John chuckled.

"If we win the Cheerio rag, we could beat Peach. John, I want to see Keller first thing in the morning."

CHAPTER 4: PLOTTINGS

While we are sleeping, two-thirds of the world is plotting to do us in. -
Dean Rusk

Steaming hot water ran down the outline of a tall, well sculpted young body with thick tree trunk legs and broad shoulders. Seaman Recruit Keller planted his hands on the wall, dropped his head to let scalding water run down his neck and body. Another figure cut through the fog and started the shower next to him.

"Morning Keller," Thompson croaked.

"Morning," Keller gurgled. He turned around and leaned up against the wall and took a handful of water and splashed his face. "What in the world, did I get myself into? All they do is yell at us. I've been so wound up that I can't even take a dump."

"I know what you mean, man. I can't eat, that chow hall food turns my stomach, every time I go in there. The powdered eggs are awful."

"I feel like I'm being beaten like a tired old mule," Keller said.

"I'm just tired," Thompson complained. "Getting up at 4:00 AM every day is sure getting old."

Keller thumped his head against the wall, "I'm not paranoid, but I think they're out to get me and I . . ."

From the thick cloud of steam a voice boomed into the showers. "Keller, are you in there?" John said.

Keller took a step from the wall and clicked his heels together. "There's no place like home, there's no place like home." He held his breath for a moment and hoped the growling commander would go away, but through the steam Keller saw John's big frame in the doorway.

"You're not in Kansas any more Toto, you're in this man's Navy now. Get your butt in uniform. Petty Officer Sievers wants to see you in his office, on the double."

"Aye sir," Keller said and shot Thompson a worried look. "What now?" He muttered to himself as he wrapped a towel around his thick frame.

Alex stared out the window of his cramped office. His feet were up on the beat up gray steel desk. He studied a Blue Jay working on its nest in a tree adjacent to his office. A knock at the door broke his concentration; he plopped his legs down and straightened up in his chair. He cleared his throat, "Come." He shuffled some papers to make himself look like he was doing something important.

The door opened and banged the wall. "You asked to see me sir," Seaman Recruit Keller said.

Alex rocketed out of his chair and exploded on the recruit, "Is that the way you've been taught to enter this office."

"No sir,"

"I'm sorry recruit," Alex said barely audible and then yelled back at him "I can't seem to hear you."

"No sir," Keller said a little bit louder.

"Louder."

"No sir," he yelled.

"Louder."

"No sir," he yelled at the top of his lungs and then his voiced cracked.

"That's better. Now do it right."

Keller backed up one step and shut the door and pounded on the door three times. "Request permission to enter the company commander's office sir."

"Enter," Alex yelled at the door.

Keller opened the door and took three paces, made a left face and stood at attention.

"Good morning Petty Officer Sievers, Seaman Recruit Keller, Company 197 reporting as ordered sir," he said as loud as he could without yelling.

"What's that? Alex yelled. "I'm having trouble hearing you again."

Keller clenched his fist and gritted his teeth, widened his eyes and shouted so loud the barracks next door heard him, "Good morning Petty Officer Sievers, Seaman Recruit Keller, Company 197 reporting as ordered sir."

Alex bristled at that one, "That's good," he said to himself.

Keller picked a spot over Alex's shoulder to focus his attention on and not look him in the eye.

"What is your second general order, Recruit?" Alex snapped at him.

"To walk my post in a military manner, keeping always on the alert and observing every . . . everything . . . uh . . .uh, around me." Keller looked at Alex for help.

"At ease, recruit."

Keller snapped his hands together behind his back and thrust his left foot out.

Alex took a moment to do a visual inspection of Cade Keller. A baby faced nineteen year old with hands like catchers mitts. His chair squeaked when he turned to look out at the bird again. "Blue Jays are loud, obnoxious, cocky birds and attract attention wherever they go." Alex whirled the chair and pounded the desk. "I want to crush a Blue Jay."

Keller swallowed hard and his face contorted in confusion. "Sir," He said puzzled.

"Petty Officer McCarthy tells me you're falling behind in your training. And after the way you recited that General Order, he's right." Alex paused. "The swim lessons aren't going so well either."

Keller pursed his lips and shifted his weight to relieve some tension.

"But there is one bright spot," Alex said slow and soft. "Athletics." Alex stood to look him in the eye. "Because of the deficiencies in your training, I must make a decision. I have to consider what is best for this company. There are three things I can do for you. You can be ASMOed back two weeks and start the training all over with another company. Or you can be discharged and return to civilian life."

Alex watched the recruit's eye twitch and turned away when his eyes reddened with moisture.

"Sir, I can't-"

Not wanting to let him interrupt Alex held up his hand to silence him and sat back down. "I'll make a deal with you. I'll let you stay in the company, if," Alex paused again. "If you lead our team in the Captain's Cup competition. You're in better shape than anyone else."

Shocked and bewildered, "I. . . I don't know what to say. I try to take care of myself. I don't chew, smoke or drink."

"Then it's done. You'll lead the team."

"No sir. I can't."

Alex stood and bored holes into Keller with his eyes. "What do you mean, no sir, you can't?" Alex said in a stiff staccato.

"Permission to speak freely sir."

"Granted," Alex said as he folded his arms.

"Sir, I. . . I don't know if I can do it. I crack under pressure. When I was a senior in High School, my football team, the White County Warriors was playing for the 8A-AAA State Championship against the Burke County Bears," Cade said. "In the final play of the game I caught the ball and was tackled on the one yard line. I stretched toward the end zone and couldn't get in. Everybody blamed me for losing that game, I even blamed me."

"So?" Alex said with a note of sarcasm. "What's the problem?"

"So, don't you see sir, I can't let them down."

"You said you caught the ball, right?"

"Yes sir, but what's that got to do with-" All of a sudden the light went on. "Anything," he said with a smile coming across his face.

"Just because you didn't get in the end zone doesn't mean you didn't make the play. It's not like you dropped the ball, you got tackled. They kept you from getting in for the score. Am I right?"

"Yes sir, that's right," Keller said.

"I'm not asking you to make a touchdown. I'm asking you to lead your company. It may require you to do some things only you can do, but that's being a leader."

"The whole company will be relying on me. I don't want to fail them."

"If you don't do it, you'll fail them and yourself. We need men in the Navy who will be courageous leaders and being willing to lay it all on the line. This is your chance." Alex gazed into his eyes and watched the turmoil and war going on inside his head.

Keller met Alex's gaze and looked into his reassuring eyes. He looked away and found the spot over Alex's shoulder again and then yielded to what he knew he must do. A smile crossed his face and he reengaged Alex's stare. "Alright Petty Officer Sievers I'll do it."

"You won't regret it." Alex thrust out his hand to him and Keller pumped it up and down.

"But what about the rest of the stuff you talked about? How am I-"

"Going to get through the rest of the training? I got that figured out too," Alex sighed. He walked around his desk and opened up the office door and Seaman Thompson stood just outside the door. "Seaman Thompson is going to tutor you and help you pass all your inspections."

Keller smiled at Thompson.

"You're dismissed," Alex said. He started to walk out the door. "Keller." He stopped and looked at his company commander. "Don't let me down."

"Y'all don't worry about nothing, Thompson and I will get it done."

Dust danced in the rays of sunlight streaming in through the wooden shudders cracked opened just a bit. Captain Callaghan, stone faced, sat behind the large cherry colored mahogany desk. Behind him, a credenza flanked by an American flag and a US Navy flag.

The US Navy flag, authorized by executive order 10812 on April 24, 1959 by President Dwight D. Eisenhower is dark blue, trimmed by a yellow fringe and bore the seal of the United States Navy and a yellow scroll with the words United States Navy imprinted on it.

On the table is a brass ship's bell from his first command the *USS Charles P. Cecil* (DDR-835) home ported in New London, CT. He received the ships bell from the crew when the ship was decommissioned in 1979 and sold to the country of Greece. His desk also bore pictures of his wife, children and grand children. Two winged back chairs stood at attention in front of his desk. In the corner a black suit coat with four gold bars a half inch wide and a star on the cuffs and five rows of ribbons, three abreast hung on a coat rack. On the top of the rack was a white combination cap with a gold chin strap attached with gold buttons, a black felt peak embroidered with gold oak leaves and acorns. The cap also bore the officers crest device, a silver federal shield over two crossed gold fouled anchors.

On the dark paneled walls, hung a United States Naval Academy diploma, awards and commendations. In the most preeminent position on the wall, a large picture of President Ronald Reagan shaking his hand at the White House.

The captain's large frame sat motionless while reading the reports on his desk. He is dressed in a white shirt decorated with black shoulder boards with an embroidered gold star and four bars. He rubbed his graying temple to relieve the stress and then picked up a crystal glass of water and then banged it on the desk. He mashed the intercom button. "Miss Wylot, have the Executive Officer come to my office immediately."

"Yes sir," the intercom squawked back at him.

He sat back in his chair, swiveled to stare outside and gather his thoughts. Captain Callaghan sighed and sat erect when someone tapped the door. "Come in."

A short young man with light brown hair, white shirt, black tie and black trousers entered the office of *Recruit Training Command's* Commanding Officer. "Sir, you sent for me."

The captain stood up and beckoned to him with his hand. "Come in. That was fast."

"Happened to be passing by," Commander Jim Talon said while sitting down in one of the wing backed chairs.

"I just received word that the Secretary of the Navy will be attending the graduation ceremony for the first class to receive the *Double Salute*. He read the article in the Navy Times about my plan to reinstate it."

"I read that too, *The Revival of Navy Tradition*. Good article. I think the writers name was Russell Geiss."

The captain continued, "He wants to personally congratulate the company that receives it. He started his naval career right here in Great Lakes. He was the Rpock of a company that won the *Double Salute*."

"Really?" Jim said.

"Really," the captain parroted back to him. "And I've got a problem. For all I know we could have a bunch of scrubs for company commanders in that class. Now I want to make sure none of them embarrass me on graduation day."

"Then what do you suggest we do about it?"

"I want you to get all the service jackets on all the commanders, review them for me and then brief me on each one of them."

"Aye sir."

A group of recruits, dressed in light blue chambray shirts with dungarees are seated on the floor between two rows of bunk beds. Alex and John stood in front of the group dressed in their all black uniforms with a black tie and red rope around the left shoulder.

"Gentlemen we are heading into the most difficult part of your training. You're going too be graded as you undergo several inspections. We can receive up to 4000 points for each inspection cycle. There are four areas you will be graded on: scholastic achievement, military appearance, athletic achievement and the most coveted, drill."

Alex backed up to the black board behind him and pointed to the picture of the 'S' flag with a scroll and a quill in the center of the 'S'. "You can earn up to three 'S' flags. You'll be taking classes on skills required for duty in the fleet, such as: Navy time, watch standing, command organization of ships and other Navy units, Uniform Code of Military Justice and in the history, courtesies, customs, ships, uniforms and awards of the Navy."

He took a step backward and pointed to the 'A' flag. Which was an 'A' enclosed in a circle. "We will definitely win all these. When we do then we will qualify for the Captain's Cup competition and a shot at the Olympic Flag and an additional 500 points to our overall score."

Alex took another step back and tapped the blackboard with his index finger. "These are the easy ones. You just have to look good for this one and fold your clothes and make a tight bunk."

Once again he stepped back and sighed when he did. "Now this is the toughest one to get of all three. The third one is called Old Yellow, but we like to call it, 'Old Yella'. He pointed to a picture of a M1 Carbide crossing a cutlass. "These are the drill flags. The entire company will have to work as one well oiled machine to snag this rag. You will move the M1 through a series of motions in complete synchronization."

Alex stepped around the table in front of the blackboard and sat on the corner. "If we can attain the highest score in the graduation class we can win the *Double Salute*." The recruits looked at each other to see if anybody knew what he was talking about. "We will repeat all the inspections three times and try to attain the best score. The *Double Salute* is given to the company that rises to the top of the class." Alex nodded at John.

John straightened and walked in front of the recruits. "What does it mean to you and why should you care about winning this award? You would have the distinction of being the first company to win it in 20 years and it also means an extra day of liberty on graduation weekend."

The room erupted in conversation. He put up his hands to quiet them down. "The Secretary of the Navy will be in attendance and what a way to start your Navy careers."

Seaman Shuster, a red hair freckled face youth of 18 years old, put his hand up to ask a question. "Shuster," John said.

"Why are they doing it after suspending it for 20 years?" Shuster said.

Alex stepped forward to answer the question. "Tradition. It is a way to instill values and to set a standard to live by. When a tradition is forgotten you float away from the standard that the foundation for a great organization is built on, like the Navy. Because of the political fall out of war in Vietnam, tradition became a casualty of the pressure to train military personnel quickly. With the dismissal of traditions, standards began to lapse and the Navy weakened. The idea is to reinstate the traditions and make the Navy stronger. Company 197 is going to be the first to claim it."

The room grew silent and Alex leaned up against one of the bunks. "You know," he said. "With all your families and girlfriends coming in for graduation weekend, I'd think you'd want to have the whole weekend instead of having to report back to the base every night."

They all laughed and started talking again.

"So let's go out there and win it."

"Yes sir," Company 197 resounded back to Alex.

Jim Talon, Executive Officer, *Recruit Training Command* sat in the winged back chair with his legs crossed and the personnel file of Wayne 'Hatch' Harris.

"You'll get a kick out of this guy, Captain."

Captain Callaghan wiggled his finger for Jim to pass him the file. "Let me see that."

"Probably will never make Chief. He's been in and out of trouble his whole career," Jim said and laughed. "Stupid things though, but the best one was when he was on the *USS Tripoli*. He welded the skippers escape scuttle shut after the captain yanked a stripe for an Unauthorized Absence (UA) charge. Took another after that little incident. The guy still managed to make E-6 somehow."

The captain tossed Hatch's service jacket back at Jim. "How'd he get in here with all that trouble?"

"I don't know sir. Maybe somebody over in the detailer's office wanted to help him salvage his career and get a fresh start."

"Definitely not him," Captain Callaghan said. "What else you got?"

Jim opened the next folder in the stack. "Electronics Technician First Class, Alex Sievers. Been in for 10 years and spent his whole career at sea until coming here. His evaluations are stellar and he has applied for LDO.

Since being here at RTC he's graduated above average companies, but never had a company finish first. He was severely burned in a shipboard fire trying to save a shipmate."

The captain rocked back in his chair. "Sounds like a hero."

"Not quite. He was found negligent of the fire and the death of the man he was trying to save."

"How? Why? That doesn't make any sense. Does it say anymore?"

"The report doesn't go into any great detail."

The captain rubbed his chin and leaned over to take the file folder from his XO. "I remember hearing about this when I was at Pearl," The Captain said as he read the report. "I talked to the skipper of that boat and well, that's not what he told me. Ah, I don't have time for that. Maybe we'll come back to him." He slid the folder across the desk and sat back. "Who else you got?"

"This guy looks pretty good," Jim said with a raised eyebrow. "He's up for chief, but because of his rating being overloaded probably won't make chief any time soon. He's graduated all his companies at the top of their class. He is being considered for transfer to MED. His record is impeccable, but his evaluations say his method is a little unconventional."

"What's his name?"

"Petty Officer First Class Rodney Peach."

The captain leaned forward in his chair. "Wasn't he mentioned in the report in the Sievers incident?" Captain Callaghan asked.

"I think so." Jim opened up Alex's folder, found the report and scanned with his finger. "Here it is. He was mentioned as a witness at the inquiry into the fire on board *Ingersoll*. His division officer says he doesn't play well with the other commanders especially Sievers."

"Sound's like we got ourselves a little bad blood in the ranks," The Captain said.

"Do you want me to have one of them reassigned?"

"No, no. Don't do that." The Captain smiled slyly. "We can use this. Let's let them duke it out and let's see who's left standing. Maybe even tilt the scales a little."

The Rpock for 197 stood motionless in his Cracker Jack blue uniform with a dixie cup white hat squared on his head. A black silk scarf tightly rolled and tied in a perfect square knot peeked out from the flap on the back of the uniform. At parade rest his polished dress shoes were in alignment with his broad shoulders. His left hand in the small of his back and his right hand holding a clip board at his side ready to record any discrepancies in Company 197's first Personnel Inspection.

The rest of Company 197 stood like statues at parade rest in front of the rows of bunk beds. Voices were heard approaching from the lounge adjacent to the barracks. When the first company commander entered the room the Rpock snapped to attention. "Attention on deck," he shouted to the rest of the company. In one united movement the company snapped to attention. The Rpock snapped the Military Training Department Inspector (MTD) a crisp salute who entered the room with Alex and John. The black uniformed Chief Petty Officer returned the salute. "Sir, Company 197, standing by for your inspection," The Rpock said in a stiff staccato.

"Very Well," The Chief said. He gave the Rpock a quick inspection by looking him up and down. "Ok, who's first?"

The Rpock led him to the front of the room to the first recruit to be inspected. The inspector gave the recruit a quick glance then focused on the white hat and measured with two fingers the distance between the cap and the man's eye brows. He nodded and then took the ends of the neckerchief in each hand and pulled it tight to see if they matched. He let it go and examined the knot to insure it pointed in the right direction. The inspector turned to Alex, "The neckerchief is my pet peeve. Not too many people can tie it right for the first inspection." He nodded to the recruit. "Good knot," he said.

Then the inspector looked at the right side of the recruit's neck and then the left, then back to the right. Then he repeated the procedure and turned to the Rpock, "Hit him on shave."

"Yes sir," the Rpock said and he wrote down 'shave' next to the man's name.

The inspector turned to Alex and said, "He needs to stand a little closer to his razor next time." The inspector took the young man's face in his hand and turned it so Alex could see his neck. "Look." Alex leaned in and played along. "There's no blood."

Alex and John snickered, shot each other a playful look and shook their heads.

After the last recruit was inspected the MTD Inspector held out his hand to the Rpock. The Rpock removed a sheet of pure white paper and handed it to the outstretched hand. The inspector headed toward Alex's office with the two commanders in tow. He took the seat behind the desk, while Alex sat in front and John closed the door to the office, also sitting down. The MTD totaled the scores, while Alex and John studied his face for any indication about how they did. Once the inspector finished, he leaned back in the chair which let out a bone clattering shriek making the two commanders cringe.

"Well gentlemen," the inspector said grimly. Alex leaned closer to the desk and relaxed his furrowed brow when the corners of the inspector's mouth turned up in a smile. "Best company I've seen all day."

Alex and John's sighed in relief. They turned and then high fived each other.

The inspector stood. "You're lucky you got me first. The next inspection won't go as well."

The puzzled look on Alex's face said what his mouth could not.

"But you didn't hear that from me."

"I don't understand," Alex said.

"I don't agree. I don't like politics," The inspector said grimly. "With what they're doing and . . . that's all I'm going to say." He pursed his lips and started to the door to leave.

"Tell me, what's going on. I won't tell anybody I heard it from you."

The inspector paused at the door and shook his head. "I can't."

"C'mon man."

"Track the scores," the inspector said and then walked out.

Alexis Althorne, typed a quick paced staccato in the Division

Commander's office. Her crystal blue eyes darted back and forth from the steno pad to the screen of the word processor. The steady click of her finger nails droned on with out missing a beat. A wide smile spread across her well made up face revealing her perfect gleaming teeth. "Alex Sievers! My this is a very small Navy. I didn't know you were stationed here."

"Hi Lexi," Alex said surprised.

She stood, came around the desk to hug him. "How have you been Alex?"

"Fine and you?" Alex said and returned the hug. "How long have you been here?"

"I'm fine. I've been here about six months."

"How come I haven't seen you around?" Alex asked.

"I was over at main side in the admiral's office and just transferred over today."

"That's great."

She took a step closer to him. In a low sexy voice said, "Maybe we can get together tonight." She raised her eyebrows, "And get reacquainted."

Alex took a step backward, cleared his throat and pointed to his wedding ring. "Only if my wife can come along."

"Wife, oh," she said like she'd been bitten by a snake.

"You remember Cathreen Jeffries?"

"My old roommate?" Alexis said. "Robbing the cradle, aren't you Alex?"

"She is only two years younger than me. We hooked up in San Diego. We dated for about a year and then got married. I thought you were getting married to that bozo, what's his name?"

"I don't know who you're talking about," Alexis said folding her arms.

This time Alex took a step closer and put his face right up to hers. "Aw C'mon Lexi. You know who I'm talking about, the jerk you dumped me for."

"If you hadn't gone to another ship after your time was up on the *Buchanan*." Her eyes flashed with anger. "Maybe we could've worked something out. I didn't want to be a West Pac widow you know."

Suddenly an idea flashed in her head, she quieted herself and moved a little closer to him. Her perfume flooded his nostrils and his face softened. "You know Alex we had something special and well maybe we can-"

"I . . . don't think so Lexi." He took a defensive posture and stiffened to her. He handed her some papers. "Give these to Commander Hendrick."

She took the papers and flashed a mischievous smile, "See ya round sailor." Alex spun on his heel and made a bee-line for the door.

CHAPTER 5: CAT CALLS IN THE NIGHT

I love the man that can smile in trouble, that can gather strength from distress, and grow brave by reflection. 'Tis the business of little minds to shrink, but he whose heart is firm, and whose conscience approves his conduct, will pursue his principles unto death. - Thomas Paine

A black silhouette stood above the refueling hose aboard the *USS Ingersoll*. The specter heaved an ax at the cable release for the refueling probe. Over and over the frantic figure clanked the ax against the cable. Fuel streamed on to the deck from the probe soaking the dark figure.

Behind the desperate man, another silhouette emerged from the blinding light. An orange glow smoldered in the mouth of the large framed dark outline. "Sievers," a sinister voice said. "You think you can beat me?"

Alex stiffened and gazed at the form. "I will win," he shouted through defiant clenched teeth.

"Win. Ha. I own you. Your destiny lies with me forever in-" The figure took the cigar from his mouth and held it high so Alex could see the cherry glow and then shot a glance at the fuel around his knees then back at the shadow. The ominous figure flicked the ember and yelled, "Hell."

The fuel flashed and Alex's clothes lit like a torch. He screamed and sat straight up in his bed crazy with panic. "Put it out. Put it out," he screamed and beat his body to put the flames out.

"Alex!" Cat yelled and grabbed him. "It's just a dream. It's me Cat."

He rubbed his head and examined the scars on his arms and tried to compose himself. He wiped the sweat from his bare chest with his pillow. "The dream, it's coming back," he said. "And it's worse."

She put her hand on his shoulder to try and comfort him. "What can be worse?"

Alex explained for about five minutes and then put the pillows behind his back. Cat propped herself up on her arm to listen. "What do you think it means?"

"I don't know. It's like whenever I get close to success things get weird."

"I don't understand."

"Success runs when it sees me coming." He held up his thumb an index finger about an inch apart. "I'm always this close and then boom."

"Boom," Cat echoed back to him.

"Yeah Boom. Everything blows up in my face," Alex said. "*Ingersoll*, is a great example. I'm suppose to be Command advanced. Boom. Blows up in my face. I can't forgive myself for what happened to that kid. I should've-"

"Should've, what?" Cat shot back at him. "How many times do I need to say this, you did all you could do. We've been over this a hundred times. Let it go, stop beating yourself up."

"No. I . . . I think there is something more to this. I've had some crazy things happen to me in my life and never had things haunt me like this. No . . . no, this is different Cat. This is a pivotal moment in my life. I hate to use the cliché, but it is going to make me or break me."

"Can you be a little more specific, I'm not following you."

"It is a fork in the road. One way is the path to greatness and the other to ruin. I feel like if I mess this up there will never be another chance."

"What's standing in the way?"

"Fear."

"You, afraid? You're the ultimate daredevil, you're fearless."

"This is different, it is almost real. It is almost alive, so alive I can touch it."

"I've always seen greatness in you Alex. You've got to embrace what happened and let it change your thought process to where you see yourself winning and attaining your goal," she said then paused "And second, you've got to let Mattingly go."

"You're right, but it's crystallized in my mind and I don't know if I can ever let it go." Alex paused for a moment. "Cat, I'm scared."

Cat probed him with her eyes for a moment, then wrapped her arms around him and squeezed him tight. "You've been very distant and I hardly get to see you." Tears welled up in her eyes. "I worry about you. It's been a long time since you've told me how you felt."

She wiped the tears with her hand and then reached over him to the night-stand for a tissue. He took her hand and kissed is gently. "Honey, I know this has been hard on you. I thought this would be the best place for us, but I had no idea it would turn into such a mess." Alex readjusted and bounced like a kid on Christmas morning. "What do you say we go away for the weekend? I'll get John to cover Friday night and we'll take off to the lake and get a suntan."

Cat slapped his chest. "Are you planning to lay out in 40 degree weather?"

"Yeah I guess your right. Bob Chambers would. We can still rent a cabin for the weekend and relax for a couple of days. The past few weeks have been grueling and is wearing me out this might help get my head screwed on straight."

"You're on," Cat said with a smile.

Alex took her into his arms and pressed his lips against her and hugged her tightly.

In the company commander's lounge Alex, John and Hatch discussed the results of yesterday's inspection.

"So, how did it go Hatch?" Alex said.

Hatch rubbed his head and furrowed his brow. "We got killed. LaRusso didn't shave, Fisco's knot was backward, Leahy didn't have his ID card in his pocket and well Adams was a total knucklehead."

"So. How did you do?" John asked.

Hatch raised a fist and pursed his lips. "One of these days Dorothy. Pow! Over the rainbow for you." Hatch turned to Alex, "What happened with you guys?"

Alex rocked back in his chair and examined his thumb nail. "We got the three rags and beat Peach like a drum."

"Hot dog, hop aboard," Hatch said and slapped Alex on the back. "Good for you Alex. I'm glad somebody is giving that arrogant son-of-a-gun a run for his money."

"Yeah, we kicked his pansy-" John stifled himself before he cussed and held up his big paw.

Alex high-fived John, "Yeah but we didn't beat him by much. Hatch, do me a favor and try to get as many commanders in the class to document their scores. Peach is up to something and I'm going to find out what it is."

"No problem. I've had an ax to grind with him, since we were on the *Tripoli*. He's the one who suggested I weld the captain's scuttle shut, then ratted me out when I did it," Hatch said through gritted teeth. "It amazes me how he's always making trouble where ever he goes, but never gets his goose fried." He shook his head.

"You didn't have to listen to him. You know."

"At the time I was so angry about losing my stripe, the idea seemed like a good one. Ah, the pitfalls of being young and stupid."

"You know if this had been five years ago, I might've taken him down to the weight room and made him into one of those Rock 'em Sock 'em Robots," John bellowed.

"Wasn't that the game, the two robots would punch each other until his head popped up?" Alex said, while he demonstrated by punching John.

"Yeah that's the one," John said to the table across the room. "And if you don't stop hitting me, I'm going to hit you so hard Hatch is going to feel it."

"Why not do it any way? What's different now?" Hatch inquired.

Alex rolled his eyes. "Oh brother, here we go."

John ignored Alex's comment. "I'm learning how to turn the other cheek," John said.

"Oh, I gotcha," Hatch said.

"John's a holy cow now."

"Holy Joe. Holy Joe. If you're going to insult me, please get it right."

Hatch laughed at the two comedians.

"Holy Joe now," Alex said with no emotion. "Please don't get him started Hatch. I've got too much to think about right now."

"Listen here transceivers, you ought to be thinking about this. You don't know when your number's going to be up and then it's barbecue city for you," John shot back at him.

Alex rolled his eyes again and put his hands in the air in surrender. "Save it John. That man I tried to rescue was a Christian. Why didn't God save him?" Alex waved his hands in disgust. "Never mind, don't answer that. I don't really care any way."

Hatch could see trouble brewing so he said, "Any who, what's next on the schedule."

Glad to change the subject, Alex jumped right in. "We're gunning for Old Yella on Monday. I've got the weekend off, so John will be working with the kiddies all weekend."

"I bet you don't know this but somebody is gunning for you," John said to Alex with a concerned look on his face. "And if you're not careful he may get you before it's too late."

A terror washed over Alex and his face went white as a sheet. His stomach constricted into a knot and he felt like someone jabbed a baseball bat in his gut.

High powered spot lights washed the fence line of *Recruit Training Command* with intense white light. Three massive drill halls where the companies practiced drilling lined the fence. A shore patrol jeep rumbled through the wooded area on the perimeter road around the base belching exhaust in the crisp spring evening. A pair of eyes watched the jeep creep away until it was out of sight. The silhouette stepped into the light and took a few cautious steps toward the fence. Dressed in recruit denim bell bottomed dungarees and blue chambray shirt the man jumped on the fence and spider-manned up it. At the top, he flipped himself over the fence and fell to the ground.

He landed hard on his right leg, "Agh." He tried to get up, but fell back to the ground in agony. He rested for a moment and hobbled to the woods just as the Shore Patrol jeep made a u-turn in the distance.

The parking lot in front of the Navy Exchange buzzed with traffic moving to and fro. The white Volkswagen Cabriolet eased through the myriads of people that walked to the main entrance to the Exchange. Cat watched a man get into his car, stopped and clicked her signal light on to wait for the space to open up. Once parked, she got out and locked the car.

"Cat, Cathreen Sievers," a female voice called to her.

Cathreen jerked her head around and her sunglasses slid down her nose. She looked over her glasses to see an attractive, well dressed woman approach her. Her face lit up, "Mary Lou McCarthy, what are you doing here?" Cat said surprised. She pushed up her glasses and greeted the woman with a hug. "You look nice today."

"Just came from a woman's breakfast at the church," Mary Lou said.

"Wow, sounds like fun," Cat said to make polite conversation. *Why did I say that?* She thought.

"You ought to come some time. We do it once a week."

Cat looked down at the ground to avoid Mary Lou's gaze. "I'm not much for church and well . . . I'm not sure . . . you see . . . I don't want to be made to wear a dress to come into a church."

"I'm sorry, did you say you don't want to wear a dress?"

"No. I said I don't want to be made to wear a dress to get inside," Cat mumbled and fumbled with her purse.

"Isn't a dress one of your uniforms?"

"Yes it is, but I don't think I should have to be made to wear one to go into a church."

"I'm sorry. I hope I didn't upset you," Mary Lou said. "It's not required.

We're not strict that way. Why?"

"When I was a teenager I tried to go into a church and one of the elders met me at the door and told me I couldn't come in."

Mary Lou's eyes widened and her mouth dropped open. "No," she said astonished. "Why wouldn't he let you in?"

"He told me that I couldn't come in because I had pants on. He said women had to be in a dress to come into the house of the Lord," Cat said, folded her arms and turned her nose in the air tapping her foot.

Mary Lou put her hand to her shocked face. "I'm sorry darling, that must've made you feel real bad, but God's not like that man. He is gentle, kind and would never forbid someone to come into his house because of what they're wearing."

"Well I'm sorry Mary Lou, I vowed to never go back."

"I'm sorry too, Cat."

Cat cleared her throat and changed the subject. "Are you going in?" She asked and nodded to the entrance.

"Uh . . . yes. I have to pick up John's new uniforms at the Exchange. Are you going into the Exchange?"

"No. I'm going into the Commissary to pick up some groceries."

"You and Alex need to come over some night."

"Yeah. Maybe."

An awkward silence came over the two ladies as they walked to the entrance and then parted inside the exchange complex. Once alone she found a place to sit for a moment. *Oooh those religious fanatics make me so mad. Thought I'd forgotten all about that.* She opened her purse and found a tissue and dabbed the corners of her eyes. *But there is something I like about her. She's always so happy. Why?* While she sat there thinking, nausea washed over her. *That's the third time today. What is going on?* She shook it off and walked into the store.

The men of Company 197 were scattered through out the barracks doing different things before it was time to get in their racks for the night. Some read others wrote letters and while others sat on the floor in groups having a few laughs. The Rpock sat in a chair in front of his rack spit polishing his shoes. When Alex stepped in, the Rpock stood and yelled, "Attention on deck."

The entire company scrambled to their feet and stood at attention.

"At ease, gentlemen," Alex said. "Gather round."

The recruits came to the front of the room and sat or stood. Behind Alex, another recruit stood with a sea bag. Alex held up his hands to quiet the company down. "Alright guys, settle down. I'd like you all to meet Kevin Galardi, he's the newest member of our company. He's been reassigned to our company and will need to be brought up to speed on what we are doing here. Rpock," Alex said.

"Yes sir," the Rpock snapped to attention.

"Find Recruit Galardi a rack and bedding."

"Yes sir," The Rpock said and led the new recruit to his rack. "Follow me."

"The rest of you men," Alex said. "Go to bed. Taps in 10 minutes and don't forget to welcome Recruit Galardi to the company."

The men broke up and headed back to their racks. Thompson elbowed Keller in the ribs, "Hey man. Ain't he the dude who jumped the fence the other night? Name sure sounds familiar."

"I have no clue. I'm just struggling to keep my head above water here. I have no time for anybody else," Keller said. "How did you find out anyway?"

"Remember the other night, when I had to stand watch. We got a message says, some dude jumped the fence and was picked up by shore patrol on the strip trying to buy some clothes," Thompson said. "I don't remember the guys name, but it sounds like the same guy."

Keller sat down on his bunk and looked right through Thompson while he rambled on.

"Don't you care?"

"Not really. I'm bushwhacked. How much longer until lights out?"

"Five minutes."

"Great, that means we can get in our racks now. See you tomorrow," Keller said and ambled back to his rack in the back of the room.

The Rpock led Galardi to the back of the room to the rack by the rifle storage unit. He tossed his sea bag up on the top bunk and bumped into Keller, who was trying to get into his rack. "Watch out man," Keller exclaimed.

"I'm sorry man," Galardi said.

"You'll have to stow your gear and put it away tomorrow. I'll help you make your rack up. Lights out in a couple of minutes."

"Thanks dude," Galardi said with a California surfer accent.

"You a surfer," Keller asked from the bottom bunk.

"Yeah dude, west coast."

"Where on the coast?" The Rpock inquired.

"San Diego," Galardi responded.

"Really. What part of San Diego?"

"I lived in Ocean Beach," Galardi said. "I lived on a hill overlooking Sunset Cliffs. Used to go down every morning to the cliffs with my board and surf for a couple hours." He paused for a moment and a lump knotted in his throat. He cleared his throat and changed the subject. "You from there too?"

"Yep. Grew up in Carlsbad," The Rpock said and then threw the blanket on the bed just as the PA system crackled.

"Taps, taps. Lights out. The smoking lamp is now out. Taps." As soon as the announcement was finished the lights snapped off.

The Rpock whispered to Galardi, "I'll see you tomorrow. If you need anything I'm up front and I'm sure Keller here can help you out. Welcome aboard." And he plodded off to his rack.

Galardi undressed, hopped up into his rack and covered his head with a pillow. He tried to keep from shaking the bed as he wept quietly in the lonely darkness.

Keller heard. *I'm such a jerk, I should've been a little nicer to that guy. Lord please forgive me. This guy needs your help, let him sleep and give him peace. If there's anything I can do let me know.*

Cathreen sat with a novel in her lap and waited for Alex to arrive.

With out warning, the room whirled around her, the queasiness she'd been feeling all day tied her stomach into a knot and threatened to explode. She made it to the bathroom in time to empty the contents of her stomach. Once her body stopped the gut wrenching spasms, she wilted on the tile.

She gathered herself off the floor when she heard the deadbolt click. After she washed her face, she checked her look in the mirror. "I've looked better," she said to the mirror.

"Cat," Alex called from the living room.

"Just a minute," she said and mustered her strength. She took another second to smooth her hair and went out to greet him.

When she opened the door to the bathroom Alex had already come in and had pulled his tie off. "Aw man, I'm beat," he said over his shoulder as he sat down on the edge of the bed to remove his shoes. "You don't mind if I go right to bed?"

"Have you eaten?" Cat said. "Do you want me to make you something?"

"No, I got something before I left the base."

Cat slipped under the down comforter, glad for the lack of conversation. The after effects of the vomiting abated, she closed her eyes, slipped into a dreamy fog and never heard Alex say good night.

The groaning of the bunk above Keller's head prompted him to ascend through the layers of the deep sleep he had slipped into. When he entered back into the world of reality, he listened for a reason for why he'd awoken. All he could hear was the steady breathing of other recruits around him.

Now awake, his bladder called for relief. He got up to relieve himself and as he entered the bathroom his mind struggled to grapple with what he saw. Seaman Galardi stood on a toilet with a sheet around his neck and the other end tied to an over head pipe. Keller's eyes widened when he saw him step off the toilet and the sheet go taught. "No," Keller said and lunged to grab the man.

Galardi pounded Keller's head with his fists. "Let me go. I want to die."

Keller reached through Galardi's flailing arms and grabbed the sheet. With all his might he yanked the sheet free from the water pipe. When the tension let go, Keller and Galardi fell to the floor. Galardi fell on Keller and continued to pummel him with his fists. Keller, being the bigger of the two, threw the scrawny little recruit off and hopped up with both fists clenched.

"What the heck are you doing, dude?" Galardi spat at him.

"Trying to save you from yourself you nut," Keller retorted.

"Well I don't want your stinking help, man. Just go back to your bunk and let me die in peace."

"Are you crazy man? You think I'm just going to leave you in here to do yourself in. I don't think so man."

"You don't care about me just like everybody else in this stinking world doesn't," Galardi shot back at him. "This whole life sucks and this Navy sucks."

"How do you know I don't care? You don't even know me."

"I don't have to know you, to know that you'll probably bail on me too."

"If the whole world hates you, what the heck are you doing here anyway?"

"My old man told me I had to come in the Navy or I'd have to leave his house."

"I don't understand," Keller said. He put his fists down and tried to make sense.

"My dad has been in the Navy since Moby Dick was a minnow. He's a Master Chief on the Air Craft Carrier Abraham Lincoln. He's been nominated to fill the Master Chief Petty Officer of the Navy's job. He hasn't been around for me much. He's spent a lot of time at sea. Whenever he is in port we just got into a lot of fights. He came back from a West Pac Cruise and I got picked up on the base for underage drinking. He goes ballistic and tells me its time for me to pack my sea bag and ship out."

"How old are you?" Keller inquired.

"Seventeen."

"Whew, isn't that a little young to join the Navy?"

"I thought so, but my dad went to the Navy Recruiter with me and signed the papers giving me permission to join. He didn't care; he joined up when he was sixteen."

"So why are you trying to commit suicide?"

"I hate my father and I want to embarrass him. I figured if it gets out that his son is a screw up then it will maybe ruin his career. I tried to go UA and they caught me in town. I thought maybe my Mom would understand and help me out with some cash or something. When I called her and told her what I did, she was appalled. She kept telling me how this would embarrass the family. I asked her not to tell Dad and she put him on the phone. He told me that if it had been time of war they could have shot me for being a deserter. I was devastated so I figured I'd do it for them." Galardi sat down on the floor and started to cry. He took a few moments to compose himself and then continued. "I didn't know what to do. I tried calling some friends, but they wanted nothing to do with me. I got picked up shortly after."

"So what did they do when they brought you back?"

"They told me I would be reassigned to another company and if I didn't shape up I'd be dishonorably discharged. And that's when I came to your company."

"So it's so bad that you want to commit suicide?"

"Yep," Galardi said flatly.

The two young sailors silently stared at each other for a few moments. Keller spoke first, "Do you want to know what I think?"

"Go ahead. Say what ever you want."

"Suicide, is a permanent solution to a temporary problem."

"What kind of psycho-babble are you trying to lay on me dude? Take your pad answer and shove it, because I don't need you or anybody else to tell me what's wrong with me," Galardi cursed him. "Now leave me alone so I can die."

Keller got up to leave and then stopped in the door way. "You are selfish twerp. This is not about your father or mother, this is about you.

Nobody cares for the little bitty baby boy. The big daddy doesn't, mama won't wipe the snot off your nose and the Navy doesn't love you either. It's all about you and you're little pity party. You against the world. Let me tell you buddy life is always going to suck if you have that kind of attitude."

After his speech, Keller turned and walked out and then returned with a *Blue Jackets Manual* and the Bible. "You are so focused on your self you have no clue what you have the chance to be part of. This company is going to make history here at RTC." Keller held up the manual. "This is the *Blue Jackets Manual* and it tells you everything you need to know about how to be a successful sailor. And this is the Bible and it tells you everything you need to know about how to be a successful person. Why don't you stop feeling sorry for yourself and be the man your Daddy knows you can be. Read these books learn them and do what they say."

Galardi glared at Keller, but no words came to his mind. After a long time, he stood up and held out his hand to Keller. "Alright, tell me all about it."

CHAPTER 6: MERCURY RISING

Secrecy involves a tension which, at the moment of revelation, finds its release. - Georg Simmel

Brilliant sunlight filtered through the Venetian blinds arousing Cathreen from her slumber. She forced one eye open to check the time, "Nine o'clock." She threw off the comforter and catapulted out of bed. Nauseam and dizziness greeted her after two steps causing her to fall back with a *poof* into bed. She rolled over and moaned, "Must be the flu. I'll sleep a little while longer. No duty today," she said and squeezed her eyes shut willing the sick feeling away.

Before she could get back to sleep, an awful taste filled her mouth and the pressure of a bladder needing to be emptied forced her into the bathroom. With eyes shut she felt for the toothpaste, but was no where to be found. She knelt and opened the cabinet under the sink to get a new tube and the nausea washed over her again. When she looked in the cabinet, she saw the home pregnancy test kit she'd bought last year. She longed for children, but the transfer from San Diego to Great Lakes was tougher than expected, so they decided to wait.

"I wonder if I'm-" she said. Cathreen rocked back off her knees, sat on the floor and stared at the pink box. She studied the box for a long time. The information the box would share with her would change her life forever. She wrestled with the possibility of being pregnant and all that went with it. Her conflicting emotions paralyzed her until a desire to know gushed from deep within her. She grabbed the box, tore it open and read the instructions. "Oh my gosh."

Cathreen proceeded to unseal the kit, followed the instructions, looked at the tester and gasped. "Pregnant."

Alex scrawled his signature on the weekly reports, until the phone jangled. "197. This is a non-secure line subject to monitoring. Petty Officer Sievers speaking."

"Alex," Cathreen said.

"Hi Honey. How's it going? Everything packed?" Alex said leaning back with a screech from the chair.

"Yes. I got everything done this morning. Are you going to be home on time?"

"Barring any problems we should be up in Wisconsin before sun down."

"Alex, there's something-"

A rat-tat-tat on the door caught Alex's attention. "Hold on a second," Alex said and punched the hold button. "Come in."

Alexis opened the door and stuck her head full of wavy gold locks in the door. "Commander Hendrick needs you to bring those reports over right now. He wants to review them before his staff meeting in twenty minutes."

"Alright tell him I'll be right over."

Lexi smiled at Alex and he returned it out of politeness. She opened the door and stepped in. "Do you got a minute?"

"Uh . . . I'm on the phone." Her crystal blue eyes pleaded with him and he couldn't bring himself to say no. "Hang on a second." He hit the button on the phone. "I'll call you back in five minutes. I got to go." He nodded. "Ok dear. Talk to you later."

Cathreen twirled the phone cord around her finger while she waited on hold. Alex came back on the line. "Alex I want to leave early. So don't be late." She took a breath to say something else. *Click.* She sighed heavily, let the phone drop to her neck, where she cradled it for a moment. After a long pause, Cathreen slowly hung up the phone. *What's he going to do when he finds out?*

Alex hung up the phone. "I'm all done, I can take them over now. I'll walk over with you."

"Was that the little lady?"

"Yeah. How did you know?"

"I didn't think you would be calling the admiral, dear."

They both laughed. Alex couldn't help noticing something was wrong. "What's the matter Lexi?"

"My fiancée dumped me," she said looking at the deck. "I needed to talk to somebody and you were the first person I thought of. I didn't know who else to talk to."

"I'm sorry, but I don't know what I can do to help."

"I just need to talk it out. I've only been here a short time and haven't made any good friends yet and I just didn't want to dump my garbage on somebody I don't know real well. You were always a good listener and I thought maybe we could go to lunch and talk."

"Look, I've already told you I'm married and it's probably not a good idea-"

She turned away. "I understand," she pouted.

"But if it would make you feel better maybe we can walk to the Exchange and get a soda."

Alexis smiled innocently. "Ok."

"Let me drop these papers off and then we'll head out."

"How long have you and Cat been married?" she inquired.

"Well it will be four years in October."

"You got married in October? That is a strange month, don't you think?"

"You sure haven't changed much," Alex said stopping in mid stride.

"You were always blunt."

"I didn't mean anything; I just say what comes to mind. May or June is usually when most people have their weddings. I was planning ours for June."

"Ours?"

"Me and Hank's. Did you think I was talking about us?"

Alex cleared his throat and didn't respond to the inquiry.

"You did think I was talking about us. I was planning a June wedding for us. Oh wouldn't it have been beautiful on the beach. I really loved Sunset Beach. It was so romantic."

"Alexis. I would really not like to talk about that."

"I understand. I won't talk about that anymore. But it would have been beautiful."

Alex opened the door for her to the outer office of LCDR Hendrick. She took the documents from him and disappeared into the inner office for a few seconds to complete the errand.

"Ok let's go," she said.

Alex opened the door for her, followed her into the corridor and took his place at her side. As they talked Petty Officer Peach greeted them. "Oh don't you two look so nice together."

"Thanks Rod," Alex said and glared at him.

"Thanks Petty Officer Peach," Lexi said. "Did you need something?"

Peach smiled a sly smile, "Not right now. Where are you two lovebirds off to?"

"To the Exchange," Lexi said.

Alex stood tight lipped not wanting to volunteer any information to his nemesis.

"Ahhhh. Have a good time," Peach said and walked away.

Alex could see the wheels in his head turning. *It is never a good thing when he smiles,* Alex thought to himself.

Cathreen sighed deeply, rested her head on her hand and started to twist her gold locks of hair with her finger again. The warble from the phone snapped her back to reality. "Hello," she said flatly.

"Hi Cathreen."

"Hi Mary Lou."

"Are you ok?"

"Just a little tired. I've been busy all day."

"Well I won't hold you for very long. I just wanted to invite you to church tomorrow night. The ladies are having a dinner and I thought you might like to go."

"I'd love to, but Alex and I are going out of town this weekend. That's why I'm home, I took the day off to get ready."

"John did mention something about Alex going out of town. I must of misunderstood him, I thought it was just Alex going. I thought you were going to be home alone, that's why I invited you to the dinner," Mary Lou said.

"No," she laughed. "We're going up to Lake Geneva. We rented a cabin for the weekend."

"How nice. Sounds like fun."

"We used to try to get away once a month when we were stationed in San Diego. We haven't had much chance since we've been here. As a matter of fact I hardly ever see him any more."

"Ditto. I understand completely," Mary Lou said. "So what do you do while he's gone all day and part of the night?"

"When I'm not working I don't do much. I don't know many people," Cathreen said with a sigh. "How about you what do you to keep yourself busy?"

"I spend a lot of time at church. There is always something going on and it's a good way to meet people."

"Like I told you, I'm not much of a church person."

"You don't have to be a church person to come. You're invited to come any time you want," Mary Lou said with genuine warmth. "Feel free to call me or come over any time you want to. If Alex's not there, that means John's probably not here either. I'd like the company."

"Thank you, Mary Lou. I appreciate the offer and I'll take you up on it."

"That would be great. Well I got to run. Have a great time. I'll call you on Monday."

"Thanks for calling. You made my day. Talk to you Monday. Bye." Cathreen hung up the phone and smiled. *That was sweet,* she thought. *I can't wait until Monday.*

Alex and John stood on the marching grinder watching the tightly formationed company run the length and breadth of the parking lot. The two commanders shivered in the unusual spring chill. "I thought all this cold weather was behind us," John said.

"Old man winter's trying to hold on for just a little longer," Alex said with his arms folded. "How many more laps they got?"

"Three and that's it for the day."

"You got everything sorted out for the weekend?"

"Drill, drill, drill," John yawned. "And then I guess I'll drill them some more."

"Perfect. Old Yella on Monday. Sounds like a great weekend. Hope you have fun."

"Look boss, I'm doing you a favor. I could've said no," John bellowed.

"But you're such a teddy bear and have a heart like a marshmallow. How could you say no to you're superior?" Alex pointed to the three chevrons on his sleeve.

"Yeah, but this subordinate teddy bear has a fist like steel," John punched him in the arm.

"Ow, man what did you do that for and why are you always punching me?" Alex said grabbing his shoulder.

"That eagle looked like it was trying to fly off your arm. And besides your attitude needs occasional adjustments." John punched the palm of his hand with his fist. "So I tweaked it a little for you."

"Well don't do it again." Alex rubbed his arm. "Cathreen and I haven't spent much time together over the last few weeks and we need it. She's been really emotional lately man and I am clueless what I can do to help her."

"I really don't mind doing it. I just like giving you a hard time, because you take things way too serious."

A red 1982 Pontiac Firebird Trans-Am snaked through a forest of pine trees. The sleek car slowed, clicked on the right turn signal. The sports car eased into the long twisting driveway, water splashed from the right rear tire. Brake lights lit up the semi-darkness and slowed to a stop, crunching rocks and pine cones under the raised white letter Goodyear Eagle G/T tires. A motion sensitive light at the apex of the cabin popped on and two doors immediately opened. Cathreen shot out like a coiled up spring. Alex eased out from behind the steering wheel and stretched the kinks out of his back. Cathreen clapped her hands together. "Oh Alex, isn't it beautiful?" She exclaimed jumping up and down like a school girl.

Alex scanned the cabin, walked around the back of the car and popped the trunk. He yanked out the biggest suitcase first. "Ugh. What do you got in here? Bricks?"

"Look how gorgeous this is."

"Yep," Alex said. He looked around for a second. "You've seen one forest, you've seen them all." And then went back to unpacking.

Without warning a snowball walloped him in the side of the head. Stunned, he looked up to see Cathreen laughing and running away from him. He picked up some snow and started to chase her. Once he caught up with her he poured the snow over head. She screamed and picked up a hand full of snow and threw it back at him, then took off running again. Alex tried to pursue, but he slipped and fell on some ice. Cathreen stopped running and doubled over in laughter at Alex's comical attempt to get up.

"Come over and help me. And stop laughing at me."

"I can't," she said. "You look so funny."

Cathreen walked with care to keep from falling and extended her hand to help him up. He grabbed her hand and pulled her down on top of him. She screamed again and tried to get away from him. After much struggle, the two of them got back to their feet. He took a deep breath and looked around. "It is pretty. Isn't it?"

"Well Mister company commander, it's just me and you for the next two days."

"Do I know you? You better not tell my wife I'm up here with a strange woman."

Cathreen slapped Alex's chest. "You'd better watch it mister."

Alex grabbed her around the waist and started tickling her. He kissed her and then hugged her. "I'm glad to be here." He smiled and then went back to unloading the car.

"Me too," said Cat. "Me too."

Outside the barracks, Company 197 stood in ranks with their M1 carbides next to their right foot and thrust out an arms length from their bodies. Each recruit's feet were spread apart and left hand in the small of their backs. Their flags whipped in the cold wind as the company waited.

The Rpock stood at attention and listened to John's orders.

"I'm going to be tied up for awhile. Take the company to chow and then come back here. We'll be going to the drill hall this afternoon."

The Rpock snapped a crisp salute at John. "Aye-aye sir. We'll be back at thirteen hundred hours."

John lazily returned the salute. "Don't get in any trouble or I'll have to mash your eyeballs out." He smiled and turned away.

The Rpock snapped an about faced. "Atten-hut," he shouted. The Company snapped to attention at his command. "Shoulder. Arms," He said in a stiff staccato. The recruits snapped their rifles up to port arms, shouldered the M1 Carbide, then snapped the left hand away. "Company. Forward. March." Leading with the left foot the company marched. "Your one, two. Three, four. Your one, two, three, four," the Rpock barked.

Companies came and went on the grinder in front of the chow hall. The Rpock ordered, "Comp-any, halt." He quickly accessed the area. "Port arms." The company brought their rifles across their chests. "Company. Fall out and stack arms."

Immediately the first six men in the front of the company peeled off and formed two groups about five feet apart and formed a tripod with their rifles. Once each of the tripods were completed the rest of the men alternated stacking their rifles around the tripods. After all of the rifles were stacked the guide-on, the person that the entire company synchronized their step with, laid his blue flag with the white 197 emblazoned on it, across the two stacks of M1 Carbides.

Company 195, marched onto the chow hall grinder. Their Rpock watched 197's guide-on place the company flag on the rifles. He maneuvered his company toward the rifles. When 195 passed the rifles, the Rpock kicked the two stacks of rifles over.

Before the guide-on from 197 disappeared into the chow hall he heard the rifles tumble over. Horrified he darted into the chow hall to inform the Rpock what had happened. The Rpock rushed with the rest of the company in tow. He examined the rifles and looked up to see the 195 Rpock laughing at him and approached him.

The two Rpocks approached each other. "Did you knock over our rifles?" Rpock 197 said.

"So what if I did?" 195 answered.

"What did you go and do that for you moron?"

"What are you going to do about it?" 195 said. "You know what I think? Not a darn thing." Then he shoved 197. "Because you're a bunch of losers like that cruddy company commander you're stuck with."

197 had enough and shoved 195 so hard he stumbled back a couple of steps. 195 ran like a linebacker back at 197. Unable to step away from the charging Rpock he caught him in the mid section toppled to the ground. The two Rpocks rolled around pummeling each other with punches. An all out brawl ensued between the two companies. Company commander's in the proximity launched into the fray to break up the mayhem.

In the quiet office, John worked on his paperwork. He glanced at the clock and grunted, because he knew the troops would be back soon.

The silence he'd been enjoying was shattered by the jangling phone. "Company 197, Petty Officer McCarthy," he said.

John's white face turned red and he bit his lip hard. "They did what!" He shouted into the phone. "I'll be right over. No, no. I'll page him. He's going to be . . . yeah. Yeah. Ok. I'll be right over."

John grabbed his hat and blustered to the door. He grumbled, "this is not good."

Alex sat at the end of a plaid brown and yellow couch, dressed in jeans and a red L.L. Bean shirt, with his hiking boots propped up on a dusty old wooden coffee table. Cathreen lay in his lap, dressed in a blue Kansas University sweat shirt, jeans and heavy gray socks. Alex stroked her golden hair and tried to clear his mind and relax.

Both Cathreen and Alex stared at the roaring crackling fire. Alex leaned his head back on the couch. "Whew, I forgot what it was like to have a day off to do nothing," Alex said. "I can't remember the last time I slept that long."

"Me neither," Cathreen said. "I can't remember the last time you stroked my hair."

"Mh," Alex said in a relaxed tone. "Lots of amnesia around here."

Cathreen sat up and looked at Alex. "When was the last time we did anything like this?"

He shrugged his shoulders and continued to stare into the fire.

"It was back in San Diego, before you deployed for the West Pac on *Ingersoll*. We went up to that little town in the mountains. What was the name of that place?"

"Julian," Alex answered.

"Yeah, Julian that's it. We stayed at that cute little bed and breakfast," She laughed, "Do you remember the apple pie and cinnamon ice cream?"

"Sure do," Alex said with a smile.

"You ate three pieces," she giggled.

"Paid for it later. Spent an hour in the head."

Cathreen slapped her leg and laughed loudly. "Ooooh, I remember.

You were hysterical."

Alex furrowed his brow and rubbed his stomach. "With all this talk of food. What's for lunch?"

Cathreen got up from the couch and headed to the kitchen. "I bought half the commissary, got all your favorites. You can have anything you want."

Alex got up, stirred the embers in the fire and it roared to life in a shower of sparks. Then went to the kitchen and rubbed Cathreen's back as she took things out of the refrigerator. "Just a sandwich will be fine. I want a big one," Alex said and stretched out his arms real wide. "I'm really hungry."

"It's chilly in here. Can you put another log on the fire?"

"Sure." He went in and tossed two big logs into the hearth, took a step back and shoved his hands in his pockets. He stared at the crackling and popping fire consuming the new fuel. The most hideous face he'd ever seen shot from the flames. Fingers constricted around his throat. When he came to himself, he'd fallen to both knees gasping for air.

An ethereal voice whispered eerily to his mind, "We own you."

"Alex," Cathreen shouted. "Alex. Are you ok?"

"Yeah," he gasped. "Just feel a little woozy."

"Maybe you should lie down."

He lifted himself up with Cathreen steadying him. "No I'm fine."

"What happened?"

"I was staring at the fire and the room started to spin. Next thing I know you're yelling my name. Weird." He took a deep breath to clear his head and shook off what he'd seen. While he had been in the hospital the pain killers did a job on his mind. *Maybe I was having a flash back,* he thought. "This cabin is a little stifling. Let's go for a walk after lunch."

"I had the same thought, besides I got something I want to tell you."

"Really. What is it?" Alex inquired. "Give me a hint."

"Nope. I'll tell you later. I want it to be special."

"Alright," He said. He wrapped his arms around her, squeezed her and shoved her off to the kitchen. Still shaken, Alex scanned the cabin and then back to the fire. "Hey Cathreen, I don't want to eat here tonight.

I say we take our walk first, go to town and check out that tourist trap we saw on the way in. Then go to dinner."

"What about all this food I bought."

"Wrap it up and we'll take it home with us."

"Alex, can you come and open this jar of pickles?"

He walked into the kitchen and grabbed a piece of pastrami off the counter and popped it into his mouth. He picked up the jar and in one easy motion twisted the top. *Thwap.* "I love that sound. The rush of air escaping from being under pressure. I'd like to escape all this pressure some time and go back to Kansas."

"Why?" Cathreen inquired while she splatted mayonnaise on a sandwich.

"Things were simpler when I was younger."

"You can't go back, only ahead, grasshopper."

"You're right," Alex said. "You ever regret getting out?"

"Nope."

"Why not?"

Cathreen turned and put her hands around Alex's neck. "Cause you're my life now and I love-" Alex's beeper warbled and interrupted her. "To hate that thing." Her hands slid from around his neck as he looked down to silence the obnoxious electronic leash. "I told you to leave that thing at home."

"You know I can't do that." He kissed her on the forehead. "John probably can't find something. No big deal."

"Do you have to call right now? Let's eat first."

"It'll only take a minute. I'll be done before you can finish the sandwiches." He kissed her on the forehead again and pulled the pager off his belt.

Cathreen turned back to the counter and knew the weekend was over.

The black telephone with the rotary dial hung on the wall. Each twist of the dial screamed as the old phone clicked off the taps to the ancient telephone relay system. The phone rang once and then an operator came on the line. "*Recruit Training Command.*"

"This is Petty Officer Sievers. May I speak to Petty Officer McCarthy."

"I will transfer you to Lieutenant Commander Hendrick's office."

Alex's face went white as the blood drained from his face. In stunned amazement he said, "Commander Hendrick's office. Why?"

Cathreen whirled around and shot Alex an intense look. "What!" She exclaimed.

Alex held his hand up to quiet her and turned his back to try to keep her from hearing the conversation. A half of a ring then Commander Hendrick's voice, "Petty Officer Sievers, it's about time."

"Sir," Alex squeaked.

LCDR Hendrick sat behind a large gray metal desk, with his hands folded and leaned into the speaker phone. The two chairs in front of his desk were occupied by John and the other by Paul Santello. "Alex we've got a problem. Your company got into a fight with 195 and I need you here to help sort this thing out."

"They did what?" Alex shouted.

John leaned into the speaker phone. "Alex this is John."

"What happened John?"

"I let them go to lunch while I finished that paperwork you left for me. 195's Rpock kicked over our rifles and Scott had a slug-fest with their Rpock. Both companies, well you can figure out what happened."

"Where's the company now?"

"Confined to quarters," LCDR Hendrick chimed in. "Captain Callaghan wants to meet with you and Petty Officer Peach ASAP. What time can you be back on base?"

Alex furrowed his brow and ran his hand over his head. Cathreen watched him with anticipation.

"I'll be there by 1800 hours," Alex said and nodded his head a few times. "Ok. Alright sir, we'll see you then." He hung up the phone and stared at it for a moment he could feel Cathreen's gaze burning holes into the back of his neck. After a deep breath he turned to face her. "That was Commander Hendrick."

She stood with arms crossed and her eyes narrowed.

"The guys got into a fight with Peach's Company. They need me to come back and meet with the Commanding Officer."

"You're cheating on me Alex."

"I don't follow you."

"This other woman you give your full affection to. The United States Navy. They call. You run. I call and you forget to call me back. Who's more important?"

"Cathreen, I know how you feel."

"No . . . no. You don't know how I feel." She shook her head. "I feel you care more about your career, than you do about me."

"I'm sorry Cathreen," Alex said and walked up to her. He wrapped his arms around her stiff body. "I'll make it up to you. I swear." Alex headed to the bedroom to start packing and left Cathreen in the kitchen shell shocked.

Tears rolled down her face. *Dear God what's happening to us? I feel so helpless and alone.*

CHAPTER 7: CONSPIRACIES

The world is in a constant conspiracy against the brave. It's the age-old struggle: the roar of the crowd on the one side, and the voice of your conscience on the other. - Douglas MacArthur

Two Halogen down lamps in the two back corners of the ceiling and a desk lamp lit Captain Callaghan's office. The captain, dressed in a white golf shirt, with black slacks sat back with his arms folded. LCDR Hendrick sat in one of three winged back chairs. When a knock broke the silence, the captain leaned forward and bellowed, "Come in."

Alex and Rod entered the office. The captain gestured to the two vacant chairs. "Sit down."

"Thank you sir," Alex said nervously.

"We'll dispense with pleasantries and cut to the chase. I'm not going to stand for this garbage on my base. I expect both of you to mete out the proper punishment. These boys need to have their eyeballs mashed out. Am I clear?"

"Yes sir," Alex and Rod said in unison.

"This type of behavior is not acceptable in this man's Navy. This is not some high school locker room. You want to beat on each other then save it for the Captains Cup. I don't mind a little spirited competition, but this is unsatisfactory. Don't let this happen again or I'll be chewing on you two characters backsides."

"Yes sir," they repeated in complete submission.

"While you are here there's another matter I wanted to discuss with you two. Your companies are the sharpest in the competition for the *Double Salute.* No one else is close. I want you to know that whoever wins will be personally congratulated by the Secretary of the Navy. So you better get your act together."

Alex and Rod looked at each other surprised.

"I want you and your companies to stay out of each others way. Can you do that?"

Alex glanced at Rod, then back to the captain. "Yes sir. I can. As long as Petty Officer Peach here can."

Rod clenched his teeth and flashed Alex a murderous look. *Jerk,* Rod thought to himself. "Yes sir. I can," he responded.

Captain Callaghan clomped his hands down on the desk and stood. "Then it's settled. May the best man win." The captain shook Alex's hand and then Rod's. "Petty Officer Peach could you stay for a minute. I'd like to talk to you for a moment."

"Yes sir," Rod said.

Alex looked perplexed at Rod and then shuffled out of the CO's office. Commander Hendrick followed Alex out and closed the door. "That was a close one. He went easy on you."

"Yes sir, he did."

"Alex I recommend you get this over with now and let the guys get a fresh start tomorrow."

"I agree," Alex said and nodded. "Sir, do you know where Petty Officer McCarthy is?"

"He's with the troops."

The two walked in the main entrance to the barracks where Commander Hendrick's office was located. When they got to the office Alex saw Alexis sitting behind her desk. "Hi Lexi. What are you doing here on a Saturday night?"

"I was bored at home so I thought I'd come in for a couple hours after lunch to finish up some work."

"You've been here all day?"

"Yeah. Because of the big mess your company made, the commander needed some help. So I stayed."

"Dedicated puppy aren't you," Alex taunted.

"Yep. You know how we pit bulls with lipstick on can be," she fired back.

Alex and the commander laughed.

"Well I got to run. I'm going to be here for a while mashing the kids."

"Have fun," she said.

The captain watched the door close to the office before he said anything else. He motioned to Rod to be seated as he sat. He reclined back in the executive chair and sized Rod up. "Did you know that the *Double Salute* competition is attracting a lot of attention?"

"No sir. I did not. I've been just trying to concentrate on how to win it."

"That's good. There's a real lot of attention."

"I don't follow you sir," Rod said.

The captain leaned forward in his chair and pierced Rod with his steel blue eyes. "There's also a panel of senators coming right after the secretary is here."

Rod stared at the captain.

"There is talk that two recruit training bases are going to be closed and these senators are part of the base closure committee."

"Sir, I don't . . ."

"I need someone to win who can make me look good and make somebody else look bad."

"Sir, do you think that I'm somebody who can do that?"

He pointed his finger at Rod. "I know about the case of Scotch and you pretending to be on business for me over at personnel."

Rod shifted in his chair as the blood drained from his face. "Sir," Rod managed to say.

"You stacked your company with the best athletes and test scores."

He squirmed in his seat and wiped a bead of sweat from his forehead. "Uh . . . I."

"You can't deny it so don't even try," The Captain growled at him.

"It's people like you," He paused to keep his fish on the line. "Who make my job a heck of a lot easier."

"Excuse me sir, I'm not sure I heard you right."

"You heard me right Petty Officer Peach. I like people who use a little ingenuity and bend the rules a little to get what they want. That's a leader and you're the one I'm putting my money on to win the *Double Salute*."

"I don't think it's going to be a problem, but Sievers could make a run at it. He's already jumped out to an early lead."

The captain tapped his finger on the desk and listened to the litany of excuses for a moment. Then rose from his chair and narrowed his eyes. If they had been lasers they would've burned a hole right through Rod. The captain's gaze made him shudder. "I don't want to hear what Sievers can do and what might happen. I want to know what you're going to do." He paused. "I also have word that there are powerful people who want this base closed. You are going to have to beat Sievers in a way that will make me look good and some higher ups look bad. If you can pull this off I've got one more incentive you might want to keep in mind."

"What's that sir?"

"Your service jacket said you are eligible for chief, but probably won't make it because too many in line ahead of you. How would you like to go to the head of the line and maybe a little farther than that?" he lowered his voice and smiled. "Master Chief maybe?"

Rod fidgeted in his seat and felt like he was going to wilt under the captain's intense stare. He looked down at the floor to gather his composure and then looked back at the captain. "I won't let you down sir."

The captain's face softened and a smile crept across his lips. He thrust his hand out to Rod. "Do whatever it takes to win."

Rod took his hand and pumped it up and down. With Rod's true to form cockiness he said, "He's dog meat sir."

"Make it happen and your career will be set."

The door to barracks 197 suffered the first blow of Alex Sievers' wrath when it crashed into the wall. Alex stormed into the room. "Suit up in your PT gear, on the double," Alex yelled then made a quick left turn into his office and slammed the door.

Alex picked up his chair and threw it at the concrete wall.

The recruits of Company 197 looked at each other in stunned disbelief and hurried to get their Physical Training gear on.

The door to Alex's office flew open and the RPock yelled, "Attention on deck."

Each recruit yanked their gear on and put their toes on the line staring straight forward.

"Flutter Kicks," Alex yelled. The recruits dropped to the deck on their stomachs. "Begin."

Each recruit lifted their torso and legs off the floor and began to swim. "Don't even think about putting those legs on the deck."

Grunts and groans, followed by labored breathing came from all over the barracks. Sweat puddled on the polished ebony floor. John and Alex prowled the floor like cats looking for prey. The groans grew louder. "Don't put those legs down," John yelled at one recruit.

"Down," Alex yelled. With a collective sigh the recruits dropped their bodies to rest.

"On your butts," he yelled. The recruits followed the order with little protest. "Twisters." The recruits raised their legs and torsos off the floor. "Begin."

Each recruit flipped their right leg over the left and twisted their upper body to the right. "One sir," the recruits yelled back.

"Twist," Alex yelled and the recruits threw their left leg over their right and twisted to the left.

"Two sir," the recruits yelled back as their gut wrenched in the movement.

Alex yelled, "Twist," over and over. Diaphragm muscles were savaged by the punishing exercise and amplified when a pause was added to the cadence. Each command, a reminder meant to sear into their minds the payment for their actions and to never do it again.

Through gritted teeth, growls and painful grunts met every order to twist. The agony of tears and perspiration intermingled in the struggle that sapped every ounce of energy from the guilty men.

"Down."

The recruits sighed and some said, "Thank you."

Alex looked out the window toward the 195 barracks and saw the lights switch off. *Peach is done already, I'm just getting warmed up*, he thought to himself.

"Petty Officer McCarthy, may I speak to you please," Alex said.

"Yes Petty Officer Sievers." John ambled over to where Alex stood by the window. He pointed out the window toward Peach's berthing compartment.

John's eyes widened in surprise. "Push ups and sit ups," he whispered and pointed to the door and mouthed, "I'll be right back."

Alex slipped out into the darkened courtyard. Taps had just sounded and the lights were turned off. With his best stealth he kept to the shadows and found an open window next to the quarterdeck. As he came up to the window, Peach emerged from the barracks door with Paul Santello.

"You're not going to mash them at all, Rod."

"Nope."

"Why? They deserve to have their eye balls mashed out."

Peach smiled his crooked smile, "They deserve a medal. They did me a huge favor. Don't worry Paul, I'm covered. Captain's going to …" Rod lowered his voice so Alex couldn't hear.

"The skipper's going to do that for you," Paul said louder than he should have.

"Shut up, you hoser. You want the whole dang base to hear it." Rod pulled Santello into him, wrapped his arm around him and headed towards the back entrance of the quarterdeck. He laughed. When the footsteps faded, Alex stole back into his companies' barracks.

John's booming voice greeted him as entered the room. "One, two, three, four."

"Atten-hut," Alex shouted. The recruits jumped to attention and stood panting. "I think we understand each other."

"Yes sir," they shouted.

"Get in to your racks, on the double. Dismissed," Alex said. He turned to John who'd come alongside him. "In my office."

John closed the door behind him, "Waz up?"

"Peach didn't even mash them."

"What?"

"Yeah, I over heard him talking to that squirt half-pint assistant of his."

"What's he up to?"

"That's not the best part," Alex said in a hushed voice. "He said something about the captain doing something for him."

"Are you kidding me, I'm going rip that bugger's head off and stuff my fist down his throat," John said as his face tried to loosen his collar.

"Not very Christian of you John," Alex chided him.

"Look, man don't go there. After the day I've had, I'm ready to rip your head off."

"I'm sorry man, I couldn't resist it," Alex said. "We've got to find out what he's up to."

John blew through his teeth and sat down. "What I don't understand is they embarrassed the snot out of him and he doesn't make them do so much as one push up. Why?"

Alex sat back, put his feet up on the desk and rubbed his tired eyes. John stroked his whiskers and gnawed on his lip and jumped when Alex clomped his feet down on the deck. "He said they did him a favor. He is the master of playing one side against the other while he slimes away."

"He sure is a slime bag."

"We can't give him the ammunition he's looking for. I want you tell the men, in no way are they to confront, say or do anything about 195, even if they are provoked."

"Hey, this reminds me of something the pastor said in church last week. He said that if someone strikes you on the cheek, you're to give them the other."

Alex stared out the blackened window and responded, "Please not church stuff." He paused for a second. "What did you say?"

"Turn the other cheek."

"That's it. Tell the men that. If we are going to win this thing we are going to have turn the other cheek. Because if we don't we are going to get our butt cheeks kicked."

John snickered and rolled his eyes. "I'm not sure that's what the pastor meant, but I think you've got the idea."

"Cat, I'm sorry," Alex said into the phone. "I can't come home tonight."

"Why?" she said her voice trailing off.

"Division Commander was so upset about what happened, he wanted us both to stay tonight in the Company Commanders Quarters and not cut them any slack for the rest of the weekend."

"I . . . I understand," she said with no emotion. "No Alex I don't understand. I am at the end of my chain and well you've got to start figuring some things out soon."

"What is that suppose to mean, figure things out?" he said his pitch rising. "I've got things all figured out."

"You sure do," she said with a sharp edge in her words. "It's late and it's been a long day and you've got to get up early. Let's talk about this tomorrow."

"Ok, but . . . I guess you're right. Please don't be mad at me babe."

"Alright Alex," she said to him. "What time are you going to be home?"

"I really can't say."

"Then I'll see you tomorrow."

"Good night. I . . . I love you."

"Uh . . . huh. Goodbye."

Click. Alex sat for a long moment and listened to the dial tone, put the phone in the cradle and stared at it. *What is going on with everybody?* He thought to himself.

Cade Keller, a two-sport sensation and member of the Army Junior Reserve Officer Training Course (JROTC) worked hard to get to the

Navy. After his first attempt at the Armed Services Vocational Aptitude Battery (ASVAB) the Army recruiter laughed and told him to get the heck out of his office. The test was meant to measure his developed abilities to predict his future academic capability and what job he could be successful at in the military. Undeterred he tried again with the Air Force and Marines but still couldn't achieve a high enough grade for acceptance. With choices shrinking, he cornered one of his unit ROTC commanders for help and they recommended he get a book on how to prepare for the ASVAB.

The Navy was his last shot, which was really his desired goal. A gifted athlete, but a poor book learner it took more mental strength to prepare for that test then it took get ready for football season. Full of optimism and confidence he drove the 25 miles to Gainesville, Georgia pumping himself up. He marched into the office on Dawsonville Highway and said, "I am ready to be a sailor."

The recruiter sat back and looked over the perfect athletic specimen, "I've seen you next door, what are you doing loitering around my office?"

"I haven't made up my mind, which to choose."

"Uh huh," Electricians Mate First Class Clark Rycraw rocked back and allowed the government issued chair to scream in protest. Rycraw stared at him a long time trying to decide what to do. Keller looked away. *I'm behind on my quota this month, I guess I'll take a chance on him*, he thought to himself. "Are you here to waste my time? Cause if you are I'm going to throw you out of here right now. "

"No sir, I want to join the Navy."

"I know you washed out on your ASVAB with the Zoomies, Jarheads and the Grunts, so why do you want to waste my time testing you again?"

"I just want to join the Navy Petty Officer Rycraw."

Clark scrunched his eyebrows and bored into him. He stood up and wagged his finger at him, "I shouldn't do this. If you bomb this I'm going to kick your-"he thought about it for a second. "butt. You understand me?"

"Yes sir, don't worry. I won't waste your time. Let me take the test and I'll show you."

"This is your last chance." He stood up to get the test from the file cabinet. "Not really your last chance, there's still the Puddle Pirates but their not even part of the Department of Defense."

Cade shot the recruiter a questioning look.

"Department of Transportation. Puddle Pirates. Coast Guard. You'd have to go all the way to Atlanta for that."

For two and a half hours of head scratching, nail biting and heavy sighs he finished the test for the fourth time.

Petty Officer Rycraw gathered up the test and sent Cade out of the room. Clark laid the template over the blackened dots on the IBM answer sheet. He smiled as he tallied up the score. "Punk did OK."

He sat down behind his desk and gave no indication by his body language of the results of the test. "I told you when you came here you better not waste my time."

Cade fidgeted in his seat and held his breath.

"Well, the United States Navy," Clark said with no emotion and then allowed a smile cross his face "would be glad to have you." He stood and shot his hand out for a congratulatory hand shake.

Keller rose and took the waiting hand. "You mean I passed."

"Yes. You passed. Not earth shattering but well enough," Clark said as he sat back down. "Welcome aboard."

Cade reflected on how that moment changed his life. As he prepared to get in his rack, the soreness from the mashing reminded him of the commitment he made to Petty Officer Sievers to be an example for the company. *I didn't do a very good job today being that leader,* he thought to himself.

"Thompson," Cade whispered to the top bunk next to his.

"What," groaned Thompson. "I want to go to sleep."

"Thompson, we let Petty Officer Sievers down today."

Thompson rolled over and propped his head up with the pillow. "This was 195's fault and we got jammed for it. How do you figure we let Petty Officer Sievers down?"

"He stuck his neck out for me and getting into a brawl wasn't the best way to repay him. Think about what he's been trying to teach us;

Strength through discipline. That was not very disciplined to let those idiots goad us into that. Even though they got in to trouble too, they still won because we lowered ourselves to their level. That's how we let him down."

"So what do you suggest?"

"We beat them where it counts. In the competition."

"Tomorrow is Sunday. We'll use our free time to study together, drill, fold blankets whatever needs to be done to be the best."

"Alright man, I'm all in. Now go to sleep."

Silence offered no solace. Darkness conjured up accusatory images. His own pulse pounded in his head like a drum beat of judgment. Unable to fight off the fatigue, sleep snuck up on him and ushered him into the courtroom of torment where he stood to defend himself against the shadows. Nefarious voices boomed the charges and rendered an instantaneous verdict.

"Dereliction of Duty. Guilty!"

"Incompetence. Guilty!"

"Murder. Guilty!"

A cacophony of voices rose in unison. "Pay the penalty." They repeated over and over, rising to a fever pitch, "Pay the penalty." Index fingers pointed at him from all around, closing in on him and suffocating him. Alex panted, his chest heaving as he fought for every breath. "Air," he said to the fingers.

Alex awoke with a start, gasping for precious oxygen, gulping it with voracious fury. After a few deep breaths, the cob webs of delirium receded into the murky blackness as the light of clear thought flooded his mind. The musty smell of the company commander's barracks assaulted his nostrils helping him reconnect with the real world.

The steady rhythm of John's breathing aided Alex in reeling in his thoughts. The many sleepless nights since the incident on board *Ingersoll* had not been wasted staring at the ceiling. A well designed plan for his life formed in his mind, in his imagination he laid the foundation and built it. Each night he would fill the rooms with his emotion and longed for its completion.

Since the battle for the *Double Salute* had begun, a fire storm of circumstances were threatening to burn down the dream he'd built. Unseen forces were dragging Cathreen and him apart. Peach had ramped up his assault on him. The looming firefighting training gnawed at him and pointed its bony finger accusing him of being a coward. Alexis wanted to rekindle a flame long since extinguished in him and the boots needed him to be strong and lead them. *How did I become the center of everybody's universe all of a sudden?*

His eyes grew heavy as sleep climbed out of its box. As the curtain of fog engulfed him a thought emerged from the heaviness, *what does no greater love mean?*

A jangling phone does not make a good alarm clock. Cathreen groaned and rolled over to snatch the menacing noise maker. "Argh, who is calling at this ungodly hour?"

"Hello," Cat said in a dull flat voice. She rubbed her tired eyes and tried to sit up.

"Cat. It's Mary Lou. How are you darling?" she said in a bright cheerful voice. "Did I wake you? I'm sorry."

"I was just getting up," she said.

"Since Alex and John had to stay at the base, I thought I'd see if you wanted to go to breakfast?"

"Don't you-" she said and cleared her throat. "It's Sunday, aren't you going to church?"

"Wouldn't miss it for the world. When John works I like to go to the later service. Just feels more relaxed to me. He likes to go early so he can get home and watch a NASCAR race or a football game or something like that. He always ends up passing out and sucking the nails out of the drywall no matter what he watches."

Cat giggled.

"So what about it? Breakfast?"

"I don't see why not. I wouldn't mind getting out."

"Alright I'll see you in an hour. I'll meet you at the Denny's on Northpoint Blvd."

Cathreen Sievers, a navy brat who'd lived in a different city every two years since she'd been born. Her favorites were: San Diego, CA, Norfolk, VA, Mayport, FL, Brisbane Australia, Auckland, New Zealand and Washington DC finally settling in the planes of Kansas. By the time she was old enough to leave home, she'd become a loner because making friends and losing them had become too difficult.

With all the heartaches of traipsing around the world, it was difficult to get out of the system. The apple doesn't fall far from the tree and Cathreen decided she wanted to discover her own world and joined the Navy too.

Not long into her world tour she bit into the apple of love when Alex came into her life. The zeal he had for life and confidence drew her like a moth to a flame. Passion set them assail on the high seas of life, but his injuries cooled their burning hearts and threatened to cast them adrift. The physical burns may have healed but the inner wounds opened a chasm between the two of them. The trauma etched deep within him may require a fire of a different type, something beyond what her love and devotion could accomplish.

Cathreen rolled her Volkswagen Cabriolet into the parking lot of the red-roofed Denny's and found a place to park. When she turned the car off, she heard a pop and puff of smoke come out from under the hood.

CHAPTER 8: OLD YELLA

Perfection is achieved, not when there is nothing more to add, but when there is nothing left to take away. -Antoine de Saint-Exupéry

U.S. Navy Regulation 1990 states that 1 day in 7 is recognized as a day for religious services and holiday routine (referred by some as the Sabbath). Commands normally specify this day as Sunday. Article 0817 specifies that daily routine on Sunday shall be modified as practicable to recognize, respect, encourage and minister to the religious preferences and the varying religious requirement of individuals.

"Alright you gun-deckers lets get out of those racks. For those of you who worship on Sunday there will be services at oh-nine-hundred hours at Drill Hall 1600. As for you pagans you may use the free time to coke and smoke or do whatever it is you do," barked Petty Officer McCarthy.

Groans and grunts were the response.

"Company 197." John yelled. "Atten-Hut."

Blankets flew off, squeaking of the bunk springs and the thump of feet hitting the deck. The recruits at their best attention, dressed only in a t-shirt and skivvies, and silver dog tags stood at attention in very short order.

"Did we forget where and who we are speaking to ladies? That mashing you went through last night is nothing compared to what you will get if you slack off one bit. You're only getting this day off because of regulations. If I had my way I'd march your butts until your boondockers fell off. Let's get this straight, Petty Officer Sievers and I took a butt chewing yesterday like we've never had since we've been pushing boots. It ain't going to happen again. Are we clear?"

"Yes sir," the company responded.

"Are we clear?" John yelled back at the recruits.

"Yes sir," the recruits responded at the top of their lungs.

"Good, because God help you if you screw this up," John said to them. "Rpock"

"Yes sir."

"Fall them out in 15 minutes for chow. Bring them back here and form a detail and march them to Drill Hall 1600 for services."

"Aye-aye sir."

"Keller, Thompson," John yelled.

"Aye sir," Keller and Thompson said in unison.

"You are to report to the dunk tank at 1400 hours for remedial swim training."

"Aye-aye sir," Keller and Thompson said.

The term *aye-aye* meant to communicate that the recipient of an order, has heard and understood the order and will carry it out.

"Sir, request permission to ask a question," Keller said.

"Go ahead recruit, fire away."

"Sir we've talked with every one in the company and decided we would like to fore go holiday routine this afternoon and would like it very much if you and Petty Officer Sievers would conduct a drill exercise."

The bushy eyebrows on John's face lifted in surprise at the request. "Am I hearing you right? You guys want to conduct training instead of taking it easy?"

"Yes sir, we do."

John rubbed the back of his neck, then scratched his head followed by a long whistle as he thought. "You're sure?"

"Yes sir, we're sure."

"Alright I'll talk to Petty Officer Sievers."

The 58,000 square foot drill hall at the extreme southwestern part of the base is where Company 197 stood in formation. Each recruit stood like statues at parade rest, with a vintage 1942 M1 Carbine at his right side thrust forward, left hand in the small of his back and legs spread apart. "Never lock your knees."

"If you lock your knees and you faint, you had better bounce twice or I'm not going to pick you up off the deck," Alex said to his company.

"Drill is how commanders move companies in simple formations from one place to another in standard, orderly manner. From these formations combat positions can be easily assumed. Drill also teaches discipline, habits of precision and automatic response to orders. It also allows increased confidence of officers, junior officers and non-commissioned officers through the exercise of command by giving proper commands and by the control of drilling troops."

Alex right faced, left faced and then about faced twice. "Drill is facing, marching and rifle commands that you are to follow in a uniform manner. All of you men are to move in unison on my command."

"The hardest flag to earn here at RTC," Alex paused for a moment and walked across the drill hall floor to where the flags each company can earn were displayed. He stood by a yellow flag with the crossed saber and rifle. He took it from its stand and held it high. "Is 'Old Yella.'"

"Not only do you have to earn it once, you've got to be tested three times and score high enough each time to earn the flag, but also the two ribbons that go with it, to signify that you've gotten it three times."

"Once you have this one, the rest of the flags are easy. Once you have this one, you're on your way to capturing the ultimate prize, the *Double Salute.*" He paused again for emphasis. "Screw this one up and you've got no shot, even if you were able to win the Captain's Cup. This is the key to even being in the conversation for best company. This is the rag we want."

"In just a few moments, all the pain and sorrow will congeal into one moment where you move together in complete harmony and nail that sucker. You're the best now win Old Yella."

"Great. What do I do now?" Cathreen said pounding the steering wheel as she looked up to the rearview mirror.

A mirror never tells a lie and this morning it was telling an awful truth. She checked her look and asked the tired eyes looking back at her, "Who are you?" She grabbed her purse and fumbled around looking for her compact. "That is a very good question," she answered her self. Turning her attention back to the mirror, she dabbed her eyes trying to mask the dark circles left by the insomnia fairy. She continued the conversation with herself, "What happened to take-on-the-world Cathreen?"

She looked long into the blood-shot eyes that yielded no answer. "Don't answer that." Drawing a deep breath she gathered her arsenal of personal items: purse, sweater and umbrella as she threw the door open it clunked the car next to hers. "Aw man."

Cat got out seeing if there was any damage. Bending down to look at the side molding of the blue 1978 Chevrolet Impala, she didn't see any dings. Licking her fingers she rubbed a speck of white paint off.

"Ahem," a baritone voice came from behind her.

Whirling around to face the challenging sound. Embarrassed she responded, "Got out a little fast."

"May I?" the tall imposing figure asked.

"Sure," Cat said and stepped past him while he examined the car.

She fidgeted from one foot to another and could not have been happier to hear the familiar voice, "Cat, hey. How are you?" Mary Lou said giving her a hug from behind. "What's going on here?" as she tried to see what the man was examining.

"I bumped his car with my door."

"C'mon lets go inside, it's starting to drizzle and I had a time of it getting my hair just right this morning." Mary Lou put her arm around Cathreen and shepherded her away from the inquisition. When the door of the restaurant opened, the aroma of bacon flooded Cathreen's nostrils causing a wave of nauseam to wash over her. She took a step back "I need to sit down," she said.

Mary Lou steadied her and guided her to a bench by the front door, "Are you OK dear?"

"Just feel a little bit dizzy, I haven't eaten anything since yesterday morning."

The host came over, "Is she ok? Is there anything I can do?"

"Could you get her a glass of water and can we have a table please?"

"Oh yes, let me get some menus."

"Can you walk Cat?"

"I'm better," Cat said standing up. "Still a little dizzy, but I'll manage."

The two women followed the host to a booth in the far corner of the dining room near a window. Cat put her sweater on and adjusted in her seat. "I've been like this for about a week now."

"Have you been to the base hospital to get checked out?"

"Mmmh . . . yeah," Cat said grabbing the silverware, unrolling the napkin. She looked down and bit her lip trying to keep the emotion at bay and not let Mary Lou see her moistening eyes.

"Have you mentioned this to Alex?"

She looked out the window, crushed the napkin into a ball and dabbed her eyes. "I tried to tell him when we went to Lake Geneva and well you know what happened." She looked down and took a heavy breath. "He's so wrapped up in the company, school and his career. I hardly ever see him any more. When I do see him there's nothing left for me."

Cathreen's shoulders went up and down as she cried. Mary Lou reached over and patted her hand. "I'm pregnant Mary Lou."

The door to Captain Callaghan's office burst open and banged when it hit the wall. A red faced, barrel-chested admiral stormed into the room wagging his index finger. "What the heck happened here yesterday?"

Captain Callaghan stood in respect to a superior, but not because of the man. "Good morning, to you to, Admiral," he said void of emotion.

"Cut the garbage, Bill. I want to know what happened."

The captain opened the report folder and read flatly. "Company 195's Rpock kicked over 197's rifles and a fight broke out. You know as much as I do."

"How is something like this possible, when we are paying men to babysit these kids 24 hours a day?"

"I spoke to the company commanders and they were not present."

"Why not?" Admiral Perkins demanded.

"At a certain point in the training we encourage the companies to go places alone. It is not necessary for the commanders to hold their hand every movement. The companies are encouraged to work as a team and to operate as a team. At a certain point it is necessary to find out if they can."

"What is being done about discipline?" Admiral Perkins said calming down.

"Since neither commander was present at the time I have given them permission to discipline their own companies at they see fit. They also assured me there would be no further trouble. These are the two best companies in the Grad Class and I wanted to insure that this did not effect the *Double Salute* competition."

The admiral sighed and stepped around the chair he'd been standing behind and sat down. "Let's drop the ranks for a minute Bill. Do you know why I didn't recommend you for a sea command when we were stationed together on the *Harry W. Hill*?"

The captain sat down slowly and felt every muscle in his body tighten. His face flushed with anger. "Is it because you didn't like me as much as I don't like you?"

"It is true, I don't like you very much, but in my position I do not have the luxury of basing my decisions based on likes and dislikes. As officers it is our duty to insure the men we promote are the best possible candidate for the job we are promoting them to. You weren't the best man for the job."

Unable to control his emotions any longer, Captain Callaghan's eyes narrowed and he rose leaning toward the admiral, keeping both fists on the desk. "Well now that the ranks are dropped Admiral. I would like to say that I did my duty as meticulously and as close to perfection as I could. I did everything in my power to insure that you looked good."

"Me look good!" the Admiral said and rose to answer the glare. "No, you were all about making you look good. You are arrogant, closed minded and try to control everything and everyone. You don't provide an atmosphere of trust, but of backstabbing and treachery. You don't inspire people to go out of their way for you. Every one of those men knew what you were about, you used them and never won their hearts."

The captain's eyes softened for a moment at the realization and with doubled fury his anger flared viciously. "Don't lecture me on heart, Admiral. Who needs hearts in battle; I need men who will follow orders."

"You are right, they would've followed your orders, but would they have fought to the death for you?"

"They're warriors; they would fall on a hand grenade for me."

"That's true, but you need to ask your self, are you willing to fall on a hand grenade for them?"

"Now honey, don't cry," Mary Lou said to Cathreen. "I'm sure he'll understand when you talk to him."

"Talk to him. How can I talk to him, I don't ever see him. He's always at the base and I can't seem to get him on the phone and if I do he's got to go. I don't want to flippantly just drop this on him," Cat said with an attitude. "Oh hi dear, how was your day and by the way I'm pregnant. What is that? I want this to be special, this is our first child."

"Cat I understand what you are feeling. I feel the same way too; my husband is standing right next to him. I want John home at night also, but I've got to see the big picture on this."

"Big picture," Cat shot back at her. "I would at least like to be in the picture. All Alex ever talks about is his career, where he's going and how he's going to get there. He doesn't talk about how we are going to get there. I'm worried about how he is going to react when he finds out about the baby. How's this going to affect those big plans of his?"

"What are his big plans?"

"He wants to be a commissioned officer."

"Why didn't he get an appointment to the Naval Academy out of high school?"

"Alex did everything he knew how to do to get an appointment, but his grades weren't high enough to be selected. He was a member of the Reserve Officer Training (ROTC) at his high school. He obtained Eagle Scout in Boy Scouts. He was active in his community. He worked very hard trying to keep his grades up, but he was more of a hands-on kind of a guy. He learned better doing things then reading about them."

"He seems to be a very hard worker."

"He is and people recognize that and admire him for being this way. That's why he enlisted."

"I thought he wanted to be an officer," Mary Lou said.

"When he wasn't accepted to Annapolis he didn't know what to do. One night by chance he ran into an old buddy of his from his High School baseball team who was home on leave from the Navy. He'd graduated two year prior to him. They got to talking and he found out the Navy had programs to help enlisted people to become officers. All he had to do was keep his nose clean, do his job well and apply for the positions when he reached a certain rank."

"Well, where's he at on the plan?"

"He was about to be command advanced on *Ingersoll* when the fire happened and that kid died. Having to be in the hospital recuperating from the burns and not getting advanced set him back about a year. The board of inquiry named him responsible for the whole thing. At first it devastated him, but he wasn't going to give up on his dream. Every detailer and counselor he spoke to told him the same thing, 'Either be a recruiter or push boots, it will help your career.' He inquired at RTC San Diego and they didn't need company commanders at that time, but they told him Great Lakes really needed some."

"That's great. What did he do next?"

"Well he found out you had to have a spotless record and he thought there would be no way he'd be accepted. When they interviewed him, the subject of the *Ingersoll* incident came up and was told someone on *Ingersoll* had personally recommended him to be accepted. We were transferred and just when he got here he got the news he'd been promoted to Petty Officer First Class."

"How did you handle the move and being here?"

"It wasn't easy for me. I was at the end of my enlistment when the new orders came through. So I decided to reenlist and use my Guard Three."

"Guard Three?"

"Yeah it's Guaranteed Assignment Retention Detailing Program or Guard. They always need Personnel people everywhere so it was a cinch to get orders here. I made second class and even got a reenlistment bonus."

"That helps I'm sure."

"I'm glad to have my job to go to, it helps spell the time."

"Did you get the place you're living in when you first got here?"

"Oh no," Cat said. "Getting a place near the base took some time, we stayed in Temporary Quarters until a place in housing opened up. We made due in our Spartan quarters and put everything in storage until we could get settled in. And that's about where we are at right now."

"Wow. That's got to be tough. I wanted to finish what I was going to say earlier," Mary Lou said. "I've been around you guys for just over a year now and I think I might be able to provide a little perspective. You've got to look at the big picture on this thing. I know Alex loves you and those plans are to make a better life for you and your family." Mary Lou paused. "By what you just told me, it sounds like he communicated all his plans to you when you first met him. Right?"

Cathreen looked out the window and bit her lip. "Yes . . . yes, he did tell me his plans."

"What did you think of them, when he told you?"

"Its part of the reason I wanted to marry him."

"You liked that take charge, I know what I am doing, kind of a guy. Didn't you?"

"Yeah, you're right. But . . ."

"No. Don't do that. Now that you are out in the deep ocean of his plan you want him to change his course. That's not very fair. You signed on for the whole journey not part of it. Why do you want to change what you fell in love with? He needs you right now, don't give up on him?"

"Look, Mary Lou I've got needs too. Why do I have to sacrifice all the time?"

"He's not sacrificing? Pushing those boots all day, going to school, studying and having a family. That's not sacrificing? I'll bet you he wouldn't mind some time off to be home with you and maybe relax a little. Maybe watch a football game."

Keller pounded the door to Alex's office three times. Alex looked up from the calculus book he'd been poring over for the last two hours.

"Come," Alex said in a deep baritone voice.

Keller and Thompson took three steps into the company commander's office and stood at attention. "Sir Seaman Recruit Keller and Thompson request permission to check out to go to remedial swimming class."

Alex sat back in his seat and looked the two recruits over. "Keller, how's the swimming coming?"

"Getting better every day sir."

"Good. Are you going to pass the test this time?"

"Flying colors sir."

"That's good. I guess then you'll be ready to anchor the swim relay at the Captain's Cup."

"I didn't say I was that good, sir."

"That's not what I hear. My friends over at the pool are telling me that you're really going for this swimming. As a matter of fact they've asked if you would be interested in taking the SEAL test."

Keller's face contorted in confusion. "I'm not following you sir."

"Keller, I was looking at your ASVAB score and that your score was high enough to be considered for the Navy Seal program. You'll need to take a swim test and have a psychological profile done on you."

"Special Forces. Me?"

"The big bad Navy Seals," Alex said and then turned to Thompson. "They're interested in you to. What about it boys, interested?"

They both smiled and responded, "Yes sir."

"Good, because that's what you're being called to the pool for. There is someone here to administer the test. Go have fun guys."

"Yes sir."

"You're dismissed," Alex said to them. "Hey guys, make sure you double time it all the way over."

"Aye-aye sir."

Keller and Thompson entered the pool area and stripped down to their bathing suits under their dungarees, sat on the first row of bleachers. Six other recruits entered the swimming area and did the same taking their places next to Keller and Thompson. A door on the opposite end of the pool banged open and a Navy Special Warfare Specialist entered with a clip board and a stopwatch around his neck.

Keller yelled, "Attention on Deck!" The recruits came to attention.

"At ease, gentlemen. I don't need any of that garbage. I'm one of you."

The men relaxed and remained standing.

"I'm Petty Officer First Class Stiles and I am a United States Navy Seal. Can any one tell me what SEAL means?"

The recruit at the end of the line said, "It's where y'all operate. Sea, Air and Land."

"Alright," Stiles said. "Now let's get down to why we are here. You guys are going to take a swim test just to see if you can meet the minimum requirements for the training. You will swim 500 yards using either a breast stroke or a side stroke. No hands out of the water. You have to do it in a minimum of twelve and a half minutes. That's nine laps."

Keller piped up, "Is that there and back?" Making an up and down hand motion. "Or one length of the pool?"

"Just one length of the pool," Stiles said.

"Alright men, lets get this started. Line up on the edge of the pool."

Stiles held up the stop watch and yelled, "Go!"

The recruits dove in the water and came up swimming spreading their arms out in heart shape strokes and kicking their legs like frogs. Pants and groans echoed through the hall. Keller and Thompson kept a good pace but by the completion of the seventh lap the pace had slowed. The recruits were no longer swimming for qualifications it was just about surviving the test and finishing.

Keller was the first to touch the wall to complete the swim followed by Thompson. Each recruit huffed and puffed their way to the finish line while Stiles matched names to times. "Out of the pool."

"Well it looks like we have ourselves a few winners," he said looking at his clip board. "Keller, Thompson and Noble. Congratulations men that will be the easiest thing you'll ever do to becoming a SEAL. I have a few more physical tests."

"What other tests?" Thompson inquired.

"At least 42 push ups in two minutes, 50 sit-ups in two minutes, six pull-ups no time limit and a mile and half run in 11 minutes. Those are the minimums; if you can do more do them that will definitely help. We just set the minimums as guidelines, but those who screen you want to see as much out of you as you can get."

"Piece of cake," Keller said to Thompson. "I did more than that in the last PFT test we took."

"Yeah man," Thompson said. "I can do that with my eyes closed."

Keller and Thompson burst through the door of the Aquatic Center jabbering and excited about what just happened. The two started to double time when they were yelled at from behind. "You two halt."

Petty Officer Peach approached the recruits standing at attention with their backs to him. "Did you leave your military bearing in the barracks recruits?"

"No sir," they responded in unison.

"Are you a bunch of chattie girls that don't know how shut your mouths?"

"No sir,"

"Define Military Bearing?"

"To behave oneself in a military manner of discipline and adhere to the utmost level of honor, duty and professionalism," Thompson said. "Sir."

"Ah someone has been studying his *Blue Jackets Manual.*"

"What is your company number and the name of your company commander?"

"Company 197, Petty Officer Sievers is our CC, sir," Keller said in a stiff staccato.

Peach put his hand up to his mouth and laughed.

"What were you doing in the Aquatic Center?"

He walked behind the two recruits looking them over.

"Taking SEAL Training qualification test, sir," Keller said.

He stopped and raised an eyebrow. "Mermaids?" said with a condescending tone.

"Give me your demerits card."

Each recruit handed him the demerits card and Peach wrote on each one of them and handed them back where they were stowed in their right front pocket of their blue chambray shirts.

"You go see your company commander as soon as you return to the barrack and show your cards. Now go on, get back to your barracks without talking. Double time. March."

The two recruits ran off and Peach smiled to himself and watched them double timing, "Big son of a guns. Where did Sievers get them from?"

"What the heck are you two guys doing, getting 30 demerits?"

"Sir we were just talking when we came out of the Aquatic Center and this Petty Officer gigs us for not having proper military bearing."

"I can't quite read the initials on here. Who is this Petty Officer that gave this dressing down?"

"I don't know sir," Thompson said.

Alex got in Keller's face, "Have you ever seen him before?"

"He looks familiar, but I'm always looking forward every where I go, it's hard to recognize people. I had seen him some where, I just can't place it. Sir, I'm sorry."

"Yeah you better be sorry. Cause if I can't find out who it was I'm going to have to send you two jokers to Motivational Training Unit (MTU) for an entire day."

"I got it. I remember where I've seen him. Last night when we were getting our eyeballs mashed out. I was looking into 195's barracks while I was doing my jumping jacks. It was their company commander."

Alex looked away from the two recruits and over toward 195 barracks. "Peach. You rotten son of a . . ." He said and slapped his hands together. "You two are dismissed."

CHAPTER 9: POSTURING

We try, we fail, we posture, we aspire, we pontificate - and then we age, shrink, die, and vanish. - George Saunders

Alex stormed into the 195 barracks and pounded on the company commander's door. "Peach I want to talk to you."

The door opened to a grinning Rod Peach. "Ah. Petty Officer Sievers, I was expecting you."

Alex stepped into the office surprised to see Lieutenant Commander Hendrick sitting there. Peach stepped around his desk and sat down "Petty Officer Sievers, we were just discussing what has happened over the last few days. Petty Officer Peach was telling me he had to discipline two of your men for unnecessary chatter."

"Yes sir," Alex said, as he wrestled down the anger raging in him. "I think 30 demerits are a little excessive for a minor infraction."

"Thirty is a lot," Commander Hendrick said and paused for a moment while Alex shot Peach a disgusted look. "But I think it will serve as a reminder to be a little more disciplined and keep their military bearing."

Peach nodded in agreement and shot back a fake look of sympathy.

"Sir, they are my men. Wouldn't it have been better for Petty Officer Peach to bring it to my attention and give me the courtesy to deal with them as I see fit?"

"It would be the courteous thing to do, but it was within Petty Officer Peach's latitude to meet out discipline as he sees fit to recruits of another company as is it is your right," LCDR Hendrick said. "I also want to remind you both, if this turns into a tit for tat war between you two I'll write both your butts up in a second and drag you before the old man for Captain's Mast. Do you understand me?"

Peach put up his hands in mock submission and said, "Yes sir."

"Yes sir," Alex said trying to hide the rage he felt. He turned and burned holes in to Peach with his gaze. *One of these days Peach I'll wipe that smug look off your face,* he thought to himself.

"Is there anything else Petty Officer Sievers," Peach asked in a condescending tone.

"No," Alex said and opened the door. "Good day, Commander." He backed out of the room, closed the door gritted his teeth and marched out of the barracks.

The door to the 197 barracks banged open; Alex went into his office, slammed the door and marched back and forth huffing, then picked up the chair and threw it against the wall. A knock at the door broke his tirade, "What is it?" he yelled at the door.

"It's me. McCarthy."

"Come in."

"Who got your panties in a wad? Somebody steal your lollipop?"

Alex's eyes flared and he held up a fist. "Look I don't need the sarcasm right now. That weasel snookered me and I want rip his head off, jump down his throat and tap dance on his liver." He marched back and forth again trying to relieve his frustration. "I swear I'm going to kill that guy."

"Take it easy, you're not going to kill anybody," John said sitting down. "What did he do this time?"

"That dirt ball set me up. He gave Thompson and Keller 30 demerits for talking coming out of the Aquatic Center. Knowing it would tick me off and I'd come looking for him, he had Lieutenant Commander Hendrick in his office when I busted in. Played me like a broken record. He sat there with that stupid smug look. Man I wanted to beat him like a red headed step child in a very bad way."

"Calm down, man. You're going to blow something up. What'd you do?"

"I stood there liked a whipped puppy, saying 'Yes sir.' While he sat there with that gotcha look he loves to do."

"What did you do to incur this joker's wrath? Did you pee in his Wheaties or something? I have a hard time believing you and him were friends one time."

"We grew up together and were pretty good friends. He started having a real bad time with his Dad after we started High School. It really messed him up, he was cool one day and a butt head the next, he would just snap and go ballistic. One time during the winter, we were out shooting squirrels with BB guns and for no reason he shot me in the foot. It hurt like that place down below you're not so fond of."

John cleared his throat to lodge his protest against the barb.

Alex continued, unfazed by the protest. "He just stood there laughing like a hyena. He is one son of gun and he always has a chip on his shoulder."

"Sounds more like a boulder," John interjected. He sat down and crossed his legs.

"Most of the guys tolerated him, because he was pretty good in sports. He wasn't a bully but he knew how to manipulate people. He dated a good friend of mine. They got into a fight one night and he slapped her. After she told me about it, I went to his house to try getting him to apologize. He told me where to go and he slugged me. I had to get seven stitches. He's always starting something. He heard I was going in the Navy so he decided to join up too."

"That is too weird sounds like a freaking stalker. How the heck does he keep ending up wherever you are stationed?"

"Man I wish I knew. I can't seem to get away from him; he's like onion breath you know, I just can't get rid of him."

"If he uses people, how come they don't get wise to him?"

"He's always plotting, it's like he is two moves ahead all the time. Before people get wise to his little schemes he's on to the next poor sucker."

"Well then we need to be three moves ahead."

"That's sounds great, but he keeps you so caught up in the thing he just hit you with that you are unaware of what he's getting ready to hit you with next."

"Let's back up and see if we can see if there is a trail to follow here and head him off at the pass," John said.

"You're right," Alex said. "He knew about the swim test because his guys were going to be there. He was waiting for Thompson and Keller."

"Back up to Saturday, he didn't mash his company after the rifle incident and he remained behind with the captain after I left."

"He spoke to the captain about what?"

"I don't know, but I think I am starting to understand. He was in personnel the day before our companies came in looking at personnel files."

Alex's eyes widened as the glimmer of understanding began to illuminate his mind. "I think he loaded his company and I think the captain is helping him."

"Why?"

"Captain wants him to win the *Double Salute*."

John's face reddened in anger. "So this whole thing is rigged in his favor. I'll kill him." He stood up.

"Hang on there big guy. We'll figure this out."

"Maybe the answer is do what we do and let him hang himself."

"He's too smart for that. I think he's tipped his hand who he wants to take out."

"Who?"

"Thompson and Keller," Alex said.

"Why them?"

"The Captain's Cup."

"Ah. I get it. They are our best chance of winning the Cup and if we don't then he's got the inside track to winning the overall competition."

"You know John, Dale Earnhardt said once, 'The winner ain't the one with the fastest car, it's the one who refuses to lose.' Peach thinks he's got us backed into a corner on the defensive. I refuse to lose. Get Keller and Thompson."

Lexi switched off the light to Commander Hendrick's inner office, stepped in to the corridor and locked the door. She turned to the click of a pair of corfram dress shoes on the highly polished deck. "Petty Officer Peach, how are you doing this evening?"

"I'm fine. Going home?"

"Yes, I have my own life to take care of. Don't you have a home or wife to go home to?"

"Nope. Just go home to sleep. This place is my girl."

She leaned into him with an upraised lip. "You're a weird guy."

"You can say that," he said. "Hey, how about I take you to Pier 525 for dinner?"

"It's getting late. It's Monday and I've got a lot to do, maybe another-"she said and then paused to think about it. "You know that's not a bad idea. I haven't been in their yet. How about it?"

"Good. You want to ride with me?" Peach asked.

"No. I'll take my car."

"Suit yourself. Do you know where it is?"

"Yep. I'll see you there."

The '24' on the apartment door held his gaze as he fumbled for his key. *I feel more like forty eight than twenty four years old after the last seventy two hours,* he thought to himself. He took a deep breath and let it out as slow as he could. The dead bolt clicked as he rotated the key and the door opened before he could turn the knob.

"Alex," Cathreen said as she hugged his neck. "I feel like I haven't seen you in a week." He squeezed her and kissed her forehead.

"I guess when the crud hits the fan; they make you clean it up. And have I've been shoveling it up," Alex said as he came into the two bedroom apartment.

"Have you had a chance to eat dinner?"

"No," he said with little emotion.

"Alex, you look awful. Have you slept at all?"

"I'm exhausted. I tried to but that five-star hotel they booked me in didn't live up to as advertised."

Cat snickered at the bad joke.

"I might have been able to sleep in between the bad dreams if John wasn't sounding like an F-14 with asthma."

Cathreen took the brief case and coat from him placing it on the sofa. "I'm sorry honey. Sit down and I'll get you something to eat."

Alex settled into the recliner and grunted. Cat helped him slip his shoes off. She watched him get comfortable, kissed him on the forehead and then scurried off to the kitchen. *Probably not a good time,* she thought to herself.

"I had breakfast with Mary Lou yesterday," Cat shouted from the kitchen. "She is really sweet. Oh by the way the car is acting up again. I'm going to take it in to have it looked at tomorrow."

"That's nice honey."

"Did you want mustard or mayonnaise on your turkey?"

Silence greeted her inquiry and she came into check on him. A steady cadence of breathing came from Alex as his chest rose and fell. She studied her husband for a long time. His hand rolled off his chest and a slip of paper fell to the floor. Giving it no thought she opened the slip of paper and read it and gasped: *Lexi - 847-688-1111 – Call me.*

It is the custom of the Navy to provide their personnel a place to go where they could get a drink or have dinner on off duty hours. The club Pier 525 was originally built for enlisted attending 'A' training schools between pay grade E1-E6. They could secure an alcoholic beverage if they liked, provided they were 21 years of age. The club also provided a full service restaurant for those who were looking for an alternative to the chow hall. After most of the funding for clubs on the base was discontinued and the popularity of clubs decreased Pier 525 became the only club at *Naval Training Center.*

"It will be about ten minutes for a table," the hostess said to Peach and Lexi.

"That's fine, we'll wait in the bar," Peach said.

Peach pulled out a stool for Lexi to sit down then seated himself.

"What'll it be?" Buddy said as he placed two napkins on the bar.

"Iced Tea, with lots of lemon," Lexi said.

"You sir?"

"Bourbon. Do you guys have Makers Mark?"

"Ooooooh. Expensive taste there Petty Officer Peach?" Lexi said.

Peach, I wonder if this is the same Peach Alex was talking about. Has to be, how many people have the last name Peach? Buddy thought to himself. "I agree." Buddy said.

"On the rocks. Make it a double," Peach said and turned back to Lexi.

"Tell me about yourself and how in the world did you get here to Great Mistakes?" Peach said.

"Well as you know I'm part of the civil service. I transferred here with my boy friend about six month ago."

Peach raised and eyebrow and shifted in his seat. "Boyfriend?"

Lexi sipped her water. "Did I say boyfriend, I meant ex-boyfriend, ex-fiancée. Get me an x-ray machine and have my head examined."

Peach snickered. "You were going to be married, and what happened?"

"Well he drags me to this God forsaken place. I mean c'mon can't the state of Illinois plant a few more trees."

"Come on, there's plenty of trees around here."

"Are you kidding me, I grew up in Vermont. They've got tons of trees there. They don't call it the Green Mountain State for nothing. To me this is like the Sahara desert. Flat, oh my gosh, I think the highest point in Illinois is 1235 feet. Sheesh, they had to build something taller than that, the Sears Tower is 500 feet higher. I'm rambling, I'm sorry. What did you ask me?"

"You were going to be married."

"Oh yeah, shoot. The marriage. Well you Sailors are pretty big talkers and Ken wasn't any different. Nice guy, but big dreams but not very wise," she said as she grabbed a pretzel and popped it in her mouth. "We met at *Miramar Naval Air Station* where I was working in the Operations Department. He was an Electronics Technician, worked in the building on the ACLS system."

"ACLS, what's that?"

"Automated Carrier Landing System. A radar that can land airplanes automatically."

"Ok," Peach said.

"He'd just reenlisted, got a great big fat bonus and was changing rates. He was going to 'A' school to be a Fire Control Technician and then to Virginia for the Aegis Radar System. He says, 'come with me to Great Lakes and we'll get married there.' Have you ever married?"

"No. Just me to please. So I do. Go on with your story."

"He hooked me and I was on the line. However, being a civil servant I couldn't just pick up and leave. I put in for a transfer and that took some time, but I was able to get this job here in the admiral's office. We weren't able to coordinate our schedules, so I had to stay in San Diego for six week before I could get out here." She paused and took a big sip of the ice tea Buddy placed in front of her.

"Well I get here, he'd started school already and was living in the barracks instead of finding a place for us to live. His school started fast and furious and he was falling behind. I'm living in a cheap hotel in Waukegan. I'm trying to get my life settled before I started my job and life is a mess."

"So what did you do?"

"He comes by the motel I'm staying at one night and wants to go to a movie. I flipped and asked him what was wrong with him? That was it. We got into a huge fight. The manager called the cops. I told him I didn't want to marry him and he got really mad. Thank God he didn't hit me but he was close. The cops came, told him to either go away or spend the night in jail. He left and I hadn't heard from him since."

"Wow. That's tough. What are you doing now?"

"Well it took me some time, but I found a nice little apartment down in Lake Forrest."

"Wow, that's nice area."

"I like nice things and nice people, so I'm done with Sailors. Their not people, they are my job. Yep, Two is enough."

"Two. What happened with the first one?"

"Alex," she said.

Buddy put the drinks down and tried to stay in earshot of the couple by clearing some empty glasses nearby.

"Alex? Oh, Alex Sievers," he said with surprise. "Alex Sievers? What did you see in that moron?" He tried not to show his disgust.

"We were engaged to be married."

Buddy swallowed hard and quickly quelled any expression. He tried to look disinterested and hoped they had not seen his reaction when the woman spoke the name of his new friend.

Cat sat down on the edge of the bed to calm her self. She tried to sip water, but could not hold the glass steady. She stood up, clenched her fist and started toward the living room, when the phone rang. *Should I pick it up or should I let it ring and wake up Alex?* When she heard Alex stir in the other room, she grabbed the phone from the cradle and whispered, "Hello." She closed the door.

"Hello, Cat. It's Mary Lou."

"Thank God you called."

"Why? What's wrong?"

"Alex just got home," Cat said.

"I know John came home a little while ago too. He grabbed a quick sandwich and went to bed. Did you get to talk to him?"

"No. He fell asleep as soon as he sat down. He didn't even eat anything. I went to get him something to eat and he was knocked out. I come back to check on him and a slip of paper fell out of his hand. It was a note from Lexi to call her."

"Who's Lexi?"

"My old room mate."

The heat of the crucible of adversity is meant to melt a man and cast him into the image of a United States Navy Sailor. One dark night the crucible had reduced another recruit to an emotional wreck. A muffled sob broke through the rhythmic breathing and snoring of the other sailors fast asleep. A heart longing for a familiar voice or place shed a tear to release the stress from the intensity of the unknowns of the daily grind of the Navy boot camp training.

"Psssst."

Gary Masters, a seventeen year old recruit, stifled the ache in his throat when he realized he'd been busted. He pulled his grey scratchy government issued blanket tighter around himself to conceal himself from the crasher of his pity party.

"Pssst. Masters," a voice called from the darkness.

"Keller?" Masters whispered.

"Yeah man. You OK?"

"Yeah," he shot back; embarrassed he'd been caught wallowing in his weakness.

"If you want to talk, I'll meet you in the head I was just going," Keller said.

All branches of the military have their own unique jargon and the Navy was no different. When a sailor had to use the bathroom they said they were going to the 'Head,' a term first coined in 1708 by Woodes Rogers, an English Privateer and Governor of the Bahamas by using it in a book called, *A Cruising Voyage Around The World*. It is a nautical term referring to the forward part of the ship or bow, where the ship's toilet was placed near the bowsprit. The bowsprit was a pole or spar that extended out from the ship. The toilet could be cleaned with waves crashing over the bow.

Keller shuffled into the head and relieved himself. While he washed his hands, Gary Masters came in and squinted as his eyes adjusted to the harsh fluorescent light. He turned around and smiled at the scrawny baby faced kid standing in front of him. "Y'all alright," Keller whispered.

Masters shrugged and looked down at the tiled floor.

"What's the matter, man? We're shipmates lay it on me."

"Well," Masters muttered. "I guess I'm kind of . . . homesick."

"Me too," Keller said. "So what's the problem?"

"I'm used to doing things by myself. Here you got people watching you all the time," Masters said as he pointed to the row of toilets without any doors. "For crying out loud they don't even put doors on the toilet stalls. People just walk by you and watch you taking a dump."

"This is better than when we were over their in the Receiving Barracks. You remember there were no walls. You can sit there and watch a guy on both sides of you. Now that's embarrassing."

Masters laughed and felt like he could open up. "Yeah you're right. That was pretty bad."

"C'mon y'all it's not about the head. What really gives?"

"This rah-rah teamwork garbage," he said as his eyes narrowed. "No matter what I do it's wrong. If I mess something up they're all over me like a cheap suit. I do something right and they say nothing. Look man, I'm used to taking care of my self and doing things my way."

"Did you play sports?"

"No. I spent most of my time reading and studying. I won awards for my academics."

"There's your problem. Your selfish and don't know what teamwork is."

"I'm not selfish."

"You are so wrapped up in yourself that you can't see what's happening here. This is about doing hard things. Hard things require teamwork. Yeah teams can have selfish players on them who are ball hogs because they want the glory for themselves. When you look at teams like that they usually don't win championships."

"I joined the Navy because I wanted to see the world. I didn't know about all this stuff they are teaching us. What does folding a blanket or recognizing someone else's rank have to do with anything?"

"Are you paying attention to anything they are telling us? If my blanket is perfectly folded and your blanket is perfectly folded then we've worked together as a team. If you recognize the insignia of an officer you will render him the respect that he is due and you will follow his orders because you will recognize his authority to accomplish a mission."

"You got all that from those classes that are so boring I thought I was going to die."

"Yes. I understand all that. Teamwork is the foundation for duty and honor. When you realize that by doing your duty no matter how insignificant it may seem, like cleaning a head, you are part of the wall of defense against all enemies foreign and domestic."

"Is that why we said that at the AFEES station?"

"Yes."

"I think I get it. So I'm the one screwing this thing up."

"Uh huh," Keller said and crossed his arms and leaned up against the wall. "If you wait for Petty Officer Sievers to come in here and pat you on the head, tell you that you're doing a good job and wipe away your tears. It's not going to happen."

"So what do I do?"

"Your duty."

"My duty," Masters said in awe of the thought. He looked at Keller who'd come to stand in front of him. "Do you know that oath we took?"

"Yeah, I do."

"Can you swear me in, like they did at the AFEES station?"

"I can," Keller said and smiled. "I'd be glad to. OK. Raise your right hand."

Masters and Keller raised their right hands and looked each other in the eye.

"I, state your name," Keller said.

"I Gary Masters."

"Do solemnly swear, that I will support and defend the Constitution of the United States," Keller said with a solemn respect.

"Do solemnly swear, that I will support and defend the Constitution of the United States," Masters repeated.

"Against all enemies, foreign and domestic: that I will bear true and faith and allegiance to the same," Keller said.

Masters whispered the same back to Keller.

"And I will obey the orders of the President of the United States and the orders of the officers, appointed over me."

"And I will obey the orders of the President of the United States and . . . and the orders," Masters said and paused.

"And the orders of the officers, appointed over me," Keller said again.

"And the orders of the officers, appointed over me," Master said.

"According to regulations and the Uniform Code of Military Justice," Keller said.

With tear filled eyes, Masters said, "According to regulations and the Uniform Code of Military Justice."

"So help me God."

"So help me God," Masters said with exuberance.

"Ssshh. You want to wake the whole company up?"

"No man. Thanks so much for showing me this. I appreciate it so much." He smiled and continued. "We're going to win that *Double Salute*."

"You bet your dress blues we are. I'll see you tomorrow." Keller walked back to his rack shaking his head. "How did I get to be the company shrink?"

CHAPTER 10: DAMN THE TORPEDOES FULL SPEED AHEAD

Damn the torpedoes, full speed ahead – David Farragut, Battle of Mobile Bay

The sun peaked over the horizon of August 5th, 1864 illuminating an eerie tension hovering over Mobile Bay. The first admiral of the reorganized United States Navy, Admiral David Farragut, made final preparations for battle. The armada of 18 Union ships marshaled at the entrance of the 31 mile inlet of the Gulf of Mexico, leading to the state of Alabama. 67 mines (also known as torpedoes) planted in the channel by the Confederate Navy, stood as the main obstacle to the pending assault on the bay. The torpedoes were clearly marked so ships would be forced to the east and would traverse the choke point under the barrage of gunfire from the 46 guns at *Fort Morgan* and *Fort Gaines.*

Farragut conceived an ingenious plan to use his four ironclad monitor warships as cover for his 14 wooden-hulled ships that bore the heavy firepower for the assault. The wooden-hulled ships were paired and lashed together so that if one became incapacitated the two ships could continue under the power of the one operational ship.

Aboard the *USS Hartford*, Farragut flew his flag and commanded his fleet into battle. "Captain Drayton," Farragut barked.

"Yes sir,"

"Direction of the wind?" Farragut said as he peered through is telescope toward *Fort Morgan.*

"Southwest, sir."

"Good, good. The smoke from the cannon fire will drift back into their faces and away from us." Farragut snapped the looking glass shut and turned to the captain. "Send the signal to the fleet, to reduce pressure in the boilers. We'll ride the tide in and if they take a hit from incoming fire it will limit the damage."

"Aye sir," Drayton said and passed the order to the signal corp.

Farragut licked his lips and scanned the 30 year old *Fort Morgan*, named for the revolutionary war hero Daniel Morgan. "My she's beautiful, one of the finest examples of military architecture I've ever seen and she's going to be mine." He snapped the spy glass closed. "Captain."

"Sir."

"Clear for action," Farragut said in a deep baritone voice. "Order the monitors to begin there run. Have the *USS Brooklyn*, take the lead of the wooden-hulls because of her forward guns. We'll follow *Brooklyn*." The fleet passed to the east of Sand Island the initial barrier island, while a small contingent of ships blockaded the entrance to Grants Pass.

At 6:47AM the *USS Tecumseh* fired the opening salvo upon *Fort Morgan* to the east which earned a response from the fort's 46 guns. The fortress also sported 18 heavy guns, 14 standard cannons, two more powerful muzzle-loaded 7" Brookes rifles and two British-made 8" Blakely rifles.

With the sustained gunfire a cloud of smoke impaired Farragut's view of the battle. To gain a bird's eye view of the skirmish he climbed the rigging of the *Hartford*. "Why is *Tecumseh* moving away?" Farragut yelled. "You're going the wrong way?"

Tecumseh, commanded by Tunnis A. M. Craven turned to port away from the on shore bombardment of *Fort Morgan* to engage the waiting Confederate Navy and wandered into the mind field and was immediately greeted by an underwater demolition device explosion which ripped open the hull below the waterline, sinking the ironclad in three minutes. Only 21 of the 114 crew were able to abandon ship safely.

Captain James Alden skipper of the *Brooklyn* slowed his advance as *Tecumseh* sank beneath the surf. Unsure if he should continue his advance he signaled Farragut for instructions.

To keep from colliding with *Brooklyn, Hartford* slowed. Farragut yelled from the ships rigging to Captain Drayton, "Why are we slowing down?"

"Sir, the Torpedoes."

Farragut responded, "Damn the Torpedoes, four bells. Do not slow down. Go around the *Brooklyn*."

Hartford veered to the starboard into the mine field putting their full faith into the Admiral's belief that the torpedoes had been submerged too long to be effective. His gamble paid off and wrought a great victory for the Union.

"We know it better as 'Damn the Torpedoes, full speed ahead," said Alex to the mesmerized group of recruits sitting on the floor of the barracks of Company 197.

"So what happened, Petty Officer Sievers?" Thompson asked.

"Farragut was right and the mines were ineffective and he was able to crush the ships defending the bay. The army secured the three forts. The Union was able to close the blockade, suffocate the Confederacy by cutting off its last major sea port and their ability to resupply themselves."

Another recruit in the back raised his hand. "Yes."

"History is dull. Why do we need to learn all this anyway? How's it going to help me when I'm out in the fleet?"

"That is a great question," Alex said. "Well, by you learning about Naval history it gives you a snap shop of what the Navy is all about, what it is like by what it has done. By knowing this you can see how you fit in it. George Santayana said, 'Those who cannot learn from history are doomed to repeat it.' History can show us where mistakes were made before and if enough people who learn where these mistakes were made then we can make sure not to step into a mess again. Admiral Farragut used history, the technology available to him at the time and courage to win the Battle of Mobile Bay. He also learned from his own mistakes he had made at Vicksburg in 1863 to stick to the plan and not make changes to it."

Alex walked into the midst of the recruits. "Men we have a plan to win the *Double Salute* and as our heroic predecessor once said, 'Damn the torpedoes full speed ahead.'"

Seaman Hayes sat in the back of the group daydreaming not really paying attention to the banter of questions the recruits peppered Petty Officer Sievers with. He thought, *I wonder what it was like on one of those old wooden ships. They must've had lots of . . .* "RAT!" he shouted as a king size rat ran across his shoe.

He jumped up on his chair at the site of the rat.

"Well get him," Sievers shouted at him.

"Get the rat . . . rat, sir?"

"Yeah get him. We get them in here all the time. He doesn't eat much and they're pretty easy to catch. Once you get him throw him outside."

Hayes eyed the monster's beady eyes staring back at him. The recruits in the back watched and chuckled as Hayes moved closer to the rodent. In a quick snap he reached out and grabbed the rat. "I got him sir."

"Good now get rid of him," Alex said.

Hayes kicked the door open and tried to keep the rat from escaping. About to make a hard left toward the entrance to the building the door to Company 195 barracks caught his attention where he saw them standing at attention. *I know I shouldn't do this but what the heck,* he thought to himself.

The mischievous recruit stole a look around, crouched and snuck toward the door. He opened the door wide enough to let the rat into the barracks, quietly closed the door and backed away from the door snickering.

"What are you doing recruit?" a voice shouted at his back.

Hayes whirled around and his eyes widened when he saw a tall black man dressed in a black uniform standing in front of him. By his blue rope trimmed with white hanging from his shoulder he recognized him as MED (Military Examining Division). "Just thought I saw a piece of trash." He stood at attention.

"OK. As you were." The MED stepped around him and entered the

195 barracks.

As the door closed he let out the breath he'd been holding and heard, "Attention on deck." He smiled and hustled back to the lecture.

The MED is responsible for the examination of all the recruit companies at *Recruit Training Command*. They conduct personnel, barracks and drill inspections. They score each company and submit these scores for flags, honor companies and company commander proficiency in training of the recruits.

"Company 195, ready for inspection sir," shouted the Rpock and snapped a crisp salute to the chief who stood at the front of the barracks with a clip board at his side. Petty Officer Peach and Petty Officer Santello stood behind the Rpock.

The chief moved to the first recruit in line on the port side (left side) of the barracks. The Rpock stood next to the MED. As the inspector moved down the line Peach would once again inspect the recruit.

As the inspection progressed the recruits waiting to be inspected stood in a silent line. The rat Seaman Hayes had deposited in the barracks decided to perform an inspection of his own, right down the center of the two lines of recruits. Both lines watched as the rodent moseyed through their ranks.

As the inspecting party approached where the rat sat, the varmint decided to inspect the shoe of one of recruits. The inspector was only fifteen feet from him, he couldn't move a muscle or it would draw his attention. The rat had found a way to nuzzle up the recruits bell-bottomed pant leg at the horror of the recruits standing across from him.

In an effort to try to get the rat out of his pant leg he ever so slightly raised the insole of his polished corfram shoe. The rat dug his claw into his leg causing the recruit to grimace and grunt. Unable to take any more, the recruit broke ranks and shook the rodent from his pants.

The inspector turned to observe the horrified recruit as the rodent scurried away. The other recruits unable to contain themselves snickered for a moment. "You're at attention," the inspector yelled.

He drilled holes into the recruit with his eyes, "Get back in ranks." He said to the rat scratched recruit and then scanned the recruits with a disgusted look. "I don't care if the rat was biting him on the butt, this is unacceptable."

The inspector turned to Peach and said, "You fail. Call me when you are ready for a proper inspection." He spun on his heel and left the barracks.

Alex and Hatch Harris sat at the back of the company commander's mess finishing up their afternoon meal.

"Climbed right up his leg during the personnel inspection," Hatch said. He roared in laughter slapping the table.

"You've got to be kidding," John shot back at him. "What did the inspector do?"

"Walked out."

"I don't believe you. That could not have happened," Alex said as the door to the mess burst open and Peach stomped in.

"Rats, how the heck did a rat get into my barracks," Peach shouted at Santello.

"Wow. Hatch you were right," Alex said, spun his chair around and in the best fake sympathetic voice, "I guess rats have a nose for their own. Do you need me to call the exterminator for you?"

Peach growled and took a step toward Alex. "Oh Sievers I thought I smelled a rat when I came in. If I'd known any better I'd say you put that rat in there."

"Are you accusing me of something here Rod, because it sure sounds like you're trying to accuse me of something." Alex stood. Hatch stood up, leaned across the table and put his hand on his shoulder to calm him down. Alex pursed his lips and narrowed his eyes.

"He ain't worth it Alex. Take it easy," Hatch said.

"As worthless as your company is Harris, that doesn't give you much room to be talking either," Peach sneered at Hatch.

Hatch stood erect, "Yeah I might have a better chance at having a better company if rats like you weren't stacking his own."

"Are you accusing me of cheating hatchet?"

"I call them as I see them. If you ain't cheating then why don't you enlighten us to how every grad class you have the biggest and smartest dudes that come in here? How come you spend so much time over in personnel just before a new class comes in? Come on mister big cheese, please explain it to us?"

"Y'all are just a bunch of losers who can't stand getting your butts beat," Rod said and then stepped in and lowered his voice so only Alex and Hatch could here him. "I'm warning you, stay out of my way," he hissed.

Peach stepped out of the company commander's mess shaking. Not wanting anyone to see him this way, he darted off to the restroom. He crashed into the head and punched one of the closed doors. "I'm going to kill that son of a gun." As he calmed down he became aware of the strong antiseptic smell stinging his nose which helped restore order to his scattered thoughts. "Sievers some days you're the bug and some days you're the windshield. Well today I'm the windshield and I'm going to squash you like the pesky little mosquito you are," he said to his reflection in the mirror pounding the sink. "C'mon Rod. Think man."

After a long silent moment he smiled at the mirror and he snapped his fingers. "You want to play games Sievers. Well I never lose. You want to put something in my barracks I'm going to put something in yours."

Peach splashed his face, rubbing it briskly trying to shake off the remnants of the anxiety he'd felt. He dried his hands and crushed the paper towel into a tight little ball and laughed to himself. "Now I've got you Sievers." He slam dunked the paper towel in the trash can and yanked on the door.

When the door closed behind him a toilet flushed.

Alex entered the empty 197 barracks and made a hard left turn into his office. Picked up the phone and punched out the telephone number to his apartment. The phone rang several times before Cathreen picked up. "Hello," Cat said in a sleepy voice.

"Hey Cat," Alex said in a soft voice. "How you doing?"

"I was sleeping."

"It seems like any time we are around each other lately one of is tired, sleepy or asleep."

"Mmmh, mmmh," she said in response.

"I was really beat last night. I'm sorry for falling asleep on you."

"Look I am going to try to get home on time tonight I thought I'd take my honey out for dinner. What do you think?"

"Are you saying your mistress is going to let you spend some time with your wife for a change?"

"Mistress?" Alex said with a fright and gulped. "What are you talking about?"

"The Navy, the Navy," she said.

"Oh I get it; you think I'm married to the Navy too. No honey I'm not, I'm married to you and am always faithful."

"You sound like a Marine."

"Marine?" he shot back at her.

"Always faithful. Semper Fidelis."

"Yeah, yeah. Marine. No I am not a sea going bell hop. Nice uniforms, but no thanks not me. I'm not part of 'The Few, The Proud, The dead on the beach.' I'm Navy through and through."

"At least you know what you are."

"You betcha beautiful. I'm going to be an officer some day. An officer and a gentleman."

"Alright, no more. I get enough commercials on TV. What time you going to be here?"

"About six."

"Love you."

"Love you too."

Alex hung up the phone and stared at it for a moment. *She sure puts up with a lot. I'm glad this almost over.* The rap on the door brought him back to reality. "Come."

The door opened and Lexi stepped in. "Petty Officer Sievers."

"Lexi," Alex said and stood up to greet her. "To what do I owe this pleasure?"

"Pleasure and business."

"I'm sorry I don't think I understand."

"Commander Hendrick has requested your presence at Pier 525 for dinner tonight to discuss the changes to the firefighting training schedule. He is asking all the company commanders for their input."

"Why can't we meet in his office during the day? Why does it need to be at the Club? What makes me so special?"

"Look I don't know I'm just the messenger."

"I'm supposed to be having dinner with my wife tonight."

"Aw that's too bad, would you like me to tell the commander that you can't make it? I'm sure he would understand."

"I see your point. Does he ever go home and see his wife?"

"Occasionally."

"What am I going to tell my wife? She's not going to be too happy about this."

"Would you like me to call her for you?"

"Ah. No, I don't think that is a very good idea. She's been a little emotional lately and all the garbage that's been going on around here. Our trip getting ruined. Coming home late every night and getting up early. I have hardly seen her at all the last week. Last thing she needs is to have her old room mate call her up and tell her husband is going to be late."

"I get the message." She stepped around the desk and reached for his neck. He winced and backed away.

"Lexi, please don't make this more difficult than it already is."

"I'm sorry. I just remember when you would get tense you always liked a neck rub."

"Tell the commander I'll be there and could you please excuse me I need to go make my wife upset."

Standing in front of the closet trying to decide what to wear, Cathreen wondered what life would be like if she'd not been married to Alex. "The justice of the peace did say for better or for worse. I sure wish we could get back to the better." She held up one outfit in front of the mirror and then another. "I don't know," she said to herself.

Should I tell him tonight or should I wait, she thought to herself. *If I wait until he finishes this company it could be another three weeks. I'll tell him tonight.*

The jangling of the phone interrupted the conversation she was having with herself. She bounced on the bed while picking up the phone. "Hello."

"Cat it's me," Alex said.

"Don't tell me."

"It's the commander; he wants to meet with me tonight to get input on the firefighting training curriculum. They found some problems in the training and they need input from all the company commanders by next week so the Secretary of the Navy can be briefed when he comes for his official visit."

"Why does it have to be tonight?"

"He has been in meetings all day with all the other company commanders and I was the last one on his list to interview. I'm really sorry. I knew about the interviews I thought that it would be tomorrow."

"Look Alex I understand, but my patience is wearing thin. When is there going to be time for us?"

"Once this boot class is over and I win the *Double Salute* then the sky is the limit. Things are going to change after I win. I'm positive. I can taste it I'm so sure and after today I'm even more sure."

"Why do you think that?"

"Peach's entire company failed the PI."

"You're kidding, how did that happen?"

"Some rat messed things up for them."

"Who's the rat?"

"No. A real rat. One with beady eyes, long skinny tale. A rodent the kind we trap and kill."

"Yuck," she said. "Poetic justice a rat takes out another rat."

"Look," he said and then something clicked in thoughts. "I got to go. I'll try to be home early. Love you."

"Love you to," Cat said. *Click.*

Alex hung up the phone and catapulted out of his chair and went out into the barracks and was greeted with an "Attention on deck."

All the men stopped what they were doing and stood at attention. He scanned the barracks for a brief moment. "As you were," Alex said. "I need to see Seaman Recruit Hayes, on the double."

Keller relaxed from attention. "What did you do man?"

"I don't know man," Hayes said as he pulled his pant leg on. He quickly tucked the blue chambray shirt in his pants and pulled his boon dockers on.

He rapped three times, entered when commanded, took three steps into the office and stood at attention. "Seaman Recruit Hayes, reporting as ordered sir."

"At ease," Alex responded. Hayes relaxed and stood with his hands behind his back. "This afternoon when I told you to get rid of that rat, what did you do with it?"

"I gave it a new home, sir."

"That new home wouldn't happen to be the barracks of Company 195 would it?"

"Ah, yes sir. Company 195 barracks would be the rat's new home."

Alex tried to hold back a smile. "As a company commander it is my duty to discipline you for your actions and provide you with proper instructional training to prevent this from happening again. Next time you decide to put a rat in another company's barracks you will be placed on report and sent to Captain's Mast. That is your proper instructional training. This talk I am giving you is your discipline for your actions."

"Yes sir."

"Off the record," Alex waved his finger at him and smiled. "Good job, but don't ever do that again. You understand? If any one ever asks I did not put you up to it. You did it all on your own."

"Yes sir," Hayes said.

"You're dismissed."

CHAPTER 11: SERVICE WEEK

A young man who does not have what it takes to perform military service is not likely to have what it takes to make a living. Today's military rejects include tomorrow's hard-core unemployed. - John F. Kennedy

The aroma of the signature fresh baked bread filled the Great Lakes Naval Station Pier 525 and greeted Alex before the hostess did. He removed his cover and smiled at the young thin brunette behind the hostess station, "Good evening sir. One?"

"No, I'm meeting someone. A Lieutenant Commander Hendrick."

"Yes. He's already here; I will show you to his table." She picked up a menu and slalomed her way through the tables of uniformed guests. Many who chose to trade their hard earned cash for a good dinner instead of a mediocre one in the chow hall. The hostess ushered Alex to the nicer part of the club reserved for officers.

From a distance Alex could see the commander engaged in conversation with someone out of view. The hostess placed the menu on the table and gestured to the vacant chair. Alex said, "Sir."

"Petty Officer Sievers, glad you could make it. Please sit down." Alex flashed an awkward look at Lexi.

"Lexi."

"Alex," she responded and returned the smile.

"Do you two know each other? I mean outside of here."

Alex shifted in his seat and sipped from his water glass. "Yes sir, we know each other outside of work."

Lexi flashed a mischievous grin and stared at Alex as she said, "Engaged to be married."

Alex choked on the water, grabbed his napkin trying not to spit it out.

"Ahhhh," the commander said. "Congrat . . ." He turned to Alex puzzled. "Aren't you married already? And are you two getting married?"

He squirmed and flashed Lexi an irritated look as she smiled and bit a bread stick. "Yes sir. I mean, no sir,"

"Which is it Alex, are you married to me or someone else?" Lexi said in a playful but serious tone.

"Sir," he said clearing his throat. "I am married yes, but not to her."

"To whom then?" Commander Hendrick asked.

"To my wife," Alex started to say but his vocal chords locked up and didn't finish what he wanted to say. He took another drink of water and tried clearing his throat again. "Cat…"

The commander amused by the answer, laughed. "You're married to a cat."

"No sir," Lexi interjected, clearly humored by this but decided it was time to end the joke. "Cathreen. Cathreen Jeffries, an old room mate of mine from San Diego."

"If he is married to this Cathreen, how are you two engaged to be married?"

"I really meant to say, we were once engaged to be married."

"Ohhhhhh. I get it. I'm sorry Petty Officer Sievers, I thought you two. Oh never mind. Alexis, you sure had me going."

"Yes sir. I did. Didn't I?" Lexi said while looking at Alex. "I'm sorry Alex. I couldn't help myself. You're too serious and it was always easy to get you into a joke like that."

"Thanks a lot. I see you haven't changed very much," Alex shot back at her.

"I can see neither have you," Lexi said and narrowed her eyes.

"Petty Officer Sievers," Buddy said. "How are you this fine evening?"

"I'm fine sir, how are you?" Alex stood to shake Buddy's hand.

"I'm good, who are your friends?" Buddy inquired with a big grin.

"This is Lieutenant Commander Hendrick," Alex said. "My division officer."

"Commander Hendrick, it's a pleasure to meet you," Buddy said extending his hand.

"You look familiar," Commander Hendrick said as he stood to take Buddy's hand. "Captain Orr, isn't it?"

"Yes it is."

"It is a pleasure to finally meet you. I've heard so much about you. Why are you working here?"

"I'm retired now and it's hard to leave a job you've been at your whole life," Buddy said and turned his attention to Lexi. "And who is this beautiful creature."

"This is Alexis Althorne, Commander Hendrick's secretary."

Buddy gently took her hand and met her gleaming blue eyes. "It's a pleasure to meet you," he said as if he'd never seen her before. "You have the most wonderful eyes my dear."

"Thank you," Lexi said, embarrassed.

"I must get back to work. It was nice seeing you again Petty Officer Sievers."

"You too sir," Alex said as Buddy walked away.

"He's cute," Lexi said.

"He's an old man and married too," Alex shot back at her. "There are enough young bucks to get your claws into."

"Ahem. Maybe it's a good thing you two didn't get married," Commander Hendrick said. "Petty Officer Sievers I called you here to get your input on the firefighting training. Alexis will take notes on our conversation so that your comments and suggestions may be added to the report she is currently preparing for Secretary Freeman."

Lexi tapped her steno pad trying to vent her anger from the hurtful remark launched at her in front of the boss.

Alex felt the pleasure, pain and embarrassment of the verbal missile he launched at her.

Commander Hendrick plowed along unaware of the cold war being waged in front of him. "We've completed about 95 percent of the curriculum for the training but haven't been able to find a way to bring it all together in a final test that is controlled but realistic enough to provide a real world experience for all the recruits who go through this part of the training."

Commander Hendrick pulled a list from a folder and handed it to Alex who'd heard nothing just said to him. "These are some of the ideas that have been bounced around. Take a moment to look at them and let me know what you think."

Alex took his time and used it to refocus his attention. He laid it down on the table. "They are all very good ideas, but I think I might have one that might be what you're looking for. But to be honest, fire and I just don't mix and well I. . ." he gulped and toyed with the corner of the paper on the table.

"I understand what you went through on *Ingersoll* was traumatic and you would probably just as soon forget it, but I need your experience. I need you to rush back into those flames again to help prevent other accidents like yours."

After a long solitary thought, Alex sighed. "Before we deployed for our Western Pacific Deployment the ship went through a series of tests. The last one was the mass conflagration drill, where we simulated the entire ship on fire. I remember thinking, how cool it would've been if the ship really was on fire. I know you have a drill planned by the same name and it is meant to test individual fire parties from different companies, what if you set it up where all the companies work together to save the USS *Landlock*?"

Commander Hendricks sat awe struck for a moment while the wheels turned in his head, "When they built the firefighting training facility around the *Landlock* the idea was to simulate many shipboard emergency scenarios including compartment fires, but I'm not sure setting the whole ship on fire can be done and utilize all the companies in the division."

"We might be able to do it on a limited scale lets talk to the training department over there and see what they can do. This could be quite a show for the SECNAV and if it is successful I'm sure funding could be gotten to improve the facility for the more ambitious training you are proposing." He thought about the idea for a moment, then nodded his approval. "Alright Petty Officer Sievers I'm sold. You develop the scenario and then run it by techies over at the school. I also want your company to lead the drill. Two other companies will train for the drill in support of your company and one other to be on standby."

"But sir, I . . . I'm not. I don't know if . . . if, I . . . I can." Alex looked to Lexi for support and back to the commander.

Lexi avoided his gaze. "If you'll excuse me I need to use the Ladies Room." She pushed her chair back. The commander and Alex both stood. The commander helped her from the chair. The two men watched her walk away and sat back down.

LCDR Hendrick sat down and lowered his voice, "Not many people get a chance to perform in front of the Secretary of the Navy. We've talked before about your career goals and I believe you would make a great officer, but you've got a few bumps on this yellow brick road you're on. You need this."

Alex stared at him in surprised disbelief. "Sir?"

"You have Service Week next week so you'll have quite a bit of free time on your hands to complete this project. I'll need you to get it done as fast as possible so we can complete the report and get it to the SECNAV."

"Yes sir, I'll have it done for you."

Commander Hendrick leaned over to Alex and lowered her voice. "Be careful with this little vixen she is dynamite that can explode in your face. I saw the way she looked at you. Just a suggestion from one friend to another."

"Don't worry sir, I love my wife and ..."

"That's nice," Lexi said as she sat down. "Are we ready to order? I'm starved."

The rest of the dinner passed with light conversation and when it was over the Commander picked up the check and the threesome headed out together. As they were leaving the club, LCDR Hendrick lead the way, Petty Officer Peach was coming in and held the door for the trio. "Hello Peach," Commander Hendrick said.

"Hello Commander," Peach responded. "Alexis, how are you?"

"Fine Rod how are you this evening?"

"Fine," Peach said and then nodded at Alex. "Sievers."

Alex and Rod mustered their most cordial 'I hate you look,' they could. "Rod." Alex said to his nemesis.

"Have a good evening …" Rod said to the door as it closed. "In hell."

Once in the parking lot, Alex stopped in front of his Trans Am. Lexi took her leave of the company, "I forgot something inside, don't wait for me. I'll see you tomorrow Commander."

"Goodnight Alexis," Commander Hendricks said to her as she shuffled away. "Goodnight Alex, see you tomorrow. Remember what I said." He turned and walked toward his car.

"Yes sir," Alex watched Lexi as Peach met her at the door of the club. "Hmmh. That's interesting."

Peach opened the inside door to the club as Lexi entered from the outside. He hustled her to the bar and quickly ordered a drink for himself, "Whiskey," he said to Buddy and then turned his attention to Lexi. "What do you have miss?"

"I'm good," she said.

Buddy turned away and busied himself with preparing Rod's drink. Once out of earshot Rod bored into her. "What's going on? What are you doing here with Commander Hendrick and Sievers?"

"I'm doing what you told me to do. You know those interviews you've been doing all week for the firefighting input."

"Yeah. So?"

"Eaves dropping, gathering information for you and trying to break up a marriage."

"Oh yeah."

"Alex was the last one on the list and the commander didn't want to do it in the office so we came here to do it. But that is not all of it."

Buddy put a napkin on the table and placed the shot glass of whiskey on it. "Can I have a glass of ice water," Lexi said to Buddy.

"Sure, doll."

"So what else is there? How did you get invited to dinner?"

"I'm the one who suggested it, because what you told me."

"What I tell you, anyway?"

"You guys have been in and out of the office all day and I didn't hear much because they were in the office with the door closed. I knew you wanted some information from Alex so I figured if we went out to dinner that he might loosen up and say something you can use. I made the suggestion and invited myself along as the stenographer so he could have a nice conversation and not have to take notes."

"Good thinking. Last time we talked you didn't tell me much why you are doing this?"

"I don't think you'd understand," she said to him as her eyes narrowed. "I told you we were supposed to be married. I wanted kids and a home with a white picket fence. He wanted a career in the Navy. So I thought if I got another guy interested in me and get him jealous he'd come running, but it back fired on me. He was pretty broken up about how it went down and my roommate moved into help pick up the pieces."

"You dump him and you want revenge. Sounds pretty twisted to me lady, but I'll take any help I can get."

Buddy watched with keen interest the animated conversation between the couple.

"Revenge! This isn't revenge, this is justice."

"How do you figure justice?"

Buddy moved to the sink closest to the two and pretended to wash glasses.

"I was doing what was best for the both of us and now he's going to pay the consequences for not seeing what he did to me. I must keep him from achieving his goals because that's what's most important to him. Sort of like you Rod, isn't that what you are trying to do? Cooking up this twisted scheme of yours to keep him from beating you."

"Don't lecture me about twisted and schemes sister. What you're doing is pretty sick and twisted."

"What's your gig, why do you hate him so much? Why are willing to jeopardize your career to beat him? Or are you just afraid of him? Afraid that he's better than you or can win honestly with out having to cheat? Is that it, you're just afraid of him?"

"I've known him all my life. We grew up together dreaming of the sea and the stars. We dreamed of being like Captain Kirk aboard our own Starships."

"Are you kidding me?" She laughed at him.

"It was kind of a ridiculous thing and stupid now that I think about it. That's the way Alex is, he makes you believe his stupid dreams are possible. Well there not. When we went to High School things were different and the fairytales were replaced with cold hard reality. There were too many darn distractions, girls, peer pressure to be cool, parents and school work. Somehow he kept focused on the dream while my life became a nightmare. I stopped listening to his foolishness and grew to despise it. I began to hate him."

Rod sucked down the shot of whiskey. It burned all the way down his gullet and he squeezed his eyes tightly shut, demanded another and a glass of beer. Buddy willingly obliged which gave him an excuse to draw closer to the two.

"My father lost his job and had to scrounge to support the family. He became depressed and started to drink heavily. He would come home at night and beat my Mom and sometimes me. I took out my anger on people and I grew to hate Alex more and more. He was the golden boy, couldn't do anything wrong. When he joined the Navy like he said he would, I remembered the dream and thought maybe it was still possible. Once I got into this dog eat dog canoe club I realized it was every man for himself. I had to take what I wanted. People liked him and somehow he moved forward."

"You envy him. You want to be him, but you can't so you want to destroy him."

"It's a little more complicated than that sister. Do you want to know what the worst part of it is?"

"Tell me."

"Don't ask me why but a small part of me likes him," Rod said as

Buddy put another shot of whiskey and a beer in front of him. "Thank you." He picked up the shot and held it in front of Lexi's face. "But a bigger part of me hates him ferociously and will do anything to see him fail."

"So you were friends with him."

"We were never friends," Rod spat at her, thrusting forward and wagging his finger in her face. After a long moment, he relaxed back into his chair. "We were more like brothers that could never get along. He was the goodie-two-shoes that everything came his way and I was the black sheep, 'why can't you be more like Alex.' Alright maybe when we were younger we were friends, but as we got older I grew to despise him. It felt good to torment him."

"You are one sick puppy."

"That I am," taking a slug of beer. "And I'm not going to let him win that *Double Salute*."

"Wow, you sound like me."

"Cause if he's going to succeed he's going to have to go through us and he's going to pay a huge price to get it. Are you in?" He said flatly. "If not, get your skinny little butt out now."

Lexi thought about the pain he'd caused her and allowed it to percolate in her for a moment. She allowed it to seethe and boil within her until it overflowed through her lips as she hissed, "I'm in."

"Alright." Peach said as he sucked down the second shot of whiskey. "What did you find out?"

The fifth week of training is known as Service Week, which is set aside for the practical training of ship board life and is devoted to giving the recruit instruction and experience similar to what they may encounter when joining the fleet. Some companies worked in the mess hall serving chow to other recruits. Others may be assigned housekeeping duties like grounds or barracks maintenance to keep the base cleaned and polished. Some are responsible to stand watch or act as message couriers.

The peaceful darkened barracks of Company 197 were brought to life with the stabbing neon lights at 0300 hours. "Rise and shine recruits, first day of Service Week," Alex shouted.

Training had become monotonous and the 0500 wake up calls were becoming routine but the shift in schedule was another of the many shocks to the system each recruit had to endure in the eight week cycle of training. "C'mon ladies get up and get your gear stowed. Got to feed the rest of the base chow."

For the next seven days the haggard recruits of Company 197 would serve 21 meals in one of the largest chow halls in the Navy. Potatoes would be peeled; hands would crack from the thousands of dishes, trays and pots that would be scoured. Pushed to exhaustion thousands of hungry faces would pass in review as these recruits would slop the hash, scoop the scrambled eggs and pass on the mystery meat to nourish their frazzled and bewildered fellow recruits.

"Company halt," the Rpock for Company 195 shouted. With one last step and a stomp Company 195 stopped in front of the *Recruit Training Command Supply Center*. Petty Officer Peach and Santello took their place in front of the company. "Gentlemen, since you are the current points leaders in the Graduation Class I was given the privilege to pick for you where you would be spending your service week. There were ten choices. Nine of them were for service in the mess hall as mess cranks. I have chosen for you the skate job of painting the RTC supply center. Now don't go thanking me for this wonderful assignment. But you will tomorrow morning when our Division mates Company 197 is up and off to work at zero three hundred hours and you'll be enjoying your nice warm bunks for two more hours."

The recruits smiled at their commander.

"The Supply Chief will be out momentarily to give you your assignments and issue uniforms for painting. We don't want you to mess up your nice new chambray shirts and dungarees. The Navy has thought of everything. Did I mention that you get off at sixteen hundred hours every day while the mess cranks don't get back to the barracks until nineteen hundred hours?"

"No sir," the recruits responded.

"Have fun. Rpock will march you to the chow hall at noon. Petty Officer Santello and I will check in with you from time to time."

Peach approached the Rpock. "Fall them out on the loading dock."

"Aye sir," the Rpock said and snapped a crisp salute, which Peach returned. "Company 195, fall out single file on the loading dock."

The recruits filed up the lone stair case and milled about and waited for the Supply Chief to give orders. Some sat on a stack of duffle bags stacked on the dock. After a few minutes, Chief Paige, a burly fat Boatswains Mate emerged from the supply center loading dock entrance with a clip board in hand.

The Rpock barked, "Atten-hut."

"As you were," Chief Paige said. "Alright gents, this is not rocket science here. We're going to paint this building the same color it is right now. The duffle bags you were sitting on contain uniforms for you to change into. I need two men to fetch the paint from the paint locker over by the chow hall."

No one raised there hands, so he pointed at the two recruits standing closest to him, "You and you. Take the flatbed golf cart over there and tell them you are from supply and that you need the paint Chief Paige requisitioned. They should have it ready for you. Rpock, come here."

The Rpock walked with the Chief into the receiving bay of the supply center. "These are the scaffolding and there is also a cherry picker for the points too high for the scaffolding. Do you know how to run one of these?"

"Sure, piece of cake," the Rpock said. "I used to work in a warehouse back at home."

"Alright, I don't want any skylarking and I'm going to be very busy so don't bother me unless it is an utter emergency. The other thing, stir the paint real good and don't worry about the color, it dries darker than it looks in the can. Do the back side first, then the sides and the front last. I'm sure you've painted before this is a no brainer. Any questions?"

"No sir," The Rpock said. "We can handle it."

"Alrighty then. Get busy."

At the paint locker the Recruits from 195 arrived at the same time civilian workers were coming into pickup a supply of paint. "Picking up a load of primer," the civilian said to the clerk behind the counter. The civilian workers handed over the requisition papers and the clerk pointed to a stack of paint cans along the wall.

The 195 recruits repeated the chief's orders to the clerk and the clerk pointed to the same wall the civilian workers took there primer from. They loaded up the flatbed and were on their way.

Back at the supply depot the two recruits unloaded the flatbed while the Rpock began to open the paint cans to stir them up. "Wasn't this supposed to be brown paint?" The Rpock asked.

"I don't know, we just took what the clerk gave us."

"He did say that the paint is real light in the can and dries darker. Let's just stir it up and get started. Who cares what it looks like any way?"

The growling noises his stomach made startled Alex in the deafening silence of his office as he scrawled notes for the idea he had pitched to the commander last night. "That reminds me," he said to his watch. "1300 I need to get some chow and swing by and see how the boys are making out."

Alex leaned back in his chair and stretched with the annoying squeal of the beast of a chair. "I'm never going to get used to that. I've got to remember to bring some oil from home."

He stood and made sure he'd gotten all his thoughts down before he took a break. Satisfied he grabbed his cover and headed out. As he entered the darkened hallway that lead out of the barracks the door popped open and in sauntered Lexi reading something and not looking where she was going. *Wham*, she ran right into the charging Alex. Unable to keep her balance, she started to fall. Unmoved by the impact, Alex lunged to catch the falling woman. He was able to keep her from hitting the deck, but her weight and being off balance he toppled over on top of her.

"Ow," she grumbled.

"Lexi, I'm sorry. I didn't see you coming," Alex said. He bounced up to a crouching position behind her and reached under her arms to lift her up. Once on her feet, she whirled around still in his arms.

"This is nice," she said to him slipping her arms around his waist. "Reminds me of old times."

"Ahh. . . Ahh. I'm sorry," Alex said and lowered his arm.

"Are you?"

"Yes. . . yes. I am sorry." He reached around his waist and took her hands from around him and put them at her side.

"Me too," she said and let out a sigh.

"I'm really sorry Lexi. Are you ok?" he said as he stooped to pick up her notebook lying on the floor.

"I'm fine. We really need to stop running into each other like this," she said playfully. "It seems like you are always knocking me down."

"You know every time we are around each other you want to talk about us. Can't we just be friends and let what happened in the past stay in the past?"

"Maybe for you it is easy just to tie up loose ends and go on your merry way. I am not built that way. I begged you to take me back and you wouldn't. Then you married that tramp of a roommate of mine. How dare you?"

"Look Alexis, I'm old school. You want to play with fire you're going to get burned. You found another guy and in my little corner of the world that means sayonara, hasta la vista baby. As for Cathreen leave her out of this you don't need to insult her."

"Alex, I did it because I loved you."

"Love. You don't know the first thing about love," Alex said. "You think I'm just supposed to come and sweep you off your feet after you betrayed me. You need your head examined."

"You hate me."

"I don't hate you. I have no respect for you and could never live with a woman whom I can't respect. So please save it, I don't want to hear it anymore. After this class, I'm going to asked to be transferred to another division."

"I hate you Alex Sievers. I hate your guts," she yelled at him and started for the door.

"What did you come in here for?"

She stopped and looked down at the shiny black tile. "Commander needs the report by tomorrow." She threw the door open and it slammed the wall and marched away.

Petty Officer Sievers entered from the rear of the mess hall where he ran into the first of his men from his company. "Hey Petty Officer Sievers, what's going on?"

"What's up guys? You getting the hang of this mess cranking?"

"I think I like getting yelled at better than this," Seaman Recruit Hayes piped up.

"I've washed more dishes today than I have in my entire life," said Keller.

"Well glad I can help you out with the little vacation from training. Where are the rest of the other guys at?"

"In the kitchen area," Keller answered. "I don't think they're going to let you in there."

"I'll just poke my head in the door and say hi. They usually don't mind."

Seaman Recruit Thompson had been assigned to assist with meal prep, since he had experience working in a kitchen as part of the banquets department in a hotel. The lead cook asked him just to be a gopher today to get his feel around the kitchen.

"Thompson I need you to empty this grease in the bin in the back."

"Aye Chief," Thompson responded as he got up and wiped his hands on his apron.

"Be careful, it's hot."

Thompson grabbed two oven mitts, hoisted the pan of grease and ambled to the back door. He slipped on the slick floor and a bit of grease splashed out of the pan, hitting an open burner and flashed just as Alex stuck his head into the room. Alex jumped back shouting, "Ahhh."

Keller leapt to help him, "Are you alright sir."

"Yeah I'm fine. Something flashed when I stepped around the corner."

Thompson emerged from the back door and saw Keller helping Alex to his feet. "Are you okay, sir?"

"Yeah I'm fine. I didn't expect to get flashed when I poked my head in there."

"Aw sir, I'm sorry that was my fault."

Alex tried to calm himself and not let anyone know he was trembling. He exhaled a deep breath and said, "Alright men, glad to see everything is in order. We'll see you back at the barracks tonight. Carry on."

"Ok sir," they responded and went back to their duties.

Alex exited the chow hall as fast as possible to get outside and gulped the fresh air fighting the waves of nausea rolling in his gut. Unable to stem the tide, the waves crashed over him and he expelled the contents of his stomach.

CHAPTER 12: BIG CHICKEN

An invincible determination can accomplish almost anything and in this lies the great distinction between great men and little men. - Thomas Fuller

Approaching the back of the mess hall from down wind John McCarthy was greeted by the rank odor of rotting garbage. "Oysh. Time to wash the dumpsters out," John said as he passed. Panic replaced the odious smell when he saw Alex steadying himself between the dumpster and the concrete blocked containment area.

"Alex!" he shouted. John rushed into the enclosure to steady his comrade. "You OK man?" He spun Alex around. As he did Alex's eyes rolled back in his head and he collapsed in his arms.

John dragged Alex from the dumpster enclosure. Spying two gawking recruits on the loading dock, he barked at one of them, "You! Get a medic over here on the double."

The recruit dashed inside the mess hall while the other came to assist. John searched for a place to lay him down. "Over by the steps where it isn't wet."

The two sailors eased Alex down. "Go check if he called medical."

John loosened Alex's tie and slapped his face, "Alex," he yelled. "Come on man, wake up."

"Ahh . . . Oh," Alex groaned. He slowly regained consciousness, squeezed his eyes shut and opened them. "What are you doing, you big oaf? Why do you have that dumb look on your face?"

"What are you doing lying on the ground you hose head?"

John helped Alex to sit up. "I don't know man. I was heading into the kitchen when this flash of heat startled me. Just scared me." He rubbed the back of his neck. "Got real nauseous and wham I'm staring up at your ugly mug."

"You ok then?"

"Yeah. Let me get up." Alex tried to get up but his wobbly legs wouldn't give him the strength he needed to stand. John strengthened his grip and guided him to the steps to sit down. As John was sitting Alex on the steps, a male and female Hospital Corpsman rushed around the corner.

"Where's the patient?" The female corpsman enquired.

"Right here," John responded and got out of her way.

Alex tried to look up, but put his head down to fend off the dizziness.

"What happened Petty Officer?"

"Sievers. Alex Sievers."

"I'm Petty Officer Angeles. Let's see what we can do to help. What happened?"

"Got nauseas and then passed out."

While the male corpsman took notes, Angeles dug out of her field pack a small pouch and ripped open a spirit of hartshorn; a mixture of ammonium carbonate and eucalyptus. "Here you go Petty Officer Sievers."

"What's that?"

"Smelling salts to chase the cobwebs away," she said waving the pack under his nose causing him to jerk away.

Strength flooded back into Alex's body and he felt like he could stand. "I think I can stand now," he said. John and Petty Officer Angeles reached under his arms and with one surge hoisted him to his feet.

John and the corpsman backed up a bit. "You Ok?" John asked.

"I'm fine mother goose."

"You scared me there for a moment."

"Are you going to be ok?" Petty Officer Angeles asked. "Do you need to go over to Medical?"

"No I'm good. Just a little weary. I got some work to do in my office

I'll take it easy for the rest of the day."

A crowd of recruits had congregated on the loading dock and caught Alex's eye. He deepened his voice and shouted, "Shows over. Get back to work."

The 197 Company Commander's office door flung open, John and Alex entered and slammed it shut. "How are going to lead the company through the firefighting exercises if a grease fire knocks you on your keester?" John paused waving his hands in the air. "Huh? How you going to do it?"

"Look John, I've got it figured out. You're going to lead the first team in and I'll follow you in with team two to provide cover for you. We'll have the other companies to support us and I can handle that much. You get to get all the glory."

"So I get to be the human french fry. Whoopie. Alright I guess that will work."

"You betcha it will work. It's got to work. You'll see when we go through the rehearsal you'll see how easy it's going to be."

"Easy. Nothing is easy. The easiest thing was to sign the contract to join up. No sir, nothing has been easy. I'm still not sure why I joined this canoe club anyway, wet nursing a bunch of civilians wanting to wear the uniform," John said. "You know you've never told me why you joined the Navy. A landlubber from Kansas becoming a sailor, that doesn't make much sense."

"Whew. That's a great question. My Grandfather was Navy during the first World War. My Dad was 17. He joined up the day after Pearl Harbor. Spent the duration of the war on a destroyer in the South Pacific. Saw quite a bit of action and when it was all over went back home to marry his sweet heart and make babies."

"Lots of babies I'd say. Eleven kids, right?"

"Yeah buddy. I'll bet your Daddy liked having you all around."

"He sure did. He sired his own work force to take care of the farm."

"That's right you grew up on a farm. I'm going start calling you old

McDonald." He laughed at his own joke. Alex wasn't amused. He cleared his throat. "What did you do on the farm?"

"I took care of the chickens. When I was young I would collect the eggs. We had about 100 chickens and I'd get about four dozen eggs every day. That wasn't too bad. But I had to give up that job to one of my sisters."

"So what did you do after that?"

"I still took care of the chickens. I had to clean the coops out. We all got up at four in the morning to do our chores. I'd go out do my chores and then come back in and get ready for school. I had to shower after chores because I stunk so bad and get ready for school."

"I bet meal times were a lot of fun."

"There was always enough, but you had to be a quick eater if you wanted seconds. When you got six older brothers it was hand to hand combat over the last few biscuits."

"Six brothers? Wow. Bet you got your butt beat quite often."

"When I was young I was seriously outgunned, but as I got older I was able to hold my own. Dad always taught us when to fight and when to run. In my house it was mostly fight or plan to be run over. Don't get me wrong, my brothers were great they weren't mean, but they always made sure you knew where you were in the pecking order."

"I'll bet having all those brothers kept the bullies away."

"Are you kidding? I had my share to deal with. I wasn't no sissy, I learned to fight my own battles, but my brothers were always around to make sure things were fair. They knew when to get involved and when not to."

"That's great. You knew you could take care of yourself, but if you needed help you always had the Calvary to call on."

"That's the way my Dad trained us. He taught us to fight to defend ourselves and the things we believe in. He's part the reason I want to be an officer."

"I'm not following you."

"My Dad loves this country very much and he taught us to love it too. Every Memorial Day he would take us to the National Cemetery to remind us that our liberty was paid for with the blood of the men who rested under those crosses. He loved to see the thousands of American flags on each of the graves. He loved the flag. We had a flag pole in the front yard."

"That's pretty cool. We only had the thing you hung from the house with the flag you'd get at department store."

"We had a beauty. It was just like the one you see here on the base. Lightning struck it one time, blew up everything in the house but didn't damage the pole. We flew a full sized flag too. Every morning before heading out to school at exactly 8 AM we would stand out by the pole with our hands on our hearts and watch as my Dad ran the colors up the pole. We would recite the pledge of allegiance too. Then we would do it again at sunset."

"That's great."

"I was the only one in Kindergarten who knew the pledge."

"That's too funny."

"My Dad is a true Patriot. I started understanding why my Dad was that way when I started studying American history. The founding of this country, the struggle for independence and the growing pains to becoming the great nation we are amazed me. You couple that with my Dad's enthusiasm and that makes for a guy like me wanting to be part of the world's largest yacht club."

"Why did you join the Navy? Why not the puddle pirates or the jarheads?"

Alex laughed. "It's not because my Dad was in the Navy, but I want to be a sea captain and command a ship."

"A captain? You?"

"Don't laugh. I was telling you about how much I love history. What I really loved was the battles. The shot heard round the world from Lexington and Concorde, Valley Forge and all the great Revolutionary War stories electrified me. However it wasn't the land battles that enthralled me, it was the Navy battles. I read everything I could on all the famous Naval battles I could find. Every one of them was chocked full of courage and feats of bravery. I was hooked."

"That one we talked about the other day was probably my all time favorite."

"Me too. You want to know what really sunk its teeth into me?"

John shook his head.

"My Dad had the complete twelve book series of novels by C.S. Forrester about Horatio Hornblower. The novels are about a young man who joins the Royal Navy as a midshipmen and ascends through the ranks to Admiral by his heroic deeds and unwavering commitment to king and country. I found out later that Gene Roddenberry creator of Star Trek based Captain Kirk on this character."

"Oh beam me up Scotty, please. You. A geekie trekkie?" John said with as much sarcasm as he could muster. "Did you sew your own costume and attend a Star Trek convention?"

"No, you jerk. I loved how Kirk commanded respect by his acts of valor and heroism. I love the way he cheated death and spat in its eye. He made me want to be a captain."

"You've always been kind of a space cadet," John said sitting down. "Ahhhh, now I understand."

"Now Hornblower, now he's a real captain. He's a dashing young, naval officer rising through the ranks by his acts of bravery for king and country."

"Ah, so that's why you are so gung ho Navy."

"John I bleed Navy blue. I love it so much," Alex said as he sucked in a deep breath. "It's all I think about. That's why this *Double Salute* is so important to me. I've got to win it, because it is a stepping stone to my dream."

"If you wanted to be an officer, why didn't you just go to the Academy and forget us enlisted slobs?"

Alex chuckled and said, "I couldn't get in."

"Man I'm sorry. Why not?"

"I told you I loved history. I could eat, sleep and breathe it. However, the rest of the subjects you need to know I am not as proficient in. In high school I was able to maintain decent grades in math, but English and science I would rather stick needles in my eyes. I hated it. Barely passed them so I could graduate, but it didn't help me get in the Naval Academy. I was told to enlist that there were appointments for enlisted members."

"Since you're married, are you still eligible?"

"No," Alex said and sighed. He turned away and looked out the window. "Cat means the world to me and I knew I'd lose her if she had to wait another four years for me so I decided to get married and follow the ROTC route. If that doesn't work out there is always the Limited Duty Officer, but I'll never get to be a captain of a ship though."

"How's it coming with that?"

"I'm supposed to be hearing real soon. I'm keeping my fingers crossed. The *Double Salute* and the SECNAV being here can be the rocket fuel that launches me to where I want to go."

The sound of John's stomach rumbling interrupted Alex.

"Can you please tell your stomach to stop interrupting that is so rude."

"I was on my way over to get some chow when I found you laid out behind the dumpster."

"I'm hungry too, let's go get some grub."

An approaching recruit saluted the two company commanders as they approached the Supply Building. "What moron painted that pink?" Alex said as they approached the freshly painted *Recruit Training Supply Center*.

"That has got to be the ugliest color I ever did see," John commented. "It looks like Pepto Bismol."

Rounding the corner, Alex and John saw a company of recruits in formation being torn to shreds by a khaki uniformed chief petty officer. "You son of guns painted my building pink. Where did you get that paint from? That's not the paint I told you to pick up," he shouted, his voice echoing.

John and Alex came to a halt to watch the dressing down. Alex tapped John on the shoulder and nodded toward the loading dock. Petty

Officer Peach and his sidekick Santello were watching as the chief took his company apart. Alex grinned and moved in behind Chief Paige and into Peach's view and made a face in mock sympathy. He smiled when Peach's eyes narrowed.

Alex waved good bye and pushed John toward the chow hall.

When out of ear shot the two commanders busted up laughing. "Poor Peach I'm sure he was enjoying getting his gluteus maximus chewed off," John roared.

"Did you see his face when he saw me," Alex said and let out a laugh. "If his eyes were lasers he would've Swiss-cheesed me."

"He is just not having a very good week."

"Poor Peach? The only thing poor about that bugger is his attitude."

Peach narrowed his eyes, clenched his teeth and wrung his hands, *I really hate that guy,* he thought to himself.

Santello leaned into Peach, "Would you like me to put a potato in his exhaust pipe?"

The thought softened Peach's face for a moment and he leaned back to him, "I've got a better idea."

Chief Paige booming voice shocked Peach out of his fantasy.

"I want you on this loading dock at oh-five hundred hours and you will not leave until every square inch of that pink is covered up. Do I make myself clear."

Company 195 responded with a resounding, "Yes Sir."

"Dismissed," Paige shouted back. He spun towards Peach, scowled and wagged his finger at him. "I ought to . . ."

Peach threw his hands in the air in surrender and mouthed, "I know, I know. I heard it already once." He shoved Santello and shouted, "Fall in."

Sounds of clinking glasses and dishes danced atop the murmur of voices locked in conversation. Waiters and waitresses darted in and out of tables pouring coffee and removing dinner plates. The aroma of salmon waft in to the rafters giving way to fresh baked cake being served to the banquet attendees.

Alex and Cat sat engrossed in conversation with John and Mary Lou McCarthy at the closest table to the platform where the banquets hosts and key note speaker were also seated. The banquet hostess, an older lady, sported a feathered hat sat next to Alex brushed his face each time she'd move her head. She leaned over him to talk to Cathreen and gave him a face full of feathers making him sneeze.

She tapped Cat and asked, "Dear, could you get Mary Lou's attention?"

"Oh. Yes Ma'am," Cathreen said. She turned quickly to Mary Lou. "Mary Lou," she whispered in her ear.

Mary Lou turned to Cathreen. "Yes, Cat."

"Miss Nancy," she said and motioned to her right.

"Yes Miss Nancy," Mary Lou said.

In a low sweet voice, Miss Nancy said, "We're going to start in about five minutes. If you would like to freshen up, this would be a good time."

"Oh yes I would," she said and popped up from her chair. She grabbed Cat by the arm. "Come with me."

Cathreen with no time to answer was on her feet hurrying behind Mary Lou to the Ladies Room.

John twisted his suit coat and fiddled with his tie. He leaned over to Alex, "I thought that monkey suit I wear at the base was uncomfortable this is almost unbearable."

"Do you believe all these people are here to support an unwed mother's home?"

"Maybe," John said nodding his head scanning the enormous banquet hall. "Mary Lou says this is the highlight of the year. They almost raise their entire budget in this single event."

"Where does the rest come from?"

"Local corporations donate a bunch and churches."

"Wow, that is amazing," Alex said with a bewildered expression. "This dinner is first class. If this is complimentary who's footing the bill?"

"You are of course. That's why you're sitting up here in front. Didn't

I tell you that?"

Alex shifted uncomfortably in his seat and tried not to let his mouth drop open. "Ah."

John threw his head back and roared in laughter. "Sucker!" He continued to laugh. "Gotcha. The Corporate sponsorship covers all this and the donations of all these people. So what happens next?"

"That's right Mr. Sievers," Miss Nancy said and linked her arm into his. "All this is donated. We have a short video, a testimonial, an award presentation and then our key note speaker. Admiral Breaux, here." She introduced the tall man who had just sat down next to her. "Admiral this Alex Sievers, he's in the Navy too."

Alex stood up, "Admiral Breaux," he said and extended his hand. "Sir, it is a pleasure to meet you. I'm Petty Officer First Class Alex Sievers. And this is Petty Officer John McCarthy." Alex released his hand.

The Admiral extended his hand to John as he stood up to reach across the table. "Sir it is a pleasure to meet you. We've heard a lot about you."

"What is it that you boys do?"

"Sir, we are company commanders at RTC."

"Ah, pushing boots. Good for you. We need more men like you to train these young boys for fleet duties. Are you currently involved with a company?"

"Yes sir, we are. Company 197, about two weeks to graduation."

"You're in that class. Ohhh," he said thoughtfully. "There's a lot of scuttlebutt going around about that. Seems your Commanding Officer decided to bring back the *Double Salute*. Yes, yes there's lots of talk about that. Going to be a lot of brass at that graduation. I was planning on attending myself."

"Yes sir."

"How's your company doing? Think you've got a shot at it."

"Yes sir, I do. We're in a dead heat with another company."

"Good for you son," the Admiral said. "You're going be the first one to try out my mass conflagration drill."

"Your mass conflagration drill?" John said cutting into the conversation.

"I designed the logistics for the drill. I came up with the concept and when I took over Naval Education it was a top priority to get that implemented." The Admiral stopped abruptly and looked at Alex. "You're Petty Officer Sievers of the USS *Ingersoll*. I saw your name on a report that just crossed my desk. I am currently trying to test your idea and a way to implement it."

"Yes sir," Alex said sheepishly.

"Son it was because of the incident you had on *Ingersoll* this drill was conceived. A rash of shipboard fire related casualties set the idea in motion, but the death of your shipmate hastened the process. I'm sorry for what happened to you and we're trying to do everything possible to correct it."

"Thank you sir," Alex said and slowly sat as Cat and Mary Lou returned.

Miss Nancy tapped the Admiral on the shoulder and said, "We're going to start now Admiral." Turning to Mary Lou, "You'll have five minutes."

Mary Lou nodded and turned to John, "How do I look?" as she adjusted her dress.

"Don't be nervous, You'll be fine," John said to her.

An usher standing at the bottom of the steps leading up to the platform greeted Miss Nancy and helped her up the stairs to the brightly lit podium. Once she was in position the overhead lights faded and dramatic music began to play. A video splashed on to the screen as the music hit a crescendo. The music cross-faded to toddler music and the video faded to a pregnant teenager on a porch swing of a large plantation style home. The short video abruptly ended and spot lights snapped on, illuminated Miss Nancy on the left side of the stage and a row of pregnant women on the right side.

"Good evening Ladies and Gentlemen," Miss Nancy said on cue. "And welcome to this years gala fundraiser for the North Chicago Unwed Mothers Home." She paused and the crowd erupted in cheers and applause.

When the applause faded, she continued, "We are here to honor you, the donors for your unselfish giving and to say thank you." Her steady, but breathy voice stilled the room and the audience hung on her every word. "Thank you for all the diapers and wipes you donated tonight. It is our second biggest need."

Seconds felt like minutes to Mary Lou as she fidgeted in her seat, longing for the introduction to be over. She watched Miss Nancy's lips move but could not hear the words. Only when she turned to where Mary Lou was sitting and said, "Mary Lou McCarthy."

A roar of applause filled the room as she stood to her feet smiling. John escorted her to the stairs leading up to the platform where the same usher was waiting to help her up to the platform. When she stepped into the blinding spot light she lost focus for a moment. She found Miss Nancy washed in the bright light and said "Thank you," and hugged her.

"As this years Volunteer of the Year, your tireless work has been an inspiration to all of us. It has helped to reenergize us and to push beyond what we thought we could accomplish. Thank you from all of us."

Miss Nancy stepped away from the platform so Mary Lou could address the audience. "Heavens. Thank you so much. Miss Nancy this is a true honor. I am truly humbled." She dabbed the corner of her eyes and continued. "I want to thank the staff. My friends, Alex and Cathreen Sievers. Last and most important, I would also like to especially thank the love of my life, my big teddy bear of a husband, John McCarthy." The spotlight swung to John and he acknowledged the crowd by standing and waving.

"Go get 'em. You big lovable Teddy Bear," Alex shouted at him as John sat back down.

Mary Lou continued with her speech and Alex lost himself in his thoughts about the mass conflagration drill.

Cathreen leaned into him and said, "Alex I'm pregnant."

The words shot through him like an arrow wrestling his mind out of the mire of self pity. The thought so abrupt, he'd forgotten where he was and said loudly, "You're pregnant!" So loudly in fact that Mary Lou stopped speaking and the room became silent. Realizing what he did, a wave of embarrassment washed over him causing sweat to ooze out of every pore in his body.

"That is my friend Alex Sievers; whose wife Cathreen just told him that she too is pregnant." The crowd stood and applauded.

"Come up here you two, so every one can see you," Miss Nancy said stepping into the microphone. Alex and Cat stepped on stage to the thunderous applause. Tears rolled down Cat's cheeks streaking her make up. Alex shifted back and forth uncomfortably. Not knowing what to do, he gazed at Cat and noticed she was glowing. He smiled then kissed and hugged her, which was greeted with a collective "Awwwww."

Alex smiled at the tree rustling in his window. "I'm going to be a father. Me a father." A rap on the door jerked him out of his musings.

"Hello daddy," John bellowed.

"I love the sound of that."

"Why thank you son," John said.

"Not from you, though," Alex shot back at him. "What do you want any way?"

"Scores are in."

"Let me see those," Alex said as he ripped them out of John's paw.

John stared at Alex as he tore the manila envelope open. Alex's pursed lips relaxed into a smile and then an ear to ear grin. "Woooo Whooooo. Big Chicken and we're number one. Yeah Baby."

"Can we tell them?" John said and swung his thumb towards the door.

"Yeah lets."

John pulled the door open for Alex as he bounded out from the office. The first recruit who saw him coming toward him shouted, "Attention on deck." Bodies stiffened, chests were thrust out and chins were held high as each recruit assumed his role as a statute.

"At ease," Alex bellowed back after the room silenced. "Everybody come here to the front and take a seat."

The recruits of Company 197 shuffled to the front of the barracks and seated themselves in front of their company commander. Every eye probed his demeanor for a clue to what he wanted to talk to them about.

Poker faced, Alex sat on the edge of a table and remained silent for a few seconds to heighten the tension. Holding up the score sheets for a brief second he steeled his countenance and straightened himself. "We've worked for a long time," he said low and slow, "to reach." He paused "A goal. These are the score sheets for this weeks round of competitions. For the first time we are number." He paused again and looked around. "One!"

The recruits erupted in cheers and chatter. They slapped each other on the back and hooted and hollered.

Alex savored the moment, took a mental snapshot and etched it in to his memory, never to be forgotten. He stood up and tried to regain order, "Alright guys. Come on. There's more."

He gave the recruits a moment to settle down. "Needless to say, since we are number one, our weekly average is high enough to add another Big Chicken. We are a distinction level company."

Again he was greeted with another round of hooting and hollering. Alex held up his hands to quiet them, "We still have our work cut out for us. All we have to do to seal this, is take the Captain's Cup and pass the Mass Conflagration Drill. Then we are a lock for the *Double Salute.*"

A recruit in the front row raised his hand. Alex acknowledged him, "Yes Seaman."

"How did 195 do?"

Alex shifted uncomfortably and hesitated for a moment. He looked at John and then spoke, "Ahh, They're two points behind us."

The recruits whistled and sighed. "Hold on guys. You didn't expect this to be easy. Petty Officer Peach has a good bunch there; they've been on cruise control up until now and underestimated us. We've been like a little terrier nipping into the big bull's lead. These results are a wake up call and that bull is ticked off. They're going to want to stomp on you. They're going to pull out all the stops, might even try a few dirty tricks but we'll be ready for them. However, lets not mirror drive this either; we need to stay focused and run like we stole it. Alright?"

The recruits responded with a spirited, "Yes Sir!"

CHAPTER 13: CAPTAIN'S CUP

Never interrupt your enemy when he is making a mistake. - Napoleon Bonaparte

A clay 1/8th mile track marked with six white lanes encircled a fitness course specially designed for fitness training of Navy recruits. Bleachers flanked the front and back stretch. Brilliant sunlight flooded the musty drill hall through the open main door. The ten companies from the *Double Salute* graduation class paraded in front of the reviewing platform. On a small table sat the Captain's Cup and a microphone stand stood nearby with a Shure SM-58 microphone.

The company commanders assembled on the platform behind the microphone. Chief Paige, tucked a clip board under his arm, bounded up the platform and stepped to the microphone.

"Atten-hut," The Rpocks shouted in unison. Ten companies of 75 recruits snapped as one man to attention.

"Morning gents," Chief Paige's voice boomed through the microphone echoing off the walls. He stepped back, scowled at the audio technician and snapped his index finger towards the deck. The audio technician quickly turned down the main audio gain of the public address system and shot the chief a thumbs-up.

Chief Paige stepped back to the microphone and spoke, "Check." He half smiled and continued. "Let's try this again. Morning gents."

With which the recruits responded in unison with a spirited, "Good Morning Chief."

"We will be starting momentarily. We are awaiting the arrival of Captain Callaghan. For now stand at ease. No talking."

The recruits relaxed, while the chief took the clip board out from his arm and turned to the company commanders. He walked to the commander of Company 191 and held it out to him. "Sign your companies in."

A distant shout from the main door, "Attention on deck!" caused every one in the drill hall to snap to attention and stand silently as the Commanding Officer of *Recruit Training Command* entered the building with his staff. Captain Callaghan was saluted by Chief Paige and was seated by one of Chief Paige's assistance on the platform.

Once the captain had taken his place Chief Paige stepped to the microphone again. "Parade rest." The companies smartly assumed the parade position. "Captain Callaghan, Company Commanders and Companies, welcome to the Captain's Cup Competition. For the next three days you will be competing for the coveted Captain's Cup. This competition will be unlike any other seen here at Recruit Training. It will not only test your brawn and endurance but also your intelligence and mechanical skills."

A gasp ejected from the companies. The chief held up his hand, "As you were gentlemen. I'll give you more details in a few minutes, but first the Commanding Officer of *Recruit Training Command* would like to say a few words," he said and paused for a moment then turned to where the CO stood. "Captain Callaghan."

The CO stepped to the microphone, "Good morning gentlemen."

The companies responded with a spirited, "Good Morning Sir!"

"Gentlemen we are bringing tradition back to RTC and this is one from times past. Our countries Navy was built on gritty, strong men who battled not only an enemy but the sea itself. Their physical regimen in basic training prepared them for the rigors they would face in the fleet." The captain turned to his left where Chief Paige stood. "Chief do you remember how difficult the physical training used to be?"

The chief nodded to the captain and smiled.

"The warriors of the past would not let the word 'surrender' past their lips. It is you against you for the good of your shipmates. As this competition progresses your body will scream at you to stop, if you want to give up, your spirit must give a resounding, 'never.' Take each event one at a time. Over the next three days stoke the embers of passion into a raging fire that will drive you past your selves to victory." He paused for a moment for effect.

"Because of the attention surrounding the inaugural *Double Salute* competition, this class's winner will receive an added honor. The entire company will have their names inscribed on the cup. No other graduation class coming after you will share that honor. The winner will also receive a commemorative replica of the cup. Good Luck gentlemen."

The recruits respond with applause to the captain's inspiring words.

"As you were gentlemen," Chief Paige said. "We've suspended the way this event has been held. A new series of events have been implemented to more closely resemble the physical requirements needed in the fleet. The events were taken from antiquity when ships were powered by the wind instead of engines and the weather could be as just as ruthless an enemy as any adversaries they faced. As Captain Callaghan pointed out, you will be tested beyond your limitations. Each event will be preceded by a short history lesson which will help you better understand why we chose it." He paused for a moment and swept the companies with his eyes. "Rpocks have your men sit in the bleachers as we get ready for the first event. Enjoy the competition."

Chief Paige spun on his heel around to the company commanders. "Listen up guys. This is all new so bear with us. The first evolution is going to be the company run, but with a new twist. We are going to run the normal two miles. The time will only be for Physical Fitness score but will not count as part of the competition. Two companies will be running at the same time. Each company will be at opposite ends of the track." He turned and pointed to the main door and then to the back door. "On the completion of the last lap they will be directed out the doors and to the back of the drill hall. There are two anchors attached to a capstan. The first column from each company will man the capstan and will drag the anchor via the capstan 25 feet and the second column will drag it another 25 feet. Column 3 and 4 will do the same thing. This part of the event will be timed. The clock will stop when the anchor crosses the finish line."

Hatch Harris piped up, "They're going to drag an anchor across a parking lot?"

"The anchors are on wheeled carts, but it will take the collective strength of each team to move it using the capstan."

Old wooden ships used capstans which are vertical-axled machines which rotated a timber mounted vertically through the hull of a ship. The capstan moved a ratchet which allowed constant linear motion in one direction by using a pawl which clicked each time it fell into the gear maintaining a constant tension to wind ropes or cables fastened to the ships anchor. The capstans were operated manually by applying pressure to levers known as bars. Deck crews would hoist the anchor from the depths in this way.

The capstan was a valuable tool that could be used to free the ship if it ran aground. Anchors were dropped from the stern and hauled out to deeper water by smaller boats. Once planted in the seabed, the crew would man the capstan and haul the ship back to deeper waters.

"Any more questions?" Chief Paige inquired of the company commanders.

All the commanders shifted uncomfortably, but no one spoke.

"The companies will face off by their current rankings. 195 and 197 you're up first. Brief your men and have them on the track in five minutes."

"Aye chief," Rod and Alex said in unison. Alex stepped in the path of Rod and the two commanders sneered at each other.

"We're going to kick your butt, Sievers," Rod poked his finger into Alex's chest.

Alex broke out in laughter and stepped around Rod. "Get serious Rod, you're too full of yourself."

Rod gritted his teeth and stepped off the platform.

Alex waved his hand in the air and smiled, "John, this competition is going to be a snap to win. I've been studying this stuff for years. We can't lose," Alex said as he walked to where his company sat. "Guys, you're going to cream them."

The company sat straighter and leaned in to hear their company commander.

"The first event is going to be the company run, like we've been training for, but with a twist toward our favor. After the run you go out that door," He pointed to the back door. "And form up behind the drill hall. The instructors will show you were to go. We're going to haul anchors."

"Hall anchors, sir?" The Rpock piped up.

"Yes. Haul anchors. There will be a line attached to a cart which will have the anchor on it. The line wraps around a capstan on the top of a platform. A team of eight men will rotate the capstan using sheer muscle the way the old sailing ships used to weigh anchor. Now here's the dirty little secret, it is all about rhythm. Each man has got to work as though they are one man. Sailors of old would sing sea shanties to stay in rhythm."

"What's a sea shanty?" Seaman Recruit Keller enquired.

"A sea shanty is when one sailor would sing something and another would respond with a similar thought. A bit like our marching songs the Rpock does to keep cadence."

"What are we going to sing?" Keller shot back at Alex.

"I don't know. We don't have time to make one up. Pick a song every one knows."

The recruits just looked at each other and couldn't decide on one. John said flatly, "Anchors Aweigh."

"Duh!" Alex said. "That's perfect. Not quite a shanty but it will do. Alright let's do this thing. Bring it in."

The company jumped to their feet, encircled Alex and John and put a hand in. "On three, 197," Alex said. "One, two, three."

"197," the company shouted and walked to their starting positions.

The drill hall buzzed with excitement as the two companies took their positions on the track. Company 197 stood at the ready on the front stretch in facing the reviewing platform where Captain Callaghan and his assistant were seated. Company 195 stood ready on the back stretch facing the opposite direction of 197.

Instructors were strategically placed on the outside and inside of the track to help companies maintain a constant pace. They also were there to keep one company from catching up with the other company.

Chief Paige took the microphone and raised a starting pistol in the air. "Companies ready. On your marks. Go!" He said as he fired the gun.

The companies bolted and all that could be heard was the pounding of track shoes smacking the clay in a quick cadence. Both companies rounded the first turn spaced evenly.

Company 195's Rpock began to chant, "Every where we go."

"Every where we go," echoed a cadenced deep baritone reply.

"People want to know," the Rpock shouted.

"People want to know," came the reply.

"Mighty, mighty 195."

"Mighty, mighty 195," echoed off the drill hall ceiling.

The guide-on for 197 shouted to his Rpock, "That is so lame. Couldn't they think of something more original than that? Hey Rpock give them a good one."

Petty Officer Peach shot the 197 guide-on a snarled faced look and shouted "Shut up and run boot."

As 195 approached Peach, he shouted at the Rpock, "Pick up the pace and wear them out." The Rpock flashed an OK sign.

He quickened the cadence call. Some of the company did not respond fast enough to the new cadence.

"Tighten up the formation!" yelled an instructor at Company 195. "You're starting to string out, tighten up."

The booming voice reached 197 and they tightened their formation also and quickened their pace. Each of the boots turned to see where there rivals were on the track. A wave of excitement rippled through the pack of bodies as the Rpock began to sing, "One. Niner." in a low voice with a slight pause between each number and then belted out, "Seven!"

The huffing and puffing recruits echoed back to the Rpock repeated it back the same way, "One. Niner. Seven!"

"One, Nine, Seven."

"One, Nine, Seven," echoed Company 197.

"We are resolute!"

"We are resolute," echoed the company again.

"To win Double Sa-lute," the cadence caller yelled.

"To win Double Sa-" echoed Company 197 and then punctuated, "lute."

"Together," shouted the Rpock.

"U-S," the company shouted and then slightly paused. "Navy."

"Bring it on down now."

"U-S Navy," lowering their voices. 197 then shouted at a pitch, "U-S Navy, Uh."

A bell rang to signify last lap.

Each huffing and puffing company rounded the last turn. The moderators shouted at them and hustled them out the door. The companies ran across the drill grinder where two massive platforms with capstans mounted to them stood. The two companies simultaneously took their positions in front of the two platforms. The Rpock's barked at their companies, "Ready halt."

Some of the recruits gasped for air and put their hands on their knees. "Stand up guys and put your hands on your heads," The Rpock shouted.

The two companies huffed and puffed and waited for orders from Chief Paige. He began to shout, "Captain Callaghan had these two capstans designed after the capstan currently onboard the *USS Constitution* moored in Boston Harbor. The *Constitution* is the oldest fully operational commissioned ship in the world. It was built as one of six frigates considered capital ships that the fledgling United States Navy was built around. These were built with heavier armor and increased firepower. George Washington named her *Constitution* after the United States Constitution so she could be a beacon of a free people to the whole world. Old Ironsides, as she was nicknamed during the War of 1812 is a thread to our past and is a reminder of the freedom we Americans enjoy because of that document."

Chief Paige paused for a moment and let his words echo off the drill hall so the whole world could hear. He swallowed his emotion hard and continued, "Each capstan has eight levers. The first eight men of the first two columns from each company will go first to drag the anchor with the capstan. An instructor will hold up a red flag when the anchor crosses the first line. The guide-on will be posted to watch for the red flag and alert the capstan crew to stop and change to the next group. The first company to drag the anchor across the finish line wins. Everyone understand?"

"Aye-aye, Chief," the two companies shouted back.

"Good. The team taking over the capstan enters on the port ladder, the team being relieved exits via the starboard ladder."

He bounded down the stairs. The lead man of each company took his place at the bottom of the port side ladder and grabbed the rails. The Rpock of 197 took the lead position and turned around to his guys behind him, "Once chief says go, start to sing the song. Stay in time with the song. Don't forget. Stay in time. We'll show them who is mighty. On three guys. 1-2-3."

"One, Nine, Seven," the group shouted.

Chief Paige took his place in front of the platforms. "Ready."

197 Rpock placed his hands on the rails of the ladder and anticipated the shot. Bang!

He double stepped up to the top of the platform and found his place on the capstan. The men filled in and when the last man took his place, he shouted, "Go."

"Anchors aweigh, my boys, anchors aweigh. Farewell to foreign shores. We sail at break of day, day, day, day. Through our last night ashore. Drink to the foam. Until we meet once more. Here's wishing you a happy voyage home." the men sang and heaved into projecting their strength on the capstan. Slowly the wheel began to turn as the men worked as one to tighten the line attached to the anchor a hundred yards away. The nylon rope creaked as the force applied to it via the twisting capstan tightened the line. The anchor at the far end of the course on a cart began to creep along.

The instructors at the far end of the course held red flags attached to sticks to signal when the anchor crossed the first marker. Just before the gun fired the team leader of 195 was distracted for a moment and when the gun went off he hesitated. The men behind him surged forward trapping him momentarily against the stairs. They shouted at him, "Go man, go. C'mon." He pushed back and by the time he'd reached the top 197 was already in place muscling their capstan.

195 set up quickly and began to push but were working as individuals instead of a team. The singing from 197 had the opposite effect on the 195 team and disrupted their rhythm. 195 grunted and groaned against the weight of the anchor. The clicking of the stress relief provided an unexpected source of rhythm they weren't looking for.

The instructor for Company 197 squatted just in front of the anchor cart and watched intently as it crept toward the chalked line on the asphalt. "A half inch to go. C'mon. Bang." He snapped the red flag into the air.

The 197 guide-on shouted to the team. "Go. Go. Next team." The first team hustled off the platform banging down the starboard side steps as team two hustled up the port side steps. As soon as all the men were in place team two leader shouted, "Go. Sing."

195 team one leader looked up in disgust as he saw 197 changing teams and unleashed a profanity laced tirade that would do any sailor proud. "C'mon men, put your backs into it."

With that push the 195 guide-on shouted, "Go. Go. Team two up." With lightning precision the team two was in place and the capstan started clicking again. After watching team one's struggles, team two avoided their mistakes and was able to operate more in sync. Their improvement only maintained a status quo with 197 and was unable to make up the ground lost by team one.

Change over to team three by both companies was uneventful. They were able to maintain the status quo as the anchors crept down the course. Keller and Thompson chomped at the bit to get their turn as the anchor team for 197. The 197 guide-on shouted, "Go. Go."

Team three bounded off the platform and team four quickly took over and began to sing, "Anchors aweigh, my boys, anchors aweigh. Farewell to foreign shores.

We sail at break of day, day, day, day."

"Owwwww," the seaman recruit outside of Keller howled, grabbed his back and fell to his knees. The capstan stopped.

Jackson said, "You alright man?"

"Yes," the recruit replied and hobbled out of the way.

Keller glanced to see 195's anchor gaining on their stopped anchor. "C'mon guys, heave." Keller put all his might in to the push and 197's anchor started to move again, but 195's drew closer and closer.

Thompson started a cadence, "Heave, 1-2. Heave 1-2."

Reenergized 195's anchor team exploded with strength. The two anchors drew even as Keller, Thompson and the team strained with every ounce of strength. The remainders of the companies were on the sidelines shouting and cheering as the two anchors inched toward the finish line. The two instructors put their noses as close as they dare to the ground. Chief Paige watched as the drama unfolded and then almost in one motion the two red flags shot into the air. For a brief moment Chief Paige hesitated as he studied a mental snap shot of the two flags. Then shouted, "197 winner!"

197 cheered and hooted. Team four jumped down from the platform. They chanted, "One, Nine, Seven." Alex slapped all the men on the back and shook their hands furiously in jubilation. He turned in time to see Rod in Chief Paige's face like a baseball manager after a bad call. The two were inches apart and Rod's head was bobbing and his arms were flailing as he argued his case.

Peach unloaded a profane assault on Paige. "I don't know what you were watching but that flag went up first. You blind fat-"

"Stop right there Peach, I'm not in the mood for your garbage today. Here's fair warning you better shut up or I'll yank 100 points off your final score."

Not wanting to jeopardize his chances for the Captain's Cup he thought it better to not saying anything else. Peach bit back his anger, spun on his heel and growled at his Rpock, "Fall them in." Trying to calm himself he took a deep breath, turned away from his company and that was when he noticed Alex staring at him. In response Peach ran up a flag of nonverbal communication.

A thunder clap exploded over the base. The companies double timed into the shelter of the drill hall and took seats in the bleachers. The sodium lights illuminating the vast structure dimmed and then went out. Chief Paige shouted above the buzz of voices, "Atten-hut."

He waited until the room fell quiet. "We will suspend competition for the day. We will resume tomorrow at zero eight hundred hours. Dismissed."

"This is great," Alex said to John. "We know what we got to do to win. We were lagging a little bit on our knot tying skills when we did that module. I want you to conduct knot tying drills this afternoon after chow. Get them back to the barracks, get them in the uniform of the day and march them over to chow. I'll meet you back in the barracks about 1:00. I've got some business to take care of."

"Aye, aye mo Capitan," John said with a mock salute. "Where you headed?"

"I've got to meet Lexi for lunch at the exchange."

"You play with fire and you're going to get burned."

"It's nothing like that. She's got some problem she needs some advice on and she doesn't have a lot of friend's here. Wait a minute. Why am I telling you this? Get a move on I want those guys tying and untying knots all day."

"Ok. But you better make sure you don't do anything to untie your pretty little knot about to have a baby knot."

"Yes mother," Alex shot back at him.

Three raps on the sturdy oak door were greeted with a stern, "Come." When Rod stepped into the semi-lit office, the smell of peppermint tobacco filled his nostrils as a cloud of smoke floated toward him. The smoke emanated from the large desk chair facing the window. "Reporting as ordered, sir," Peach said to the back of the chair.

A fresh cloud of smoke arose in response. More silence. This kind of torture unnerved even this master of head games. The chair started a slow turn with a fog of smoke. "Peach, I am growing weary of your excuses. Don't even offer me one for your failure today. I don't want to hear it."

"Yes sir."

"Who's the guerilla?"

"Seaman Recruit Cade Keller. I passed him over because his ASVAB scores were border line. I didn't want somebody with half a brain in my company. Sir it is just as important to graduate as many men as possible and I wasn't taking any chances."

"Fine. That's not the issue here. Do you know if he's their choice for the iron man competition?"

"I would guess it will be him or the other one."

"Other one? There's another? Peach I thought you went through and gleaned all the best built men out so this would not be an issue."

"Well. . . I . . . did, sir," Peach said in response.

"I guess I'll have to listen to your lame excuse for not getting this other person they may choose for the iron man competition."

"Thompson, sir. His name is Seaman Recruit Thompson. He was set back two weeks at the beginning of his training because of medical problem. He had to start his training all over with a new company. Medical transfers are assigned by a different department at Admin and I don't know any one there so I wasn't able to snag him."

"Did you know about him?"

"Kind of sir."

"Kind of? Look Peach," the Captain said as he lowered his voice. "You don't understand what's going on here. This is a lot bigger than you. If you screw this up I'm going to put your head on a platter."

"Yes sir," he eked out.

"If Keller runs that competition you've got a huge problem."

"I'm not too worried about him. We've got O'dell who will …"

The captain's face contorted in rage, balled his fist and slammed it down on the desk. His voice pitched, "You better be worried. That Sievers isn't such a push over after all. He's leading you in the points and now he's leading in the Cup competition. I guess you're not as ruthless as I've been told. You know he's applied for Limited Duty Officer and if he wins this competition he just might get it. You better watch out Peach, you may have to salute him one day."

A guttural growl shot from his gritted teeth, "I'll get him sir. You can count on me."

Captain Callaghan sat down in his chair. "Good. That's what I want to hear. Dismissed." He smiled and turned back toward the window to nurse his pipe.

Peach spun on his heel and ripped the door open.

CHAPTER 14: TREACHERY

Tricks and treachery are the practice of fools, that don't have brains enough to be honest. – Benjamin Franklin

The Navy Exchange is a retail stored located on Navy bases and ships. These systems of commercial hubs are operated by Navy Supply Personnel and provide popular brands and services to sailors worldwide at discounted prices and no sales tax. The modern convenience of a state of the art Navy Exchange is a far cry from the bumboats of the 1800's. Peddlers of merchandise would come alongside the old wooden ships and sailors would lower exorbitant amounts of money in buckets for inferior personal items they desperately needed.

For families operating on meager military pay the Navy Exchange also provided the added benefit of commissary services. This allows families to secure quality food at lower prices.

The candy apple red Trans Am slithered through the busy parking lot of the Navy Exchange looking for a place to park. "Alright," Alex said as he happened upon a maroon Toyota minivan pulling out of a space three rows from the door. "Looks like a Mars rover," he said as he slipped his hot rod in to the parking spot. The engine growled as he revved it then cut it off.

Walking to the entrance, the slick ice blue Datsun 280ZX parked in the first stall caught his eye with the green Vermont license plate with 'LEXI 1' framed in a white rectangle. The sunlight reflecting from the chrome dazzled his eyes for a moment. As he came around the driver side, he saw her still in the car with the window rolled down. "Lexi," Alex said.

Lexi turned with a fright, "Alex. You startled me."

He opened the door and took her by the hand to help her out. His face flushed and he felt a burst of emotion when the enticing aroma of her perfume flooded his nostrils. *Wow!* He thought to himself as the feeling subsided. *Whew, that's some powerful stuff.* He smiled at her for a long moment. "You look nice and . . . and what is that crazy perfume you're wearing? It's great."

"You like it? It's Opium."

"Yeah. Love it," he said. He heard his sloppy words and jerked himself back to reality and turned his attention back to the Datsun. "When did you get the rice burner?"

"Flew home last month to see the folks and decided to drive it back. I was getting tired of relying on others to get me around."

Alex crouched down to admire the inside. "Whew, who. She's a beaut," he said gliding his hand across the polished fender as he walked around to the front of the car. "Bet ya she really goes."

"Got it up to over a hundred and twenty a few times while driving her up here. Want to take it for a spin?"

"I better not. I got to get back to the company."

"Alright let's go have lunch." She held out her hand to him and grabbed his arm.

Alex stiffened and walked awkwardly toward the building. "So Lexi. What did you want to talk about?"

"I'm lonely Alex," she said as she flashed her baby blues and patted his hand.

"Ah. Lexi I've already told you that I . . ."

"No. I'm not saying that. I'm just saying I need somebody to talk to with skin on. I call my friends back home and those in California, but they're just so caught up in themselves and what they're doing. I even called up your mama to talk to her."

"What? You're calling my mom," he said and threw her hand down.

She threw her head back and laughed at him, "No I'm not calling your mom. I used to when we were dating."

"You were calling my mom. I didn't know that. Why would you do that?"

"I swore her to secrecy. Didn't you ever wonder how I learned to cook all those great meals? You even said one time, the pumpkin pie was just like your Mama's. Don't you remember? That's because it was your Mama's."

"Lexi you little sneak. I ought to."

"You ought to what?"

Alex waved his hand at her and tried to change the subject, "Why do you like to come here and eat?"

"Alex, I would've done anything for you. Don't you understand?" Lexi said with moistening eyes.

Alex took a step closer to her and lowered his voice, "We've been through this all a hundred times this side of Sunday. Why won't you stop hammering me with this? You make mistakes and you have to live with the consequences. You burned me pretty bad Lexi."

"I know Alex. I am sorry. Can you ever forgive me?"

"I'm here. Aren't I? You're still my friend and friends help each other out."

"That means a lot to me Alex," she said and wrapped her arms around his neck and planted her lips on his.

Paralyzed by the conflicting emotions and unsure what to do he took her arms and pulled them down to end the situation. "I'm sorry Alex. I was so glad to hear you say that."

"Look Lexi. Please restrain yourself. This is a public place and I don't . . ."

Click, whir, click whir, click whir. The unmistakable sound of a 35mm camera with a auto winder. However not close enough to be heard by the principles being photographed because of a powerful zoom lens. When the two figures disappeared into the door of the Navy Exchange, the tan Ford LTD slunk out of the parking lot.

The pink princess phone on the white laced end table jangled. Mary Lou hurried into the living room, while trying to pin up her hair. "I'm comingggggg," she sang to the phone. She picked up the phone and in her sweet telephone voice, "Hello."

"Mary Lou, this is Cathreen. You busy?"

"Hello sweet heart. How is the mother to be feeling today?"

"I'm fine. Baby's fine. Do you have a few minutes? I really hate to bother you."

"I am getting ready to head out the door to the ladies meeting at the church. But why don't I swing by and pick you up and we can talk on the way."

Cat hesitated, bit back the tears and then finally spoke. "Alright. I guess that will be fine. How long before you get here?"

"Thirty minutes I've got to stop by the exchange to get John's uniforms."

"Ok. What should I wear?"

"Not to casual not to dressy."

"Alrighty then. We'll see you in a few," she mustered up the fake cheerfulness.

Mary Lou hung up the phone and sat quietly for a moment and bowed her head. "Oh Lord give me wisdom."

Alex and Lexi emerged into the brilliant sunlight from the exchange laughing and carrying on. "Do you remember the corn dogs they used to sell down on Newport Beach? I just loved those things. The exchange has the closest thing to them, that's why I try to get over here every now and then to get one," Lexi said tossing her hair out of her face.

Alex stared at her an admired her beauty. Bit by the bug of guilt he pried his eyes away from her. "I got to go. We got a lot of work to do this afternoon getting ready for tomorrows competition. Take it easy and I'll see ya around the campus," Alex said as Lexi slipped into her car and he closed the door with both hands. She put one of her hands on his and he pulled them out from hers and backed up a step.

She started the engine, waved good bye and pulled away. He watched her car disappear and was jolted back to reality when he heard his name.

"Alex."

"Mary Lou," he said surprised to see her. "Ah. What are you doing here?"

"Picking up John's uniforms at the cleaners."

"Oh good. I was just heading back to the base to tie some knots with John and the boots."

"I see. Was that Alexis Althorne?"

"Yes. Yes it was. Good guess. Do you know her?"

"No, but John has told me about her. I saw her license plate as she pulled off. It said 'LEXI 1' on it. I figured it was her. Nice car."

"Yeah wasn't it. Brand new Datsun 280ZX. She's the Division 12 secretary. We're friends. She's from Vermont. We knew each other before I started dating Cat."

Mary Lou sniffed. "Is that perfume I smell?"

"Yeah it is. I was checking out some perfume samples for Cat in the Exchange. Anniversary is coming up. The samples get all over you. It was good seeing you Mary Lou. I got to run, those knots are calling my name."

"I do to. I'm picking up your wife in a few minutes."

"My wife? Where y'all going? I thought she was working today."

"She had the afternoon off, something about some construction in the office. I asked her to go with me to the ladies meeting at church."

"Church? Cat? Those two things don't go together."

"You ought to try it some time, might keep you out of trouble."

The comment stung. He swallowed to keep his composure and tried not to show any reaction. She was probing him, he could feel it. To avoid any further interrogation he decided it was time to shove off. "I really got to run. John's expecting me."

"And your wife," she said. Paused then added "me. Take care Alex. Say hi to John for me."

"I will. Bye. Send my love to Cat."

What kind of mind games was she playing? He tried not to hurry to his car because he felt naked and wanted to hide. He quickly unlocked the door, got in and took a deep breath. *I don't know what she knows but she knows something. It's tough playing poker with a woman.*

"What is it with your wife?" Alex said as he stormed into the company office.

"My wife?" John said.

"I just ran into her at the Exchange."

"Aw man. You didn't?"

"Yeah. Just as Lexi was pulling away, she snuck up behind me."

"Oh man. You're in trouble. They don't call her the human X-ray machine for nothing."

"What?" Alex said as he pulled the plan of the day from the 'Incoming," box on the wall and gruffly sat down behind the desk as John moved out of the way.

"She's got X-Ray vision she can see when something is not right. She's always been that way. I can't get away with nothing. If I do it's because I'm not doing anything wrong."

"How do you live like that? I'd been gone a long time ago."

"No man it's really cool. It's not like she is a-know-it-all or anything like that. She never confronts me on anything I do wrong. She's got this knack for getting me to come clean with the problem and when I do I feel better about myself. She's just sweet and that's why I love her so much. I don't expect you to understand."

"I don't. She's picking up Cathreen and taking her to church with her. Do I have reason to be concerned?"

"That's great!"

"Look John, I'm not a holy roller and don't plan on being one. But if Cat wants to go to church that's up to her."

"Listen Bub. I know that already but I think you're making a mistake."

Alex lunged forward and held up a fist.

"Take it easy X-lax. I understand. As for Mary Lou she won't spill the beans, she's not the type. She's going to ask a lot of questions to get her thinking though."

"Oh great," Alex said throwing his hands in the air.

"What happened at the Exchange?"

"Lexi was being Lexi. She can't let go of things. I'm married and expecting a child and she still is coming on to me. We're talking and she's got me like putty in her hands when she starts talking about how lonely she is. How much she misses me and how sorry she is. Then she turns on the waterworks and I try to say something nice and she gets all gushy. She leans over and plants one right on the kisser."

John rocked his chair back against the wall and whistled. "Ohhhhhh Boyyyy. I told you not to go over and mess with her."

Alex shot out of his chair slamming it against the back wall. "I'm not trying to do anything. Everyone else around me is doing something. I'm just trying to get this company through basic training and win that *Double Salute* so I can go be an officer. What does everyone want from me?" He paced back and forth in frustration.

"Alex, I'm your friend. I'm not going to get in you way, but you're so focused on what you want that you're forgetting about what everybody else wants around you. If you're going to be an officer, then you have to always keep the goal in front of you but not at the cost of your own soul."

"John I told you I don't want to talk about religion."

"Who's talking about religion? I'm talking about you," John said as his voice pitched. "You're so obsessed getting to the goal on your own strength that you've forgotten you need the right people helping you."

"What are you talking about?"

John stood up, leaned over the desk and wagged his finger at him. "Lexi Althorne. She and that dead sailor they're like a dead weight around your neck dragging you down. She dumped you man, don't let her play these mind games with you. You got a good thing going. Don't screw it up."

"I guess you're right."

"Darn straight I'm right," John huffed back and stared at him. He pointed his fat, long finger at him and said, "Remember what I said. I don't want to have to kick the tar out of you."

Bustling voices filled the still barracks. "Get them tying their knots."

Closing her eyes, Cathreen lifted her face to the sun allowing it to warm her weary brow. The crisp air of the cool spring day filled her lungs invigorating her. The smell of new life softened her anxiety as she patiently waited for Mary Lou. She lifted herself on her toes and strained to identify the little Volkswagen Cabriolet. She backed up abruptly when a 1975 white Laguna S-3 rumbled up in front of her. The engine sounded like it wanted to stall. The passenger side window rolled down and a familiar voice beckoned to her, "Cat."

Cat bent down to see Mary Lou leaning over the console. "This isn't your car. Yours looks like mine."

"This is John's car. He took mine and was going to get the oil changed after work."

Cathreen pulled open the long heavy door giggled when she saw a swivel bucket seat turned toward her. "How do I sit in that?" she inquired.

"You back into it and then rotate it forward when you get in," Mary Lou said. "I think they're crazy but John likes them."

Plopping down in to the seat, Cathreen gasped, giggled and then whirled it around. The handle of the big door was too far away so she had to lean out of the car to yank the door shut. "What is it with men and these hoop-dees?"

"I don't know. John calls it a muscle car."

"Yeah I've heard Alex use that term also. What does it mean anyway," Cat said as she slammed the door shut.

"Hard to explain, better to show you. Fasten your seat belt dear."

"Why?"

"Part of the demonstration."

Click. "Ready for blast off?"

"Hold on," Mary Lou said as she punched the accelerator. The car leapt away from the curb, growled and picked up speed fast.

"Ahhhh. Yikes."

"That's why they call it a muscle car. A guy thing I guess. If it makes him happy I don't care. It fits his personality. I really don't like driving it. It's not a ladies car."

"You can say that again," Cat said trying to calm her self after the adrenaline rush. "I wanted to talk to you because I need some advice."

"What is it?"

"I'm leaving Alex."

Mary Lou slammed on the breaks and looked for a place to pull the car over. She signaled, pulled into a service station and put the car in park. "Why do you want to do such a thing?"

"He loves his career more than he does me. If he doesn't have enough love for me, what about this baby? Is he going to have any left over for him or her? That note from Lexi, what's that all about anyway?"

"Have you said anything to him about this?"

"No. He comes home at night exhausted and falls asleep while I'm talking to him. Mary Lou I'm all alone. It wasn't so bad when I was not pregnant, but now I've got to think about this baby and what's best for it. You don't have kids so you don't understand what I'm talking about." She put her face in her hands and started to cry. "I didn't want to start blubbering," she said.

Mary Lou reached over and gently turned her toward her. "I do understand. This is a very rough time for the both of you. I know how much you need him right now, but unfortunately he has no choice. The Navy expects. No actually the Navy demands he do his job. I've counseled a lot of women at the Pregnancy Center and I know exactly what you are feeling. Feelings of insecurity and the need to cling and clutch to something."

"So I'm just being a big baby about all this."

"No. No. Your feelings are valid. There's nothing wrong with what you are feeling, but what is wrong is the way you deal with them. Leaving Alex is not the answer. That will make the problem worse. You need something else to help cope with the problem."

"What can help?" Cat said with a note of sarcasm.

"It's not what, but who."

"Aw no. I don't need more people in my life."

"Not people Cathreen. It's Jesus."

Cathreen blinked back tears and stared into Mary's Lou's compassionate eyes.

Mary Lou continued, "People are like sheep. Sheep lose their way easily and need help to find their way. They need someone to protect them from the wolves that lurk in shadows ready to devour the unsuspecting gullible little sheep. They need a shepherd. Jesus is the Good Shepherd."

As Mary Lou spoke, Cathreen's eyes softened as the light of understanding began to fill her soul. A slight tug in her heart spoke to her and she knew what Mary Lou was saying was true. "This Good Shepherd can be what Alex is not?"

"Alex can't be everything even if he was there when ever you needed him. I learned a long time ago John can't fill me up completely I needed more. It was wrong of me to expect him to be that way. Only after I allowed Jesus to be my shepherd did I start to find I didn't need to depend on any one else but him."

The tugging became a little bit stronger as each word fell like water on a dry and thirsty soul. Cathreen turned to stare out the window and let the words sink in. "What do I have to do?"

"One thing."

"What's that?"

"Surrender. By surrendering you are saying that he's in control and you're not."

"That's not easy."

"It is easy if you want to let go and trust. That's why it is so much easier for a child to understand this concept, because it is a lot easier for a child to surrender in complete trust. My Daddy used to fling me in the air and then catch me. Not once did he drop me. I trusted him. Can you trust Jesus to shepherd you?"

With tear streaked cheeks Cat turned to Mary Lou and said, "I can." As soon as the words left her lips a hundred pound weight lifted off her shoulders and she gasped.

Puddles of tears formed on the console between the two women as both of them wept in joy together. Mary Lou reached across the console and hugged Cathreen as best she could.

"I feel like I can breathe," Cat said when the two parted.

"That's good. That's very good."

The tan Ford LTD pulled to the gate of *Recruit Training Command* where he was greeted by a sentry in a dress blue uniform. The uniform was augmented by white leggings, duty belt, gloves and an ascot. The guard bent to speak to the driver who had no sticker on his car to gain admission to the base. "How can I help you sir?"

An elderly man with a gray mustache wearing a fedora with a feather in it leaned out of the window. "I have an appointment to see Petty Officer Rodney Peach. Division 12."

The guard pointed past the guard shack. "You need to make a U-turn and go to the Pass and ID office, building 6130 located at the main gate. Take a right on to Buckley Road go under the Metra rail overpass and turn right onto Sheridan Road. Go about a quarter mile ahead at the next light, just north of the main gate. Show your license and registration they'll issue a temporary parking pass. Bring it back here and we can let you in."

The old man touched his hat and pulled away from the guard shack. "Thank you, young man."

The guarded nodded at him and turned his attention to the next vehicle.

The old man returned shortly to the gate and the sentry explained where to go. As the LTD glided into a visitor parking space the break drums squeaked in protest as the asbestos covered break shoe ground against it. The driver side door creaked when opened and the old man with minimum struggle exited the car.

Upon entering the barracks main entrance, he lost his bearings and tried to remember what the guard had told him. Alex came out of his company berthing area and saw the old gentleman standing in the foyer. "Can I help you sir?"

"Yes young man. I'm looking for … for," he stuttered and looked down at the faded brown 8 ½ by 11 envelope he was holding. "Rod Peach."

"That's his company barrack right there. That's a restricted area. I can get him for you."

"If you would, please."

Alex opened the door, paused for a moment and asked, "Can I say who is calling?"

"Mr. Rossatini."

"Thank you sir. It will be just a minute."

Alex entered the barracks of Company 195 and made his way to the company office and rapped on the door. "Come," a voice said from within.

Peach looked up from his desk. When he saw Alex he sneered, "You Sievers," Peach said in disgust, "what do you want?"

Not wanting any confrontation he didn't take the bait and sidestepped the rude comment. "Someone hear to see you on the quarterdeck."

Peach got up from his desk, got right in Alex's face and lowered his voice, "Easy to be smug now you pathetic piece of garbage. We'll see how smug you'll be when it comes time for the conflagration. Are you going to be chicken like you were on *Ingersoll*?"

Alex's eyes narrowed, he balled his fist and fought for every ounce of control he could muster. "You're the one who lied to the board of inquiry?" The vein on his neck pulsated and strained.

Rod laughed, "No I just repeated what you said."

"I said?"

"You said it was entirely your fault."

Alex grabbed Peach by the shirt and through gritted teeth said, "That's a lie. I never said it was my fault to you or any one else."

Peach looked down at Alex's fist holding his shirt and then back at Alex, "Oh but you did. I was manning the Repair 3 locker when the fire alarm came in. I was the first one on scene and you were mumbling that it was your fault. Since you obviously couldn't share this information with the board of inquiry, I did you a favor and shared it for you."

With a surge of fury, Alex yanked him closer and raised his fist to hit him. "You snake! I ought cut your heart out." A flash of sanity shot through the insane cloud enveloping him and he shoved him against the wall.

Straightening his uniform, Peach stepped around Alex and said, "Conflagration is coming Scarecrow," and laughed as he walked away.

Peach stepped on to the quarterdeck. "Ah Mister Rosatini. How are you?"

"I'm fine Petty Officer Peach. I have finished the job you requested and have the information here for you. I will accept full payment at this time and we can conclude our business."

"May I examine the information?"

Rosatini handed Rod the brown envelope to examine. He removed the three eight by ten photographs and studied each picture for a few seconds then placed them back in the envelope. "Fine work Mr. Rosatini. I am completely satisfied. Did you say the payment was $400?"

"We agreed to $500."

Rod smiled and said, "My mistake. Who do I make the check to?"

"Rosatini Private Investigation."

"I have my check book right here." He tucked the envelope under his left arm and extracted the check book from his back pocket and a pen from his right breast pocket. He looked up while writing the check and inquired, "Did you tell the petty officer who greeted you, why you were here?" He proceeded to finish writing the check.

"No sir. I never discuss with anyone my business."

Rod tried to hide his apprehension.

Rod handed him the check with his left hand and shook his right.

Alex left the 195 barracks, skirted down an interconnecting corridor to his company's barracks. John was at the opposite end of the barracks instructing the company on knot tying. He went behind the recruits as he walked up he could see through the windows to the quarterdeck and saw Peach taking the envelope from the old gentleman he just announced.

When Peach disappeared into his company barracks Alex stepped out on to the quarterdeck and watched the old man get into the tan LTD with a strange Illinois license plate: RENTAPI.

Wanting to think about the two strange situations he just witnessed he headed back to the Company Commander's Lounge to get a cold drink. At the far end of the corridor he saw Peach showing Lexi something. Her face turned sour and she said something he could not hear and she stomped off to her office. Peach turned and saw Alex staring. He smiled at him, tipped the documents to his forehead and disappeared into his company's barracks.

CHAPTER 15: FIRE THE CANNONS

And all I ask is a tall ship and a star to steer her by – John Mansfield

During the Golden Age of Sail tall ships harnessed the wind in their sails with the skills and strength of their crew. These warriors of the sea not only battled enemies of state but the sea itself. They faced elements so harsh, with one rogue wave, the ship and its crew could be plunged into Davey Jones' locker. To navigate the sea and control the power of the wind each crewman had to master his job and those of his mates to insure safe passage.

Hands or sailors as they are better known skipped through the rigging of a mast like monkeys in trees. Each member of the crew, including the officers learned to be comfortable high above the main deck manning yard arms furling and unfurling sails. The modern day ships still use masts for communication and radar antennas so it is still important to learn how to handle themselves on the yard arms.

"Welcome back gentlemen for day two of the Captain's Cup competition," said Chief Paige. "Our first event will be the mast climbing. Instead of using a parachute harness with a climber safety device we are going to climb the old fashioned way. We're going to use rope ladders. You'll dash a hundred yards, climb the rope ladder, ring the bell at the top and then you descend using the rope climb. Use a hand over hand motion coming down so you don't get rope burn." He demonstrated by placing one hand over another. "Each company choose a five man team and then take your places."

Peach stood in front of his company and chose five men by snapping his arm each time he pointed, "Campanelli, Mongillo, Gabrielle, Moscato and Grzesik." They huddled around Peach. "You guys are the best guys I got. We're going to beat them with muscles. You guys were the fastest up the rope when we were practicing."

"Yeah, but sir that was up the rope and we didn't train on a rope ladder," Gabrielle said.

"Look!" Rod said, grabbing Gabrielle's t-shirt yanking him into him. "I'm not here to be your mama and listen to your tired excuses. Just get up there and win. We're just behind them and if we win this event we'll get them."

A distracted recruit caught Peach's eye. "Mongillo! Are you paying attention?" he snapped.

Seaman Recruit Mongillo smiled and pointed behind Peach. "Get a load of that."

Peach turned around as did the other four recruits and all started to smile. Company 197's team was made up of the smallest members of their company.

"What kind of team do you call that Sievers?" Peach said, mocking the team Alex had chosen. "Looks like a bunch of munchkins."

Alex just smiled and nodded.

"Alright guys you got this one. Mongillo you go first since you are the fastest. We'll get a big lead on them and not look back. You'll demolish that runt brigade," Peach said. "Let's bring it in." He placed his hand in the center. "Let's take them. 195 on three. 1-2-3."

"195," the team said in unison and took their places at the starting line.

Team 195 and 197 found their places at the end of the track. The smallest member of the Company 197, their guide-on Seaman Recruit Sanchez took his place at the starting line. He stood all of five feet nothing and was dwarfed by the six foot four frame of 195's Mongillo.

Sanchez mumbled something and distracted Mongillo for a split second. When the gun fired Sanchez screamed and scurried away. Not expecting either to happen, Mongillo hesitated for a split second. He could hear Peach cussing at him and bolted after Sanchez. He quickly drew even with him and moved ahead but was unable to put any real distance on him.

The two recruits leapt at the rope ladder and started the tedious climb up the ladder. Sanchez being smaller and more nimble opened up a gap on Mongillo. The rope ladder creaked as the two competitors ascended. Sanchez bested the ladder first and rang his bell and started down the rope. About two seconds after Sanchez rang his bell Mongillo rang his and down the rope he went. Sanchez hit the floor first and the instructor thrust a red flag in the air.

The second runner, Seaman Recruit Shuster not much bigger than Sanchez shouted and dashed down the clay track toward the rope climb. Mongillo was unable to close the gap and hit the ground about two seconds behind Sanchez. Campanelli leapt out of the block like a deer, but was unable to make up any ground on Shuster. The gap widened a bit on the rope climb. Shuster was able to ring his bell first and descend down the rope and hit the ground ahead of Campanelli.

Not to be out done, Seaman Recruit Hayes let out a blood curdling scream as he rocketed off the line. He put his head down and his short little steps look like a cartoon character running down the track. He timed his leap perfectly and never slowed down as he scurried up the rope ladder opening up a huge gap back to the struggling Seaman Recruit Gabrielle huffing and puffing up the rope ladder. Hayes clanged the bell with all his strength at the summit. Then he gracefully descended the rope to the floor below.

Peach yelled at Gabrielle, "C'mon you lard butt get over here." The recruit walked over to where Peach was standing. "I thought you told me that you could do this."

"Yes sir. I . . . I did, but."

"Never mind the excuse. You better hope we can pull this out some how."

Seaman Recruit Masters fired off the line like a cannon shot and flew down the track. Like the three recruits before him he ascended to the top with ease. About three rungs to go his leg cramped, which made it difficult to climb. The pain grew more intense and he pulled himself with his arms to the top.

"He's hurt. He's hurt," Peach yelled to Seaman Recruit Moscato.

Moscato looked up and with renewed furry attacked the ropes and like a spider in a web quickly closed on his prey. He drew even at the top and they rang the bells simultaneously. The two descended the rope with Moscato leading. When the two recruits hit the deck, Seaman Grzesik the anchor for 195 exploded off the line leaving 197's Galardi yelling to his back as he came off the line. Galardi chased Grzesik's back down the track and was unable to close the gap.

Grzesik timed his leap perfectly and hit the fourth rung of the rope ladder. Galardi only hit the third rung and scrambled up the ladder, but still was unable to close the gap on the surprisingly nimble giant next to him.

Peach sensing victory got his company to urge their team mate on by chanting, "195."

Grzesik rang the bell with a short ring and leapt on to the rope and hand over handed down furiously. Galardi followed right on the heels of Grzesik. Unable to close the gap and sensing defeat, desperation took hold of Galardi. He stopped the hand over hand motion and slid down the rope just in time to snatch the victory. Company 197 erupted in cheers and started chanting, "197."

Keller ran and grabbed Galardi bear hugging him. "Y'all did it. This was what I was talking about. You did it man. Great job," Keller said and squeezed him again. "Your Dad would be proud of you."

"Thanks Cade. That means a lot to me."

The company swarmed him and when the cheering died down. Alex smiled and held out his hand to congratulate him. Bleeding and stinging, Galardi held out his rope burned hands.

"Aw man," Alex said. He grabbed the Rpock. "Get someone to take him to the dispensary and get his hands treated. Immediately."

He turned toward the recruit and said, "You didn't have to do that."

"It was my duty to the company. I had to win."

"Good job. I'm proud of you." He gently pushed him toward the

Rpock and just shook his head. *Wow*, he said to himself. He turned in time to hear Peach speaking to his team.

"You morons are worthless. You some how keep snatching defeat out of the jaws of victory."

"Alright gentlemen. We'll be starting the next event soon, but first I would like to announce the winner of the Mast Climbing event." He paused for a moment and said flatly. "197."

Company 197 exploded and started to chant again, "197."

Chief Paige held up his hand to silence the celebration. "After two events 197 leads with 195 not far behind in second. We have three more team events today and we will conclude with the Iron Man Competition on Friday."

Paige looked down at his clipboard and checked off a few items. He flipped up a page and studied for a few moments, adjusted his glasses and looked up at the assembled recruits.

"This next event has to deal with ordinance. Ships were built around their weaponry and cannons were the weapon of choice on the mighty sailing ships. Some of the largest ships had up to 120 cannons with three decks of guns. This proved to be ineffective in battle and the ideal ship of the line carried 74 guns. The cannon ball weight was used to determine the size of the gun. Some cannonballs weighed up to 42 pounds. They were stored in racks bolted to the deck with holes cut in them called shot garlands. We have constructed a shot garland which will contain a 24 pound cannonball that was used in 5.5 inch cannons."

Chief Paige paused for a moment and took a sip of water.

"We call this The Carronade Relay or The Cannonball Run. A carronade is a type of cannon used by the Royal Navy in the 17 and 1800's. This will be another race of teamwork, endurance and strength. Cannonballs will be taken from the shot garland by one team member and handed to the first runner. The runner will run the cannon ball a hundred yards to the cannon. The runner will transfer the ball to the gunner who will load the cannon. This will be repeated five times by five different runners. The team that can load five cannonballs and push the cannon 25 yards across the finish line in the shortest amount of time will be the winner. Company 190 through 194 will compete first and 195 through 199 in the second heat."

The first five companies took their places on the starting line. "On your marks," Chief Paige said with the gun raised in the air, did a quick scan of the teams to see if everyone was set. One of the teams in the middle wasn't quite set and he dropped the gun to his side. "C'mon Harris lets get that team ready."

Hatch trotted over to his team, "Just a second chief I'll see what going on."

"What's going on guys? How come you're not on the line?"

"Everybody wants to run and nobody wants to be the handler or the loader?"

"Are you kidding me?" Hatch grabbed the guy closest to him, shoved him toward the shot garland and shoved another guy toward the cannon. "Bagnoli, go hustle down there on the double. You guys are looking like a bunch of rocks out here. Let's go win this one," Hatch said clapping his hands as he backed away from the team.

Hatch jogged back to where the other company commanders were standing. "Alright chief, just a little communication problem. They're ready."

Chief Paige growled at Hatch, "Gentlemen. On your marks," The chief surveyed the teams one more time. "What's he doing now Harris?" The first recruit to run for 192 was still not in position. The other recruits waiting to start the race grumbled at Company 192, "C'mon you morons lets go."

Hatch cupped his hands and yelled, "192, get ready."

"Can we start now Harris?" Paige said.

Shaking his head and smiling sheepishly Hatch said, "Sure chief, go ahead. What's the problem?"

"Rrrrrr," responded Paige. "Gentlemen. On your marks. Get set," he shouted and then shot the gun into the air.

The companies cheered their teams on as five recruits ran down to the shot garland to get the first 25 pounder. The runner from Company 190 eagerly held out his hands to take the cannon ball and was unable to make the proper transfer and dropped the cannonball. In unison, Company 190 groaned. The recruit yelled, "Sorry."

Meanwhile the recruits from 192 had found a groove and had already placed the first cannonball into the cannon. The instructor waved the red flag signaling the second runner to go. He darted to the cannonball rack and made a smooth transfer with the handler and waddled the 25 yards to the cannon holding the ball with two hands between his legs.

Alex laughed and turned toward Hatch. "It ain't pretty but whatever works," Hatch said with a grin.

With the second ball loaded Company 192 kept showing the way. The third runner was in full stride when he became distracted by the commander from 191 yelling, "No dummy you're suppose to carry the cannonball to the cannon not roll it." He could see as he approached the garland in the next lane a recruit rolling the ball down toward the cannon. The 192 recruit snickered as he took the ball from the handler, tucked it under one arm and hustled to the cannon.

The companies and their commanders were laughing and cheering watching that fiasco. Even stone faced Peach cracked a smile. The mortified Company 191 commander turned unable to watch. All the while 192 was putting distance on the rest of the field.

The fifth recruit from 192 slammed the last cannonball into the cannon. The entire team got behind the cannon truck and pushed the 1500 pound cannon toward the finish line.

As the teams of the first group finished, Chief Paige stood up and barked at the other five companies, "Take your positions."

"Look guys," Alex said as the seven recruits walked with him to the starting position. "These guys are bigger and maybe faster. Don't look at what their doing during the race. Concentrate on your race. Even if we can't win we've got to do our best and get the most points we can. 192 had a blistering time. We may not win this battle but we can still win the overall competition. Stay focused."

"Alright Petty Officer Sievers we got you," Keller said.

"You and Thompson push as hard as you can," Alex said. "It's all you two guys."

"Yes sir," the two recruits echoed back.

As before Chief Paige started the competition with the shot of the gun and the teams were off.

Alex walked back to the observation area and saw Peach standing behind the recruits talking with someone. The stranger handed Peach a slip of paper, he unfolded it, read it and for a moment he uncharacteristically looked frightened. He slowly folded the paper slipped it in his pocket as the stranger walked away.

Rejoining John, Alex whispered, "Peach is up to something."

"Please tell me something I don't know," John said watching their first recruit run to get the cannonball. "Why? How do you know?"

Looking at the recruits running with cannonballs but not seeing them Alex played what he just saw in his mind and repeated it to John.

"Just now?" John said while clapping for his guys. "C'mon guys we can do this."

"Yeah. Right over there," Alex said looking over to where Peach was standing. Like Alex he was looking at the competing recruits but was not seeing them. He looked distant, deep in thought, almost shaken. Alex had known Peach for a very long time and never had seen him like this before. "He's in trouble John."

"Good for him. Maybe he is finally reaping what he has sowed," John said and turned to take a quick glance. John's smile flattened. "I've seen that look before. He's not only in trouble, but that is a look of desperation. You don't want any part of that."

"Whatever he's in to and why it is happening is probably because of us. No I'm not going to steer clear as a matter of fact I'm going to play chicken with him. We'll see who blinks first."

"You're taking a huge chance. Desperate men will do desperate things. Even kill if they have to."

"What was that quote by Thomas Paine? 'I love the man that can smile in trouble that can gather strength from distress, and grow brave by reflection. 'Tis the business of little minds to shrink, but he whose heart is firm, and whose conscience approves his conduct, will pursue his principles unto death.'"

"Are you willing to follow that conviction into the conflagration?"

Alex blinked back at him unable to answer the painful question.

The cheering of all the companies signified the end of the competition.

The companies reassembled in the Fitness Center Drill Hall. Holding up his hands, Chief Paige silenced the murmuring recruits waiting for the results of the Cannonball Run.

"All right gents. The winner of the first Cannonball Run to no one's surprise Peach's guerillas that manhandled the field and easily took first place. Company 192 took second by a razor thin margin over Company 197. The overall standings show 197 still in first by a whisker over 195 who has closed the gap dramatically with the win but was unable to overtake them," Chief Paige said. "We will reassemble on the *Camp Porter* drill grinder at thirteen hundred hours after chow for the next event."

News of the reformatted Captains Cup competition had spread around *Naval Training Center* and attracted many spectators. Local media also requested credentials from the base public affairs office to cover the competition.

Television cameras followed Chief Paige as he took his place between two small boats.

"Good afternoon ladies and gentlemen. I see we are drawing quite a crowd. Just to give a brief explanation of what we are doing here. *Recruit Training Command* has endeavored to improve our modern day training with the traditions of the past. Normally our Captain's Cup competitions were companies competing against each other in boring physical fitness exercise. We've added a twist to the physical fitness by adding to it activities traditional sailors of old were required to know when sailing old wooden ships."

Pausing for a moment to take a sip of water, Chief Paige continued. "Modern ships like their sailing counterparts used smaller boats to transport crew and supplies to and from shore when suitable port facilities were unavailable and ships would anchor in the harbor. Sometimes it became necessary to remove the boat from the water and transfer it to another body of water for some other mission. The act of moving the boat over land is called portaging and was performed by the crew. Other boats that were used are cutters, whaleboats, gigs, jolly boats, launches, dinghies, and punts. These two boats to my left and right are called gigs. They were crewed by four oarsmen and a coxswain who would pilot the boat. In this competition you are going to portage this boat back to the track at *Camp Moffett*."

"That's all we have to do is run this boat over to the other side of the base?" asked a recruit.

"No that is not all you are going to have to do with it. You are going to take a detour via the pool. The boat will be placed in the pool and the whole team will have to get in the boat and row across the pool, then get it out of the water and then to the finish line. As in all the competitions these are timed events. Best time wins. Pretty easy. Huh?"

The recruits gasped and whispered amongst themselves.

"Alrighty then. Odd number companies stay here and even number companies form up and march back over to the Fitness Center. We will begin the first heat in 5 minutes. Dismissed."

The companies started to form up when Chief Paige yelled, "May I have your attention please. Since 197 and 195 are leading the competition they will go first. That is all. Good Luck."

"This is great," John said to Alex. "This really levels the playing field. I can tell it is driving Peach bonkers. He's becoming a stark raving lunatic. We can't lose."

"Don't pick your peaches before they're done fuzzing up. He's not beat yet and this event favors him more than it does us," Alex said.

"What?" John said and laughed. "Where did you hear that?"

"Andy Griffith. It looks like the fuzz is growing on the inside of your head and tickling your brain."

"You're too much. I'm ready to pick that Peach though and eat him for lunch," John said pointing toward where Peach was briefing his company.

Alex huddled the men together participating in the event. "Alright guys the playing field is pretty level on this one. Y'all are in good shape and those boats aren't that heavy. Run in step and you wont have to fight with the weight of the boat that much. Rpock since you are running this, call a cadence when running. The pool might be the hardest part, but it's going to be hard for them too. Don't forget to breathe and everything will be ok. I'm counting on you guys."

The recruits broke the huddle and took their places next to 195. Cameras were rolling as the two teams faced off.

"You guys ready?" Paige asked them.

A spirited, "Yes sir," was the response.

For drama and the television cameras Chief Paige slowed it down "On your marks." Pause. "Get set." Long Pause. "Go!" he yelled and fired the starting pistol.

The two teams lifted their boats and dashed away toward the pool. The Rpock began a raspy voiced cadence. "One, Two." A short pause. "Three. Four." Then repeated it.

The two teams reached the pool at the exact same time. The instructors guided the teams to the head of the pool. 197 tossed the boat in and jumped in after it. Once they were in the boat, oars were being tossed at them. The Rpock got them in another cadence by shouting, "Stroke."

Meanwhile, one of the 195 team slipped and fell into the pool while trying to get in the boat and the team was not able to receive the oars until the last member was in the boat. As soon at they started rowing Team 197 had already reached the far end of the pool and extracted the boat from the water.

Company 197 had a good lead heading back toward *Camp Moffett* and the fitness center. The sound of the running shoes clomping down in cadence as the huffing and puffing sailors were swallowed up by the darkness of the tunnel. 197 burst from the shadows first but the fast moving company 195 closed the gap as the last corner was rounded.

The Rpock yelled, "Pick it up boys." Team 197 surged forward and tempered the advance of 195. With the finish line growing closer the gap between the two teams tightened. 197 found just enough to hold off the charging 195 and cross the finish line first.

Heading back to the platform Chief Paige nudged Alex, "I'm glad to see your guys hanging tough," he said and smiled.

"Thanks chief," Alex said then turned back to John. "Did you find a good knot nut?"

Laughing, "A knot nut?"

"Yeah a knot nut. Somebody who can tie knots real good."

"Oh yeah. I got somebody."

"Who?"

"I got somebody. You'll find out," John said.

"I'm not liking this. Tell me who did you pick or I'm going to tie you in a knot."

"Ssssshhhhhh," John put his index finger to his lips and pointed at Chief Paige coming to the microphone with his other finger.

"This is the final competition of the day. Like the tall ships of old we still use rope or lines in the operation of ships. A seaman must know what knots or bends to use to secure a line or splice two lines together. The ancient sailor was expected to do his job under the worst possible conditions. In heavy weather he may be asked to go aloft and secure a line with heavy wind and rain pelting him while the ship pitched and rolled underneath him. One member from each company will be expected to tie five knots under similar conditions. We're not going to put you aloft, but we've built a simulator that's going to rock and roll with a wind machine pelting you with water, all the while you're trying to tie the five different knots. This is a timed event. Points will be deducted if any of the knots are tied wrong. Any questions?"

"Yes sir," a recruit in the front row said.

"Go ahead. What's your question?"

"What kind of knots will we be tying?"

"Thank you. You'll start with the square knot. That's the knot that you tie your neckerchief on your dress blues with. The bowline, sheet bend, timber hitch and a carrick bend. This time we will start worst to first. 197 you will be going last."

The instructor checking the knots from the recruit representing Company 195 held up four fingers. Chief Paige, "Alright gents we've completed nine companies. We have two companies tied in a dead heat Company 192 and 195 with four out of five knots each. No ones been able to get that carrick bend just right. Well let's see what 197 can do."

Seaman Recruit Shuster stood up to take his place in the simulator. Alex punched John in the arm, "You picked Shuster. He's more hosed up than Hogan's goat."

"Yeah he is, but the other day when we were getting ready for the Personnel Inspection I noticed everybody going to him to tie their neckerchiefs for them. He was pumping those babies out with his eyes closed. I asked him how he got so good tying square knots. He told me his Dad owned a sail boat and taught him how to tie all kinds of knots."

"You better be right about this, because we can put some daylight on 195 if we win this one."

"Don't worry boss. He's good."

Shuster took his place in the simulator and took the line in his hand and closed his eyes. Chief Paige yelled "Go." The simulator started to pitch and roll. A fire hose sprayed into the wind machine and pelted Shuster unmercifully.

Unfazed by the elements Shuster whipped through the knots. First the square knot. He took two ends of the cord in his fingers and flipped the right over left and then the left over the right and yanked it tight, then dropped it out of the simulator. He took the next cord, laid it in his left hand made a loop. He brought the free end up and passed it through the eye from the underside. "The rabbit comes up out of the hole," he said to himself. He then flipped it around the standing line and. "Goes around the tree." Then passed down into the loop. "Goes back down the hole." Then yanked it tight and dropped it out of the simulator. "The sheet bend," he said. "To join two different ropes of different sizes together." He took the two different ropes, looped one and passed the free end of the rope to be joined under the loop. Then wrapped it around the original rope and passed it under itself. He yanked it tight and dropped it to the ground.

Inside the simulator a poll had been placed for the timber hitch to be attached to. Shuster took the segment of line and wrapped it around one time and brought the free end around the standing line, then brought it over the loop, wrapped it three times and yanked it tight. The other end of the rope he wrapped around the pole the free end drawn through the loop and then around the pole again and through the loop and yanked tight.

The drops of water propelled by the wind machine felt like little needles in his face. Shuster methodically tied each knot unmoved by the distractions. "Just the carrick bend and I'm home free" he said. He took the first rope and looped it and laid it over the second one. He then passed the working end of the second rope over the first, then under and over. Then under itself and back over the loop of the first and gave a good yank. He raised his arms in the air to alert the instructors he'd completed the task.

"Wow!" Chief Paige. "That was quick. Now the question is, did he tie them correctly?" Paige put his hand over the microphone and coughed as he waited for word from the instructor inspecting the knots. The instructor thrust his hand in the air with all five finger extended. "Five for five. 197 winner."

Company 197 exploded with hooting and hollering. Peach dropped his head, wheeled around and pounded the bleachers.

"Alright gentlemen. With the victory Company 197 is solidly in first place. 195 holds down second and still has a shot at victory with a win in the Iron Man Competition. We'll see you all back here on Friday for the completion of the Captain's Cup competition."

Alex punched John as hard as he could. "Ow. What was that for?"

"For being right you big oaf."

"I just kind of have a knack for these things."

"If you know so much, get these guys back to the barracks. We've got to finish working these guys on the fire fighting techniques. They're not quite getting it and the walk through is tomorrow."

"You sure you don't want to go into the broiler with me and get chicken fricasseed tomorrow?"

"This is going to work man. Don't worry about it."

"You pick this stuff up so much faster and you're good at thinking on your feet if anything goes wrong in there I might not be able to react as quick as you do."

"No worries man. You'll do just fine."

John came busting into the barracks. "Alright guys lets go get some chow, fall out."

The company hustled out of the barracks and assembled on the grinder. John stood in front of the company as the last recruit took his place in the formation. John peered through the ranks to the back row and walked in between the columns. "Hey slick, did you forget something?"

"No sir, I don't think so," Seaman Recruit Shuster said.

John patted him on the head and said, "How about your cover?"

Shuster tried to look up and put his hand to his head. "Oh my gosh. I'm sorry sir."

"Duh. Go get it," John yelled at him.

Shuster bolted away and John yelled at him, "Shuster!"

He stopped and turned back to John with his hand on his head to keep his head covered. "Sir."

"You may be able to tie knots real good, but you need to untie your brain and use your head for a little more than a hat rack."

The company giggled. "Whew," John said. "He'd be dangerous if he only had a brain."

The company laughed again. John smiled, but caught a glimpse of Lieutenant Commander Hendrick approaching and didn't want his company get caught skylarking. "Alright you guys," he bellowed at them. "Knock it off you're in ranks."

Seaman Shuster burst into the barracks and startled an unauthorized guest just emerging from in between two bunks. Shuster stopped to examine the stranger. The stranger turned to look at him and darted from the room.

Shuster paid no mine, proceeded to secure his dixie cup sailors hat from his locker and bolted from the barracks to join the company.

John stood at attention as Commander Hendrick approached and snapped a crisp salute. "Good afternoon sir."

"Ah Petty Officer McCarthy. Congratulations on your victory today."

"Thank you sir."

"Where's Petty Officer Sievers?"

"He had some personal business to attend to."

"The men look good," Commander Hendrick said as he turned toward the company. "Keep up the good work gents and you'll be hoisting that cup and maybe the *Double Salute*."

Shuster rejoined the company.

"Straggler?"

"Yes sir. Forgot his cover."

"There's one in every company. Good Luck tomorrow Gents."

"Thank you sir."

CHAPTER 16: I HAVE NOT YET BEGUN TO FIGHT

I have not yet begun to fight – John Paul Jones (Father of United States Navy)

The base gymnasium after knock-off buzzed with activity. The stale smell of sweat filled the room and took some getting used to. Alex and John sparred in the ring while others worked speed and punching bags.

"You're pounding my hands in to hamburger," John said as Alex hit the punch mitts.

"Just blowing off some steam big guy. Pressure is getting to me. This makes me feel better."

"Doesn't make me feel too good. Reminds me of a joke I heard the other day. This sailor comes up to a Marine hitting himself with a hammer. The sailor asks him why he was hitting himself with the hammer. The Marine says, because it feels good when I stop."

Alex snickered and whacked the mitt again.

"Oww man, lighten up, will ya?" John complained.

"Sorry was just thinking about somebody."

From behind Alex, "If it isn't the loser himself," Peach said.

Alex looked over his shoulder to see who was talking to him. He turned his back on Peach and whacked the practice mitts with a left and a right. "Isn't that funny Rod, I was just thinking about you." *Whack. Whack.*

"Take it easy man," John said.

Rod stepped into the ring behind Alex and John. "Don't worry McCarthy this loser can't hurt you." He shoved Alex in the back.

Alex whirled around and jumped right in Rod's face. "I'm not sure but I think you're the one losing right now. We lead you," Alex huffed at Rod.

"Care to go a few rounds loser?"

"I wouldn't mind taking out my frustrations out on your punching bag head," Alex said and moved to the opposite corner to rest for a moment while Rod laced up his gloves.

"Are you crazy man? He'll knock your head off."

"This is the way Rod rolls. This is his way of playing head games. I've been down this road with him before. He thinks it works, but it never does. Besides I used to box in those Smoker competitions on the ship. I did pretty good, even against bigger guys like him. Besides if he gets too rough with me I'll just tag you and you can finish him off for me." Alex smiled a big toothy smile and patted John on the head.

"That's what I'm afraid of. Don't get yourself killed."

John helped Alex tighten up his gloves. He turned around in time to see Rod heading toward the center of the ring. He stepped toe to toe poker faced with him. After a long stare, "You ready."

"I'm always ready to kick your butt."

The two competitors tapped gloves and just as they did Rod unloaded a cheap shot to the face. "How's that feel punk?"

Stunned by the sucker punch he took a step back and allowed the shock to change to anger. Alex moved in with hands raised and circled his opponent. Rod took a few light jabs at the raised hands and circled him. Alex steeled his will and stepped in with a few quick punches, easily parried by Rod and then offered a retaliatory flurry of punches.

The two combatants continued searching for a weakness in his opponent. With out warning Rod attacked with a right which Alex avoided and countered with a left jab to the midsection. As the blow landed it stunned Rod, he dropped his gloves for a brief second and was rewarded with a combination of a right hook and a left to the head. Unloading another volley of hay makers Rod locked arms with Alex for some relief.

Rod pushed Alex off and head butted him, stunning him. He took a step backward to regain his senses only to be greeted with punches to the face. Alex locked arms with Rod to stop the barrage of punches.

John leaned on the ropes and yelled, "Get out of there. Get away from him." He put his hand over his eyes, not wanting to watch the beating Alex took.

Alex backed into the corner taking another round of punches. He rallied the strength to push Rod away backing him up. Alex feigned helplessness kept his hands to his sides. He watched Rod sneer and move in; over confident he dropped his hands. When he was in range Alex hit him with a bone jarring punch to the face causing his nose to explode like a tomato. The blow stunned him and he dropped to one knee.

Rejuvenated by the shifting of momentum Alex lifted his hands and circled Rod still down on one knee. "Ready for more Rod? I got a lot left in me," he hissed through his mouth piece.

Rod gritted his teeth and deep from him began to growl. "I'm going to kill you." He lunged at Alex, grabbed his arms and launched a wild frenzied attack. The boxing match turned into a brawl. John and the other spectators jumped in the ring and pulled Peach off. Alex tried to lunge back at Rod but was restrained by the spectators.

Unable to reach each other they traded word punches. "What wrong with you? You freaking psychopath."

"This isn't over punk. Watch your back cause I'm going to be all over it. You worthless piece of garbage."

Rod calmed down and as the hands holding relaxed he muscled himself away from them. Snarled at Alex, grabbed the towel someone offered and left the ring. Alex followed him with his eyes to the door. "What is his problem?" he said to nobody in particular.

Fire is the number one enemy to a ship and is dependant on its crew response. It is important for the crew to be proficient at their firefighting skills so further damage can be prevented and damaged areas repaired and brought back to full operation. Basic training on how to fight fires is taught at the firefighting training center. This high tech modern building constructed to simulate shipboard fires and make things as realistic as possible so recruits will be trained on real world scenarios.

A mock up of an actual Navy ship would be used to simulate a mass conflagration where the entire ship would become engulfed in flames and the recruits would be responsible to extinguish the raging inferno.

EN1 Willie Nixon is the lead firefighting instructor at RTC and has overseen thousands of simulations and training exercises. This graduation class will be the first recruits trained in the facility and is a very special honor.

Company 197 entered the facility for the walk through for the Mass Conflagration drill scheduled for Monday when the Secretary of the Navy will be on station for the first of its kind. In the walk through, the recruits would be instructed what will happen in the final drill.

"Hi Willy," John said as he came up to a group of instructors discussing the agenda for the day. "How's it going?"

"Hey! Big John, how's it hanging? I thought Petty Officer Sievers was coming in to do the walk through."

"He was, but something else came up and I had to take his place."

"Yeah. I heard about what happened to him out in the fleet. I could see why he would shy away from this."

"He didn't shy away. Look we're here to eat some fire. Are we ready?"

"All the gear they need is over there. Let's get started. Line your guys up over there. We're only going to be doing single compartment fires today so your boys can get the feel for the big event." Willy said. He pointed to the front of the simulator.

"Got it," John responded.

The recruits lined up on the red line and donned their equipment.

"We will be breaking the company down in to teams of five. Each team will don an OBA, Oxygen Breathing Apparatus and then enter a burning compartment and the door will be sealed behind you. You will access the situation and get the fire out as quick as possible. Either I or another instructor will be going in with you as a safety observer."

The A-4 Oxygen Breathing Apparatus (OBA) is a self contained unit and is used in environments lacking oxygen, or containing harmful gases, vapors, smoke or dust. Oxygen is supplied by chemicals that purify exhaled air. The wearer of the OBA's breath is circulated through the chemicals which react to the carbon dioxide and moisture which produces the oxygen. The caustic chemicals in the canister last up to about 45 minutes, causing the canister to become extremely hot making it necessary to remove with asbestos gloves.

"Are there any questions?" Petty Officer Nixon asked

"No Sir."

"Good. I want team one to move toward the entrance to the simulator."

Unknown to John, Alex slipped into the control to observe the drill.

"These are the hoses we are going to be using," John said to the first man in line as he guided the team into the simulator to give them a feel for it before the drill began. Two 1 ½ inch hoses were secured to the wall and attached a water main with a wye gate so two hoses could be used at one time. They entered a well lit compartment inside the *USS Landlock*. After the last member of the team entered, John dogged the door closed.

To the left of the hose, battle lanterns hung from their mounts. "After the lights go out the battle lantern is your only source for light. Stay close to your buddy, because you need to rely on each other. In a real situation that may mean life or death."

A recruit shot a question at him, "Where will the fire come from?"

He pointed to another compartment, "The fire will erupt in the next compartment over. It will be your job to enter that compartment with this equipment and put it out. Before the fire flashes keep your head down it will go over the top of us. Listen up people, there ain't no fooling around in here. This is some mean stuff and it can hurt you so stay on your toes and try to remember everything we talked about."

John pulled down one of the hoses and handed it to the closest recruit. "You are the nozzlemen for the number one hose team which is the attacking unit and number two hose team is the back up. If you are not a nozzlemen than you are hosemen your job is to lead out the hose from the fireplug, remove kinks, sharp bends and tend to it by helping the nozzlemen move the hose into a fire."

"Any more questions before we get started?"

John looked at the somber faces. "Don't worry guys it's not that bad. You'll want to do it again. Nozzlemen, make sure you keep a tight grip on that hose, because when you turn it loose, it's got a real kick to it. You got it."

"Aye sir," the two nozzlemen said. "Alright light up your OBA's and let's kick some fire butt."

John keyed the squak box, "Fire team ready."

"Acknowledge," came the reply.

"When the fire flashes, turn the nozzle on, point it at the base of the flame and sweep the hose in a back and forth motion."

"Aye sir." The fire team hunkered down and prepared for the flash.

"Fire team this is control, fire in 10 seconds," the voice said from the squak box. "3-2-1"

The fire flashed with a rush of heat and light in the adjoining compartment and rushed over the top of the recruits. Startled by the abrupt flash, nozzlemen one fell backward and pushed the handle of the hose forward. The sudden high pressure wrenched the hose from his hand and smacked John slamming him into the back bulkhead. He fell to the deck unconscious and landed awkwardly on his left arm fracturing it.

In a heroic effort Seaman Recruit Keller grabbed the wild hose and directed it at the fire. Nozzlemen for hose number two did the same thing and extinguished the fire. "Fire is out," Keller yelled, ripped his OBA mask off and keyed the squawk box. "Man down in here. Petty Officer McCarthy is unconscious."

Alex ran from the control room and un-dogged the hatch to the simulator. He went to John and checked his pulse, "He's breathing, get an ambulance down here right away."

The instructor in the door way said, "They're already on the way."

With the weight of the world on his shoulders, Alex slowly entered the 197 company barracks. The quiet room came to life with the presence of two shore patrol waiting in his office. "Petty Officer Sievers," said the Hull Technician First Class.

"Yes, what can I do for you?"

He handed him a sheet of paper, "We have orders to search one of your recruit's lockers."

Alex read the document carefully and gritted his teeth to stifle any emotion he was feeling. He nodded his head in agreement. The recruits shuffled into the barrack, "I'll get him for you."

The First Class said, "Alright."

Stepping out of the office he watched the men filing in from the back door. He bellowed, "Seaman Recruit Keller, front and center."

"Aye sir," he heard faintly from the back of the room. Keller hustled to the front and stood at attention in front of Petty Officer Sievers.

Alex stepped around Keller and barked an order. "Rpock take the men to the recreation room. On the double."

"Yes sir," The Rpock ran to the back of the room and hurried the men out of the back door. Once the door thumped closed, the two Shore Patrol stepped from the office into Keller's view. He swallowed hard at the site of the two ominous figures.

Staring towards the end of the barracks Alex said, "Seaman Recruit Keller, the Shore Patrol have orders from the *Naval Investigative Service* to search your locker for the presence of a controlled substance."

"Sir I have no drugs in my locker. I've never-"

"Silence!" Alex barked. "You will speak only when addressed. I'm sorry Keller. Orders are orders I have no control over this."

"Aye sir," Keller responded, did an about face and marched to his locker with Alex and the Shore Patrol in tow.

"Open it up Keller," Alex said sharply.

"Yes sir."

Keller took a breath and opened the locker a plastic bag of marijuana tumbled out and fell to the deck. Keller's face twisted in agony, his mouth dropped open and a gasp escaped his lungs. His body quaked as his brain tried to process what was happening. "It's not mine," he eked out.

"I swear it. I've never seen that before in my life."

He shook his head in denial and squatted to retrieve the bag. "Aht, aht," the Shore Patrolmen said.

Keller turned to Alex. "Petty Officer Sievers it's not mine…"

The First Class Shore Patrolman took Keller by the arm and hand cuffed him as Keller pleaded with his eyes for help.

"Where are you taking him?" Alex inquired.

"To medical for a urinalysis and then to the brig."

"Will you advise me of the results?"

"Your Division Commander will be notified upon release of the results."

"Thank you."

Keller looked over his shoulder as the two Shore Patrolmen took him away. Alex shot him a reassuring look. They escorted him to the back door of the barracks and out the main doors in full view of the entire company.

Alex watched through the doors as they ushered him in to a van marked SECURITY. He turned to his right and entered the recreation room and motioned to the Rpock to come to him. "Rpock, have the men come in and sit in instructional positions in the front of the room."

"Aye sir," the Rpock said. "Company instructional stations."

Alex slowly walked to the front of the room and plopped himself down on the table as the weight of the entire world crashed down on him. The recruits entered the room talking amongst themselves; he rubbed the knot out of his neck from the tension he'd been feeling. The room silenced and he probed the faces of each of the men whose eyes searched him for information.

"We've had a very busy day," Alex began. "I'm sorry to say that it has not gone well for two of the members of our group. I just got word that Petty Officer McCarthy is going to be fine. He's resting and should be back to being is ornery self making your lives miserable in no time at all."

The group sighed, smiled and mumbled amongst themselves.

"Hold it down," Alex said. "Seaman Recruit Keller is another issue. He has had a minor misunderstanding that we are going to get to the bottom of. Word has come down that the Iron Man race has been rescheduled to Monday. We've got a great shot of still winning. We will use the weekend to focus on areas we can use to our advantage to win the competition. Don't worry men adversity makes us stronger."

"Rpock," Alex said. "Take them to chow. There will be no training tonight. You guys can take it easy."

"Thank you sir," several people said.

"Alright guys," the Rpock said. "Let's get changed and line up on the grinder in five minutes."

Another day Alex would like to forget is at an end. He dragged himself up the stairs to his apartment. He slid the key into the lock, turned it and slowly opened the door. He juggled his briefcase, keys and jacket with the mail under his arm as he entered the dark living room. Light flooded in from the kitchen. Cat yells, "Is that you Alex?"

Alex looked around to see who else it would be and responded with, "Yeah, it's me." He snapped on some lights, placed his briefcase and jacket on the couch and tossed his keys and the mail on the table.

"How was your day?" Cat said in her upbeat voice.

"Fine. How come you didn't get the mail?"

"I completely forgot about it. I was really busy today."

"It's dark in here, why don't you turn on some lights." He flopped down in to his easy chair, rubbed his head real fast and clomped his feet down on the coffee table. Cat walked into the room wiping her hands and kissed him on the head.

"I was thinking. Since you have the day off tomorrow we go to the swap meet."

"Can't. Got to work," he replied.

Cat threw down the rag and her face contorted in anger. "What is with you? Are you allergic to relaxation? Every time I want to spend some time with my husband that job gets in the way."

"John's in the hospital."

"I'm sorry. I didn't know," she said. Her face softened. "Is he OK?

What happened?"

"One of the recruits let a fire hose go and it smacked him in the face. Knocked him out and gave him a concussion. He also has a broken arm."

Cat moved to hug him and comfort him. He stood up and hugged her. "I'm sorry Alex, I didn't know."

"We also lost our best chance at the Captain's Cup. Seaman Recruit Keller was busted for possession of a controlled substance. He had a bag of it in his locker."

"I'd say you've had a pretty rough day."

Wringing his hands, "I blame myself for this. I shouldn't have let John go in there."

"You're just trying to protect yourself."

Alex stood with all the frustration and anger rising up in him. "Protect myself? Is that what you think? I am trying the best I know how to help this company win the *Double Salute*."

"Is that what this all about?" she fired back at him. "That honor is more important to you than your own honor. Let's face it Alex, you're afraid. Now someone got hurt again, because you won't face your fear."

"How can you understand," he said as his voice rose a notch. "You don't know what it is like to face danger. Have most of your body burned and be responsible for a shipmate losing his life. And now this."

Cat moved closer to Alex. "Alex when are you going to see what this is doing to you, me and now a baby? It's killing me to watch you be eaten up from inside."

Unable to control his rage any longer he swiped the nick knacks, keys and the mail off the table in a burst of rage.

"I don't know who you are any more. You've turned into a rage-aholic." She bent down to collect the items on the floor. She picked up a manila envelope addressed to her. "What's this?" She turned it sideways to look at the return address: **Rossatini Private Investigation.** "Why would a Private Investigator be sending me something?" Her curiosity quelled her anger and she unsealed the envelope as Alex face when ashen. She pulled three black and white 8 by 10 pictures from the envelope and gasped when she saw the first one. Her eyes narrowed and she shouted;

"Now the truth is known."

"What truth?" Alex said sarcastically. "What have you got there?"

She thrust the picture of him being kissed by Lexi in his face. Alex's mouth dropped open as he examined in stunned silence himself in the embrace of another woman. "This is not what you think it is."

"Don't make me laugh. Is that the best thing you can say? C'mon Alex. It's not what I think it is, and then what is it? You're kissing her in broad day light in front of the Exchange."

"Exactly. Why would I be kissing Lexi in front of the Exchange in broad day light? Huh? Why? If I was going to purposely cheat on you, do you think I would be kissing in front of the whole world? Look at me I'm stiff as a board; I don't have my arms around her or anything. She's been pestering me for weeks, she set me up."

"I don't know if I believe you Alex. You come home late all the time, you leave early. I found a note with Lexi's phone number on it. You want me to believe nothing is going on with you and her. What are you doing all those hours at the base? I don't know what to believe any more."

Alex put both his hands on her shoulders. "Cat you've got to believe me." It hit him like a lightning bolt. He snatched the envelope out of her hands and read the return address again and studied it, "Of course, Rossatini. He was the old man in the barracks the other day. Cat look, I think Peach did this."

"Peach did this. Alex that's not Peach kissing Alexis Althorne, who has been a thorn in my side since the day I met her."

"This guy Rossatini, he brought this envelope to Peach the other day. I even went to get Peach for him."

"You're kissing her Alex."

"I know Cat, but you've got to believe me I would never do anything to hurt you purposely."

"I don't know Alex. I need some time to sort this out. I need to get away for a few days. I'm going to fly home and visit your mom for a few days." She opened the door to the bedroom and removed her suitcase. "I was hoping I wouldn't have to do this, but I think you need some time to get your priorities straight. You need to take a good look at your self and work this out inside you. I've tried to play the good little Navy wife, but I can't help you."

She put her coat on and turned and walked out leaving him in stunned amazement. He plopped back down in his chair, rubbed his head furiously and sat for a long moment. The phone caught his eye. He grabbed the receiver and punched in a telephone number with a stiff staccato.

"Hey Hatch could you meet me at the NCO club at 9:00?"

"Sure I'll see you then."

Alex slowly hung up the phone and eased back into his chair allowing it to swallow him up.

Friday night patrons rolled into the NCO club to enjoy life and blow off some steam. The stench of beer punctuated the smoky air. Alex on the other hand was trying to forget about life. He stared at the single shot of whiskey sitting on the bar in front of him. When the moment arose to brave the shot, he threw it back with the intensity of a man on a mission to let alcohol erase the day from his memory. He requested two more and threw both of them back with the same intensity.

"Wow," he said to himself. "It's been a long time since I felt this way. Hey bartender can I get a beer please."

"Sure," Buddy said stepping in the way of the other bartender.

"Buddy, I didn't know you were here. How are you?"

"I'm fine Alex. Where's the misses tonight?"

"Left me. Went home to mother," Alex said slowly. "How much I owe you?"

"Seven," he replied. He raised an eyebrow and shook his head. "God help this boy," he said under his breath.

Alex slapped a ten on the bar. "Keep the change."

"Hey sailor," Lexi said to his back.

Buddy sighed deeply. "Not the answer I was looking for God."

Alex rolled his eyes. "Buddy. Is there a really fine looking woman standing behind me?"

"Yep."

"That's what I was afraid of," Alex said as he slowly turned around. "Oh, hi Lexi. How are you and how's it feel being a home wrecker?"

"You got the pictures, huh?"

Buddy gritted his teeth and slowly wiped the bar waiting for a chance to intercede.

"You may hate me and that's fair. But you've got no right to hurt Cathreen. What's she done to hurt you? Nothing! She's been nothing but good to you. She was your friend."

"Friend? Huh!" she spat back at him. "She took you away from me and that makes her an enemy."

Alex stepped in and lowered his voice. "You need to get something through that thick blond skull of yours, you broke the relationship. I didn't and Cathreen didn't. She found me in the wreckage of what you did. She even encouraged me to go back to you. I said no."

Lexi's eyes softened and she looked away unable to hold his gaze. "I didn't know she did that."

"Yes. She's a first class woman and that's more than I can say about you. She loved you very much and she was heart broken by what you did."

"Alex I'm sorry. I really am."

"Sorry isn't good enough. She's left and gone back to Kansas."

Hanging her head Lexi stared at the floor. A long pause hung in the air. "Alex . . . I . . . I really am sorry about everything. I was very angry at you and wanted to get even. Peach approached me about doing this and I . . . I went along because I wanted to hurt you as much as you did me."

"You hurt me, you accomplished what you set out to do, now go away," Alex said and turned back to the bar to nurse his beer.

Lexi put her hand on his shoulder. "A. . . Alex. I'm truly sorry. Please don't turn your back on me."

Buddy watched with a keen eye and stood ready on guard to keep Alex from being seduced by the siren's call.

He looked at her hand on his shoulder and turned back to her. He softened his tone as the whiskey did its bidding. "You set me up, when

I was trying to be your friend. You need to move on and stop trying to control and manipulate your circumstances and the people around you to get what you want. Dog gonnit. You need to respect other peoples feelings-" He stopped short as the light penetrated the fog enveloping him of what Cat has been trying to communicate to him.

"Alex, could you ever forgive me?"

"Yeah sure, but it's not me you need to ask to forgive you, it's Cat," Alex said as he sat back down on his bar stool.

"Thanks Alex," she said, relieved and leaned over to kiss him on the cheek. "You're the best."

"Please don't do that any more," He said to her. "Is there anything else we need to talk about? Cause I really need you to go away."

"No. I understand. I'll see you on Monday," she said, smiled and skipped away as a plan percolated in her head.

"Bye, bye." Alex said not turning to look at her. A table of Navy Seals whistled at Lexi as she sauntered out of the club. He drained his beer glass and slapped down on the bar. "Yoe Buddy, can I get another?"

"Is this a good idea?" Buddy asked him.

"It's not a good idea," Alex slurred. "It's a great idea. Look Buddy, everything blew up today and I just figure I might as well blow up with it. That woman who just left she's dynamite."

"She's dynamite alright. You got that right and you need to steer clear of her."

"Yeah she's dynamite and she blew up in my face sending my beautiful little wife scampering off to Kansas. Peach put that dynamite in her hand and lit the fuse. My assistant is in the hospital. My best chance at winning the Captain's Cup was arrested. I got nothing better to do so I decided to drink a lot."

Buddy's eyes narrowed and he grabbed Alex by the shirt, "Listen to me Alex. I've been where you are, ready to toss in the towel. You are a United States Navy Petty Officer and there is always a way to win. Find it."

Alex stared back at Buddy through the thickening alcohol induced fog trying to grab hold of the pearl of wisdom he was being offered, but could not find the strength to do so. Buddy released him and Alex settled down on the stool. "Find it. Sheesh. Find what another kick in the teeth? When. . ." Alex hiccupped. "Pardon me. When the ground collapses under you. . . you. . . you fall into the pit. I'm in the pit, Buddy and I don't see a way out."

The other bartender returned with another draft beer, Alex stood up pushing his stool back. Plucked a five dollar bill out of his wallet and slapped it on the bar. Not being used to alcohol the room started to spin. He tried to sit back down but no stool was there to greet his derriere and he toppled to the floor. A group of Navy Seals sitting at the table across from him roared in laughter. Gathering himself off the floor, Alex took the beer from the bartender holding it out. He staggered over to the table where the guys were laughing at him. "Who are you guys?"

"Alex," Buddy called to him. "Don't do this."

Alex put his index finger in the air, "Hold on a minute Buddy, I'll be right back."

"We are Seals here for some training," one of them piped up.

Buddy grimaced and picked up the phone. His mind scrambled for an answer as he painfully watched a train wreck happening in front of him.

"Ahhh," Alex feigned awe. "Underwater Demolition Team Navy Seals. Wowwww. Are you real live Navy Seals or wanna bes? Cause we got a lot of wanna bes around here."

The most muscular of the group piped up, "Oh we are real ones. It might be a good idea for you to go back over to where you were sitting and get your girlfriend to come back and take you home."

"Alex," Buddy called. "This is not a good idea."

"It's ok Buddy. I'm fine." Alex staggered a little bit closer and looked up and down the closest one to him. "Good because I've always wanted to see the seal show at Sea World, but never had the chance. Could you clap your hands together like this?" Alex put his beer down on their table and clapped his hands and grunted like a seal, then picked up the beer and tried to balance it on the seals nose. "And maybe balance a beer mug on your nose."

The seal closest to him swatted it away spilling it on the guy next to him. The group of three seals bolted out of their chairs and grabbed Alex by the jacket and threw him through the front door. Alex rolled down the steps right at the feet of Hatch Harris.

"I think you boys ought turn around and go back inside before the shore patrol throws you in the brig." Hatch pointed to a pair of Shore Patrol walking their way. "Now you don't want that do ya?"

The largest seal said, "We don't want any trouble. Keep that piece of trash out of our way."

"Boys, let me get you another beer," Buddy said as he coaxed the seals back into the club. He turned and watched Alex get to his feet with the help of his friend. "Is he ok?"

"He's fine." Hatch bent down to give Alex a hand to help him up. "What kind of trouble are you making for yourself? I thought you didn't drink."

"He ok?" the Shore Patrolmen asked.

"He's fine, tripped coming down the steps."

"Alright. We don't need no trouble," the Patrolmen said.

"Thanks for your concern," and gave him a friendly wave.

"I don't," Alex replied standing up with some pain. "That hurt." He straightened his jacket.

"Let's walk."

"John got hurt today. He's going to be in the hospital for a few days and won't be coming back to finish the training."

"Yeah I was at division when the word came in. That sucks. Who's going to help you out?"

"There's a new class coming in and no one to spare. Sailing solo on this one," Alex said and then sucked a long deep breath in through his nostrils and then belted it back out. "I love the smell of spring."

"What?"

"I love the smell of spring," Alex slurred.

"No. Not that. The other thing you said."

Alex stopped and looked at Hatch for a long time and hiccupped. "Excuse me," Alex said and paused again. "Oh yeah. I remember now.

Keller got busted for smoking pot. SP's found a nickel bag of marijuana in his locker. NIS received a tip from an unnamed source Keller had been smoking pot."

"That's crazy. That guy is dumb as a box of rocks."

Sucking in another deep breath. "And top it all off Cat left me."

Hatch whistled. "Sound's like you had a pretty rough day."

"Yep, you can say that. Somebody sent some pictures of me kissing Alexis Althorne. Says she needs some space to think about things." Alex started to walk again looking down at the ground.

"Do what?" Hatch said.

"Lexi is an old girlfriend of mine, you know the division secretary. Peach and her conspired to get a picture of her kissing me then sent it to my wife. They succeeded and now Cat is on her way to Kansas to have a talk with my mother."

"Why your mother and not hers?"

"She likes my mother. Everybody likes my mother. I like my mother. Maybe I should go see my mother too. Do you like my mother?"

"I like your mother."

"So I thought I would drink a little to forget my troubles."

"Did it help?"

"Nope."

"I see why you didn't mind letting those seals use your head for a punching bag."

"Just figured if I hurt physically then I wouldn't feel this terrible aching inside." Alex stopped again and swayed a bit trying to keep his balance. "Maybe I should change my rating to Signalmen, because I got run up and down the yard arm so many times today I feel like a signal flag."

"Alex, do you wonder why this is all happening to you?" Hatch asked.

"I don't think the man up stairs likes me too much. Maybe he's punishing me because I got one of his followers killed on the ship," Alex said flatly. "I don't know."

"Do you really believe that?" Hatch shot back at him.

"I really don't know what to believe any more," Alex said, took a step closer and raised his voice. "Answer me one question. Why would God let that kid die if he was one of his followers? Huh? Answer me that."

Hatch stood dumbfounded, unable to answer Alex's question.

Tears welled up in Alex's eyes. "Then leave me to hold the bag. I tried to save that kid," he yelled. "I got burnt up and the kid still died. What kind of God is that?" he said through muddled tears. "What kind of God is that," he repeated. "Not one I would want to serve. I tried to save that kid."

"Look Alex, I . . . I don't have an answer. Things happen in this world for a reason, but we always don't know the reason."

"Hatch," Alex said in a very soft voice and put his hand on Hatch's shoulder to steady himself. "He said the strangest thing to me before he died. He said, 'No greater love that a man has then to lay down his life for his friend.' What does that mean?"

"Alex you are a great guy and lots of people like you because you care about them. Because of that lots of people like you but there are those who hate you too and would like to see you fail. You ran into that fire to save your shipmate and you gave no thought to yourself. You're a hero."

"Please Hatch, hero smero, I'm no hero. I'm just a regular guy."

"Hero's are regular guys doing heroic things."

"I'm not following you."

"You did what you always do. Your duty. You were willing to lay down your life for your friend. I'll bet you, if that had been Peach in that fire, you would've charged in just the same."

"I'd have to think about that one."

"Alex I've known you long enough to know, you would've. You remind me of another man I know. He did the same thing, but he lost his life in the process."

"Who?" Alex inquired.

"Jesus."

"Jesus?" Alex said with a note of sarcasm. "Come on. He's just a goody goody, everybody likes to say 'Jesus loves you.'"

"Man is born with sin and sin is like a chain that binds him to a certain way of living. To be released from these chains and be free it requires someone to do it for them. By dying Jesus released mankind from doing things the wrong way and freeing them to live the way they were created to live."

"So this Jesus stuff is not about being weird and talking like a lunatic."

"No. He is about making one right with God so he can live the way God created him to live and be in relationship with him."

"You're saying Jesus can make me free. Free from what?"

"Doing things your way. These things that happened today are for a reason. God is trying to get your attention."

"My attention. Why does he need my attention?"

"He wants everyone's attention. He's got a plan for you. You've been walking in his plan all your life. Now he wants to be part of what you are doing. He wants you to acknowledge him and that it is him that is leading and guiding you."

"Whoa. Whoa. Wait a minute Hatch. I'm the captain of my own ship. I don't need some God telling me which way to steer my boat. I've been doing just fine."

"Be serious. This is not fine. This is a shot across the bow. Wake up."

Alex stared and blinked at Hatch for a long time. *I must be a stark raving lunatic. But somehow it all makes perfect sense.* Alex thought to himself. He pointed his finger in Hatch's face. "Alright, you and him have got my attention. I give up, what do I have to do?"

"I'm not really good at this. At church they got this little prayer they say, but I'm not into formulas. I think you've already did the first thing, by surrendering. Now you really just need to ask him to help you out and acknowledge that he is the son of God and that he died and rose from the dead."

"Get out of here, he rose from the dead?"

"Yep that's what the bible says."

"Look I'm tired. I'm out of gas and I barely have a company and who knows how that's going to turn out. All my plans are up in smoke now. I give up; you, John, God and the bible win. I surrender."

"Well good than I think that's all you got to do. Do you feel any different?"

Alex cocked and eyebrow and took account of his faculties. He jerked his head to look at Hatch. He slapped his chest with both hands. "As a matter of fact I do. The gnawing pain in my chest is gone." He jerked again and looked at Hatch with a bewildered look and laughed a big boisterous laugh. "I'm sober." Alex snapped his fingers. "I was stone drunk a minute ago and just like that my mind cleared. I feel lighter almost like I got air in my shoes."

"That's great. Why don't you come and stay at my house tonight? Theresa would love to see you. As a matter of fact, I'm not on duty tomorrow. Why don't you take the day off, get your head screwed on straight and I'll go in and baby sit the kiddies for you."

"No. I don't want to impose on you."

"It's no problem. Besides I'd rather you do that then having those seals use your head for a punching bag."

A wide smile spread across Alex's face and he started to laugh. "Alright. I'll do it. I feel good, you know I feel really good!"

CHAPTER 17: NO GREATER LOVE

Greater love hath no man than this, that a man lay down his life for his friends. - **John 15:13**

The red Pontiac Trans Am wound its way down the tree lined roads of rural Wisconsin. The signal light popped on when it approached the tourist trap on the side of the road. Alex switched the car off, "The tourist trap Cat wanted to visit, but never got to," he said to the cool brisk air. The crisp smell of the fresh air invigorated his ailing mind. He took several deep breaths clearing his head. The 'Open Sign' winked as he approached. Opening the door a bell tinkled to announce his arrival and in which he was greeted by the smell of chocolate candy. "Now that smells good," he said.

"Hello," a voice hidden behind the counter said.

"Hello," Alex responded. "Beautiful shop you have here. It smells good in here."

"Thank you. Can I help you find something," a frail old woman said in a breathy voice.

"No. I'm just browsing."

"Take your time. If you need anything I'll be right here."

"Thank you," Alex said. He took all the trinkets lining the shelves. Nostalgic wooden toys occupied a small area. Different types of rocks filled one shelf. Candies and scrumptious treats cluttered the front counters. Towards the back of the store Alex found glass figurines. Cat loved to collect them, so he was naturally attracted to them. A glass sailor caught his eye and sucked him into a whirl wind of images.

For a brief moment he was aboard the *Ingersoll* as the fire flared from the refueling station. Then the picture shifted to the two Shore Patrolmen escorting the handcuffed Keller from the barracks. Then another scene of Rod Peach leaning into him and his words echoing, "You're never going to win that *Double Salute.*" The day dream continued, with John being carted off on a stretcher. Then the final scene of the dream, Cathreen standing in the door way staring at him and then turning to walk away.

The breathy voice of the sales lady brought him back, "That is a beautiful piece. It would make a lovely gift."

"Huh?" Alex said.

"Are you interested in purchasing that figurine?"

Alex looked down at the figurine and twisted it in his fingers to gain a different perspective. "Oh yes. It's a gift for my wife."

"That's lovely," she said. "It will give her a whole new perspective of you."

"What did you say?"

"Gifts like that give people a whole new perspective."

"Does she collect them?"

"Oh yes, she loves them."

The lady slowly moved toward the counter and took the figurine from him and wrapped it up for him in gift paper. While waiting to pay, he noticed cigarettes behind the counter. The thought hit him like a freight train. *Keller doesn't smoke. How could someone say they saw him smoking pot if he doesn't smoke?*

"That will be 48 dollars."

Alex handed her a fifty dollar bill, picked up the figurine and didn't wait for the change.

"Sir. You forgot your change," the saleslady called after him.

The emerald colored rolling fields of Kansas were fully thawed and the rich honey-rose like peonies mixed with the strong heady scent of lilac filled the air. The mid spring day was exploding in color and beauty.

The warmth of the rising sun bathed the musty old upstairs bedroom of the Sievers farm house in the brilliant sunshine. The dazzling light coaxed Cathreen from her slumber.

A gentle knock on the door and a muffled voice, "Cathreen," brought her to full consciousness. "Dear are you awake?"

"Yes Mrs. Sievers," Cathreen responded in a sleepy voice.

"Breakfast in thirty minutes."

"Thank you. I'll be down right away."

"There's towels on the rocking chair if you would like to shower," Maureen Sievers said. Cat listened to the sound of her shoes shuffling over the hard wood floors until they faded back into the silence.

Cathreen threw back the covers and shivered as the morning cool air greeted her. She crossed her arms and shoved her feet in to a pair of slippers to insulate her feet from the cold hard wood floor. She had been given the guest room with a bathroom attached. She grabbed a towel and ambled off to get herself ready. She looked long at herself in the mirror, "Ahhh," she said to the image. "Could you please not scare me in the morning like that?"

I wonder what Alex is doing? She thought to herself. *Why am I thinking about him? I need to think about myself and this baby.* She looked around the cozy bathroom with all the frills and knick knacks. *I love this place.* She started the shower and drank in the warmth of the humidity. A warmth filled her inside and the thought came from deep down inside, *Don't worry I'm in control, be at peace.*

Cathreen bounded down the creaky wooden steps and made a u-turn down the hallway and entered the epicenter of the Sievers home, the kitchen. "Good morning Cat," Maureen said, hugged her and pecked her cheek with her lips.

"Good morning Mrs. Sievers."

"Why do you still call me that?"

"I don't know. I feel like you're Alex's mom and I don't want to be disrespectful. Actually I've never really known what to call you. We've hardly spent any time together because we hardly ever see you."

"Then call me mom will you. I like that much better. Everybody calls me that."

"Alright mom," Cat said with a shy smile.

"What are you going have to eat? Anything you want?"

"Really?"

"Really."

"I like blueberry pancakes," in a raspy voice. She cleared her throat to chase away the thickness of her vocal chords from the nights rest.

"Blueberry pancakes coming up."

Maureen turned and opened the big refrigerator and extracted the necessary ingredients for the pancakes when the phone *jangled*. "It never stops around here." She wiped her hands on her apron and a bead of sweat from her forehead. The phone *jangled* again, "I'm coming," she said. She snatched it from the cradle and in a lovely voice said, "Hello," paused for a moment and smiled. "Alexis, how are you? Long time no talk." She paused for another moment as she listened. "That's good. He's good. Yes they are all very good."

Cat studied Maureen's face in consternation at the sound of her enemy's name. *I hope she doesn't know I'm here.*

"Cathreen? Yes she's here. Would you like to speak to her?"

Waving her hands to Maureen to communicate she was not interested in talking to her. Maureen only smiled and nodded her head. "Yes dear. I'll put her on."

Cat rolled her eyes and looked at the ceiling.

"Yes. I would love to see you too. You're welcome any time. Bye-bye," Maureen said and then looked to Cat handing her the phone with a warm smile.

She took it against her will and looked at her mother in law returning to her task of preparing blueberry pancakes. Mustering her formality she put the telephone to her ear. "Hi Alexis."

The warmer days allowed for windows to be opened to air out the barracks during the Saturday field day cleaning. The spring breezes are welcomed to chase away the stale winter odors after being sealed up for six months. The recruits of 197 had finished their cleaning and were seating themselves for some tips and preparation for the final inspections they would undergo as they prepared for their last week of training.

Hatch Harris sat on the table in front of the room cradling an M1 Carbide rifle. As the men settled he slowly scanned each face. "Alright guys. I'm Petty Officer Harris; y'all know me as the company commander for 192. Your CC had some personnel business to attend to, so I'm filling in for him. He asked me to work on drilling and I . . ." He paused as a thought hit him. "Rpock."

The Rpock stood and Hatch tossed him the M1. "Stow this for me please. I got something else I want to do."

"Yes sir," Rpock replied and walked to the back of the room and stowed the rifle. He waited for the Rpock to return and then continued. "You guys have been together for a while now and have gotten to know each other pretty good. Am I right?"

The recruits looked at each other and mumbled, "Yes sir."

"Who knows Keller?"

"I do," Thompson said raising his hand in the air and stood up.

Hatch motioned to him to come up front. "Come up here, please." As Thompson made his way forward Hatch asked him, "So you know Keller pretty good?"

"Yes sir," Thompson replied. "We've been buddies ever since the swim test. We both went to the remedial swim school and we took the SEAL qualifying swim together. I taught him how to fold his clothes and tutored him with the class room stuff."

"In all your conversations, did he ever say anything about liking to smoke pot?"

"Once he told me how some kids got caught smoking weed at his high school and how they got in so much trouble. He doesn't smoke or drink. Him being from the south I thought he'd do a little chew, doesn't even dip. He's a work out fiend and talked a lot about taking care of his body."

"I understand he's from Georgia."

"Yes sir, He's from Cleveland."

"Sir," a voice spoke from the sea of faces.

Hatch scanned the group for the source of the voice. A scanty Seaman Recruit Shuster held up his hand when Harris looked his way. "Yes."

"I don't know if it is of any importance. The other day I forgot my cover and came back in to the barracks while Petty Officer McCarthy and the rest of the company waited for me outside." He paused for a second.

"So?"

"When I came in to the barracks there was another recruit in here that wasn't from our company."

"Did you report it?"

"I was so flustered about forgetting my cover that I didn't think anything of it until just now."

"If you saw him again, could you identify him?"

"Yes sir I can."

Hatch stood up abruptly and almost knocked the desk over. He put both his hands out and excitedly dashed into the company commander's office and slammed the door. He picked up the phone and dialed as fast as he could. The phone clicked and his wife Theresa came on the line. "Hello."

"Theresa. It's me. Hey, is Alex there?"

"No. He went out early and I haven't seen him all day."

"If he comes in, tell him to call me immediately."

"Ok honey," Theresa said and hung up the phone.

Just as he hung up the phone, he heard Alex's voice. "Hey guys, how y'all doing?" He smiled as he scooted behind the racks toward the office. Then he changed his tone, "What are you guys sitting around for we got a *Double Salute* to win."

"Yes sir," they shouted and cheered.

The door knob disappeared as Alex reached for it and Hatch popped out of the office with a big tooth grin. "You're not going to believe what I found out."

"Keller doesn't smoke."

The corners of Hatch's mouth relaxed. "How did you know that?"

"He told me. When I almost booted him out of the company, we talked about him being the anchor for the Captain's Cup competition and we talked about his work out regiment and how he takes care of himself. He went into every gory detail but I specifically remember him saying he didn't smoke and most of all he never touched drugs or alcohol."

"He's a boy scout."

"As a matter of fact he was one of those too. He's not a pot head. I don't buy it for a second."

Hatch backed into the office and Alex closed the door behind him. "That recruit Shuster, he saw an unauthorized person in the barracks the day before."

"Ahhhhh. The plot thickens my dear Mr. Harris. Can he identify him?"

"Yeah, he can."

"That's all I need, lets get the commander on the horn and get this all straightened out." Alex stepped around the desk and dialed Commander Hendrick's office.

The commander picked up on the second ring. "Commander Hendrick."

"Sir this Petty Officer Sievers, do you have a few minutes? Petty Officer Harris and I have some most urgent business we need to discuss with you."

"I was just heading out, but if it is urgent than I think I can see you."

"Thank you sir, we'll be there in a minute."

Alex clapped his hand and rocketed out of his seat. "Alright. We got him on the hook, lets do it." Hatch yanked the door open and marched out of the office with Alex in tow. He paused for a moment before he turned to leave the barracks. "Rpock. The men can Coke and smoke until we return." He did not wait for a reply and shot through the door Hatch was holding open.

After rapping on the Division Commanders door he waited a brief moment to the response, "Come." He opened the door and allowed

Hatch to enter first.

"Thank you," Hatch said smiling at Alex.

"Ah Sievers, Harris. You two gents look like the cat that ate the canary. What can I do for you?" Commander Hendrick said, sitting behind the large desk dressed in a teal green golf shirt.

"Sir. New evidence has come to our attention about Seaman Recruit Keller."

"He is scheduled to go to Captain's Mast on Monday. There's not much I can do . . ."

"Once you hear the evidence that we've uncovered you may be able to help us."

"Petty Officer Sievers, your recruit was found in possession of a bag of marijuana, there is not much that can be done regarding this. His urinalysis came back negative, no trace of marijuana in his system. However that doesn't excuse him from having that bag in his locker. What can you offer that requires my assistance?"

"He doesn't smoke and his buddy in the company says he never discussed anything with him about pot."

"I still haven't heard anything that can help your man."

"Yes sir I know, Petty Officer Harris was talking to the men today and well. . . You tell him Hatch."

"The day before Seaman Recruit Keller was arrested, Seaman Recruit Shuster saw an unauthorized recruit in the barracks. It's possible this recruit was from Company 195."

The room fell silent. When the commander leaned back in his chair it complained with a loud groan and then fell silent. "That was the same day I talked to McCarthy and there was a recruit who had forgotten his cover. If I authorized him to walk through the 195 barracks could he identify this recruit?"

"Yes sir," Hatch said emphatically.

"We think Peach set up Keller to keep him from winning the Iron Man competition."

"Pretty strong words, can you back it up?"

"Sir, do you remember the fight between our two companies?"

"How could I forget? The captain dressed us down for that. What's that got to do with anything?"

"The captain brought up the *Double Salute*. We were both in contention for it at the time. Right after the meeting he asked Peach to stay behind."

"I do remember that and I thought it a bit odd."

"I also find it amazing that we've been winning competitions pretty good and 195 continues to run either a close second or leads. This doesn't make much sense. Unless Peach has got some latitude and is being helped. I'm convinced Keller was set up."

"As the Division Commander I can cancel the mast request for Keller. This does change things. I'm going to do some investigating. I need you to send that recruit over to my office immediately I want to talk to him. Don't worry we're going to get to the bottom of this thing."

"I'll send him over right now. Thank you sir."

The aluminum doors of the Drill Hall were open and the sun blazed in to the dank physical fitness facility. Anticipation electrified the air with excitement as the ten companies waited for the commencement of the final competition of the Captain's Cup. One representative from each company prepared to compete in the Iron Man. A race of endurance consisting of a modification of the five events the entire company participated in. Chief Paige whispered some final detail to one of his aids and started up the steps to the platform. At the front of the platform he tapped the microphone. *Thud, thud.*

"Gentlemen, welcome to the final day of competition. In just a few moments we will be starting the Iron Man," Paige said with a rasp in his voice. He stepped away from the microphone and cleared his throat. "The participants in this event will be tested in endurance and stamina. They will begin by swimming the length of the pool in the Aquatic Center in *Camp Porter*, then jump up into a dinghy at the other end of the pool then row it back to the other side. Then dress and run to the next station."

Chief Paige covered the microphone, coughed and cleared his throat again.

"They will run to the fire fighting school where they will don an Oxygen Breathing Apparatus, grab a fire extinguisher and run a hundred yards and extinguish a torch. Remove their OBA's, roll up a fifty foot, inch and half fire hose then stow it. Then run back over here to *Camp Moffett* where they will pick up a cannon ball at the shot garland and run with it to the cannon and deposit into the cannon, then get another one and run it in to the Drill Hall. They will climb up the rope ladder, ring the bell and hand over hand back down the rope. Then proceed to the knot tying station and tie the five knots with water being sprayed in their faces. Then run two laps to the finish line. This is a timed event. Whoever finishes with the best time wins the Iron Man. We've placed cameras at each station so that you can watch the progress."

To heighten the tension Chief Paige kept 195 and 197 for last. He stepped to the microphone, "While the final two contestants make ready let me introduce you to them. Representing Company 195 from New York City, Seaman Recruit Greg Lisak."

Company 195 responded with a deafening cheer for their shipmate as he moved to the edge of the platform of the swimming pool. One of the instructors walked across the platform and tapped Paige on the shoulder and handed him a slip of paper.

"Alright guys settle down," Paige said as the cheering faded. "There has been a change for 197. Representing Company 197, from Cleveland Georgia. Seaman Recruit Cade Keller."

A surprised roar shot from the dejected company. Peach's jaw hit the deck, spinning around he stood in stunned disbelief and gazed at the monitor as Keller stepped to the edge of the platform. He approached the stage unloading a string of profanities. "He is not eligible, he is under arrest," he shot at Chief Paige who leaned to hear his protest over the din of shouting recruits.

"That's not my problem Peach. You'll need to talk to his company commander."

Bewildered, Peach whirled around to a smiling Alex Sievers. Alex made the shame-on-you sign by rubbing his right index finger on his left index finger. Peach's eyes narrowed; balling his fists he forced himself back to the bleachers.

"Alright guys," Chief Paige said to take back control. "Let's get this thing started. Iron Man contestants, can you hear me?"

On the screen, the two recruits nodded to the camera.

"Then get ready," Paige said. The two recruits crouched in anticipation. "Get set. Go."

On go the two recruits leapt in to space over the pool and fell into the crystal clear water below, plunging to the bottom. Simultaneously, powerful legs pushed off the bottom and rocketed to the surface. Breaking the surface arms flailed in to orderly strokes propelling their bodies to the boats at the opposite end of the pool. Neither swimmer able to put any distance on the other and both hit the boats at the same time.

Grasping the gunwales of the boat they pulled their weight out of the water and flung it into the boat. The two oars smacked the water with fury propelling the boats along the churning surface. Keller began to open a slight gap as he slapped the water with ferocity. Once at the edge, the two boats were vacated in a frenzy as the two sailors ran across the nonskid surface to the bleachers where their uniforms waited.

The two wrestled uniforms over wet skin. They pulled a snow white T-shirt over their heads and gave it a quick pull. Then each of the two fumbled with the buttons on the blue chambray shirt. Each yanked on their dungarees, then a zip of the zipper and the *ting* of the belt buckle. Keller took a pause to check his gig line to insure it was straight as Lisak sat to pull on his socks. Keller quickly drew even with him and the two stomped their boon docker boots on.

The Iron Man combatants exploded out of the aquatic center and ran a blistering pace to the Damage Control Training building. Keller opened up a lead and reached the Firefighting School first huffing and puffing. Entering the building with the intensity of competition on him, he about tore the door from the hinges. The instructor pointed to the waiting Oxygen Breathing Apparatus and Keller ripped the OBA from the rack. He inserted his head in between the body harness and the breastplate, tightened the straps and pulled the face piece over his head. The instructor handed him the CO_2 fire extinguisher and pointed him to the other instructor with the lighted torch at the opposite end of the room. He pulled the pin on the extinguisher and lifted the horn as he ran. He squeezed the handle on the extinguisher emitted a cloud of CO_2 and doused the fire. The instructor yelled, "Fire's out."

Keller ripped the mask off of his face, loosened the restraint holding the OBA and ran it back to the rack. He immediately turned his attention to the inch and half hose laid out on the deck and furiously rolled it. He squatted to gather it up on his shoulder and raced it across the room to the stowage locker. The instructor gave him the thumbs-up; he rocketed from the room and slammed the breaker bar of the doors to the outside. About thirty paces from the door, he heard his pursuer smash the door open.

The two recruits flashed by the administration building and headed for the tunnel. Keller disappeared into the ink blackness first with Lisak trying to reel him. The coolness of the tunnel blew across Keller's face, but he was unsure if the beating he heard was his pulse pounding in his ears or his rival making up ground. He shot out of the blackness of the tunnel in to the brilliant sunlight like a bullet from a gun. Rounding the corner, Keller sprinted to the shot garland and grabbed the closest cannon ball and hoisted it upon his right shoulder. Slowed by the off balance weight he lumbered toward the cannon at the opposite end of the course.

Not looking back at his competition he gauged his distance from him by the sound of the cannon ball being extracted from the shot garland. Lisak had made up some ground on him, but that could be because of the slowed pace of the weight of the cannonball. Keller focused his sight and will on the approaching cannon. Five feet from the cannon, he lowered the iron ball from his shoulder and slam dunked it in to the mouth of the cannon.

Keller whirled around and sprinted toward the shot garland to coral another cannonball. Then he lumbered toward the drill hall with the cannonball. He exploded through the main door as recruits shouted cheers. His muscles rippled and screamed at him as he ran the few yards to the rope ladder where he dropped the cannonball. Ignoring the pain he leapt on to the ladder. A surge of strength coursed through his body, being urged on by the cheers of the recruits. As he reached the apogee of the ladder and rang the bell he looked down to see Lisak starting the arduous climb. The two passed about half way down as Keller hand over handed to the floor down the rope.

The fan and water were spraying the ship simulator as he climbed into its cockpit. He began the knot tying and calmed his mind as he whipped off the square knot, then the bowline and the sheet bend. He wiped the water out of his face with his shoulder and tried to remember the timber hitch. Once he'd finished the carrick bend he hit the afterburners.

"Two more laps," Alex shouted at him as he came out of the simulator dripping. "You can do it."

Sucking air like a vacuum cleaner, he summoned all the energy he could muster. He ran on to the track to make the final two circuits to victory. His lungs pleaded for oxygen as he huffed and puffed his way around the track. He glanced over his shoulder to see about a straightaway separated him and Lisak. He gritted his teeth as the lactic acid built up in his left leg causing it to cramp. He forced himself forward and grimaced with each step.

Keller grabbed his leg to help alleviate the pain of the stiffening muscles. A half a straightaway to go he resolved himself and vanquished the pain from his mind.

"Lisak, he's hurt. Go. Go." Peach yelled as his guy passed him. He surged forward with a renewed vigor.

Keller picked up his pace as best he could. With the finish line in view approaching footsteps beat in his ear. Alex stood in his lane, cheering and pumping his fists as he approached. Lisak just entered into his periphery as he surged toward the line. Keller's muscles strained and spasmed as he collapsed in to Alex's arms.

"You won, you won," Alex screamed in his ears as the rest of Company 197 mobbed him.

The company chanted, "197, 197, 197."

Peach snapped his body around, threw his hands in the air and kicked a nearby garbage can. The rest of 195 in stunned disbelief watched the celebrating Company 197. Captain Callaghan who'd been sitting on the platform stood, turned toward Peach, shook his head and left the building.

A steady breeze caressed Alex's wearied face as he peered from the window of his office to the court yard below. He squeezed his eyes shut, inhaled the fresh air and struggled to settle the growing anxiety in his gut. The day he had dreaded since the beginning of the training cycle had fully risen upon him. "God I'm new at this praying stuff and I'm not sure I'm doing this quite right, but could you help me out here?"

The edge he'd been feeling eased, softening his furrowed brow and relaxing his reeling heart. He smiled, slowly opened his eyes and allowed the warmth of the sun to chase away any feelings of negativity. A confidence filled his soul, unlike any he'd ever felt before. "I'm ready."

He picked up his combination cap and stared at it for just a moment. The emblazoned symbol of the USN on the hat reminded him of his duty to country, family and now God. He turned to the mirror on the wall and slowly placed the cap on his head. After adjusting it, he stared at himself in the mirror for a moment. "You look different Sievers."

Grabbing the door knob he yanked the door open with vigor and expectancy. "Rpock," he bellowed in a deep baritone voice. "Fall them out. Let's go do this thing."

The Rpock snapped to his feet and saluted and responded with a spirited, "Yes sir." He spun on his heel and belted out the command. "Company 197. Fall out on the double."

Company 197 hustled out the door and emptied the barracks in very short order leaving Alex to stare at the bunks that stood like silent sentries over the barracks. He stiffened his back, steeled his will and marched to the door to take his place in front of his company.

CHAPTER 18: MASS CONFLAGRATION

There is one quality which one must possess to win, and that is definiteness of purpose, the knowledge of what one wants and a burning desire to possess it. – Napoleon Hill.

A specter opened a tan door marked, FIREFIGHTING SIMULATOR EQUIPMENT ROOM: RESTRICTED AREA. The shadow slipped into the labyrinth of overhead cable runs, equipment cabinets and the shrill of fans whirring to keep the compartment cool. The dark figure pulled the pins on the halon bottles, unlocked one of the cabinets, quickly flipped a switch, and with equal speed shut it. With the deed done, the silhouette made a quick egress and stealthily shut the door erasing any trace of ever being there.

Company 195 filed out of the firefighting simulator as 197 filed in. Peach approached Alex and said, "Good luck scarecrow."

Ignoring the barb, Alex proceeded to check in with the firefighting instructors. The recruits took their seats in the instruction area and made quiet conversation.

Alex returned with a clipboard full of details and procedures needing to be explained. "Ok guys, listen up. We've got a lot to go over in a very short time. First, our company has been chosen to be the first to do the Mass Conflagration drill and we get to do it in front of the Secretary of the Navy. So we've got to be on our toes. The Mass Conflagration drill is going to simulate a ship threatening fire. The company will be broken into two fire parties. The first party will begin the drill and the second party will finish. This is an exercise to see how well an enduring fire can be fought exhausting the first team and having to be relieved by a second team. Are there any questions?"

"Sir," a recruit in the back said. "If for some reason we are unable to extinguish the fire what happens?"

"Good question. They have a back up system that can extinguish the fire and keeping it from doing damage to the facility. Let's hope we don't get to that point. Is there any more questions?" Alex scanned the group for hands. "No. Ok. We already know our assignments. Everybody don your OBA's. Team 1 prepare for action. Team 2 you retire to the repair locker and wait for orders to engage."

The recruits from team 1 broke up into two hose teams: attacking and backup teams while the scene leader took his place. Another recruit donned the sound powered phones which were part of a closed circuit with the repair locker and the control room.

Within the control room instructors seated at their stations readied to launch the drill. One of the instructors yelled, "Attention on deck," as Captain Callaghan entered the room escorting the Secretary of the Navy. The lead instructor showed the captain and the secretary to two chairs prepared for them to observe the Mass Conflagration drill.

The intercom squawked from the control room, "Recruits, Mass Conflag drill will begin in three minutes make your final preparations."

"Ok guys lets get those masks on and light off your OBA's," Alex said as he pulled the mask over his sweaty brow. He pulled the handle on the front of the OBA and punctured the canister which initiated the process of changing the exhaled carbon dioxide into oxygen. He set the timer and inhaled the stale oxygen.

"Fire in the hole in one minute," the speaker squawked.

A gnawing in the pit of his stomach rose and his breath quickened. The longest 40 seconds of his life past waiting for the final order, "Twenty Seconds, fire in the hole." Alex shot a shaky thumbs-up to the control room. The lights dimmed and red light illuminated the compartment,

"Ten seconds." Bile rose in his throat as he anticipated the flash and back draft. Sweat poured into his mask, fogging the clear plastic lense. "Five." Alex rubbed his gloved hands together. "Four." Valves opened, making a low hissing sound. "Three." He cocked his head and clenched his teeth. "Two." The hose teams crouched and readied for the flash. "One." The mockup of a US Navy ship exploded into a massive firestorm. The fire rushed at him with a hateful fury thrusting him backward. The intensity of the explosion threw Alex against the back bulkhead, pain shot through him as he dropped to one knee. He furiously beat at his body, thinking he was on fire.

Willie Nixon shouted, "That was too strong. Chief that shouldn't of happened."

The captain and the secretary rose to their feet.

The control room chief yelled, "Abort. Abort. Shut it down immediately."

Willie tried to shut the gas jets fueling the fire. "Chief, they won't shut down."

"Dump the Halon and put that fire out. Immediately."

He flipped the switches of the emergency extinguishers, they did not activate. "Chief the extinguishers are off line."

"What the devil is going on?" he said scanning the control station. "Nothing is working all the systems are failing."

After the initial burst of energy from the fire past, Alex recovered enough of his senses to realize he had not been on fire. His senses sharpened and quickly became aware this was not part of the drill by the frenzy of activity in the control room. Thick smoke flooded the compartment obscuring his view of the control room. He pressed his mask against the glass to ascertain what might be happening.

Alex flashed a quick glance to see how the recruits were holding up. Like seasoned professional the recruits of 197 had recovered from the initial flash and attacked the raging inferno. The brave recruits stood unyielding against the merciless flames. Confident his guys had things under control he again peered through the control room glass to see what was happening.

"Chief since we can't turn the valves off remotely, we're going to have to do it manually."

"How are we going to do that with the fire burning in there?"

"The valves are located on the underside of the ship."

They couldn't look at the captain who was boring holes into him. He turned to look inside the simulator and saw Alex at the window. "Petty Officer Sievers can get to them."

"I think you're right." Willie got Alex's attention and pulled his finger across his throat to signify cut and pointed to the far end of the room to an access hatch at the forward most part of the burning ship. "Cut off the gas there," Willie mouthed to Alex on the other side of the glass.

"Chief," the other technician shouted. "The temperature is rising. This fire is going critical. If it gets too hot those gas mains could blow."

"That means the entire facility could go up then," the Chief said. He turned to the captain and the secretary. "Sir. Mr. Secretary this thing is getting out of control. I suggest you leave."

"Yes I believe you're right," Captain Callaghan said.

"We will most certainly not," said the Secretary. "I will not leave while those men are risking their lives."

"Sir," the Captain insisted. "We need to leave."

"No!" the Secretary said emphatically.

Willie motioned to Alex furiously to move quickly.

Alex acknowledged Willie with a head bob and pointed to the forward part of the ship. He grabbed the sound powered phone operator and yelled over the roaring of the fire. "Call Team 2 and tell them to get in here and bring extra hoses. This is not a drill."

Team 2 entered the room and tied their hoses into the fire main. "I need the attack hose to cool that area there." Alex pointed at the team leader to where the access hatch was. The attack hose nozzelmen shoved the handle of the nozzle forward and moved toward the target area. "I need the backup hose team to keep water on me so I can get into that hatch with out getting burnt."

"Aye sir," the recruits shouted at them through their OBA masks.

Alex ran up behind the attack hose, while the back up hose doused them with water. Temperatures were almost unbearable near the hull of the ship. After a minute of concentrated spraying by the attack team Alex moved toward the hull. He tried to touch the access door but was still too hot. He backed up and pointed at the door and the hose team hit with another blast of water. The scene leader had secured some asbestos gloves from the repair locker and handed them to Alex. This time he wrestled the door open and was greeted with a *woosh* and a flash of fire knocking him backward. He lunged foward when the force of the supporting fire hoses hit him in the back.

Once inside he waved at the hose team to continue to cool him with the water. The ferocious heat threatened to suffocate him as he searched for the valves in the pitch black darkness. Unable to feel for them he came back to the door and shouted to the team leader, "Get me a battle lantern."

The team leader went to the closest bulkhead and felt around in the smoke obscured compartment for a battle lantern. His gloved hand found the yellow box shaped light hanging on the wall. He switched it on and the lantern light reflected off the smoke. He found his way back to the hatch of the ship and handed it to Alex.

He quickly found the eight valves controlling the gas which ignited the fires. One by one Alex shut them down. His head swam as the asphyxia from lack of oxygen. His eyes clouded, a heavy curtain of blackness filled his head and then nothing.

With the restoration of consciousness, awareness of his surrounding became more acute. He could see light through his eyelids as he forced them open. His blurred vision sharpened. Faces, concerned faces were before him. Captain Callaghan, a familiar face of a civilian and Willy, the firefighting instructor. He weakly pushed away the oxygen mask from off his mouth.

"Petty Officer Sievers, are you ok?" Captain Callaghan asked.

"I think so. What happened?"

"The OBA canister discharged. You ran out of oxygen and you passed out."

"The fire?" he said becoming fully aware.

"You got the gas valves turned off which extinguished the fire."

Trying to sit up he grabbed his head. "Oh gosh my head feels like it's going to explode." He looked around to see he was outside on the ground in front of the firefighting school.

The Secretary of the Navy stepped forward, "You did an incredibly brave thing in there son. We need more men like you in this Navy. Good job."

"Thank you sir."

Alex stood in the back of the barracks talking to Keller and Thompson. "Good job today. You guys have done everything I expected of you and more. You guys will make great Navy Seals. Congratulations."

"Attention on deck," yelled the Rpock.

Lieutenant Commander Hendrick entered the barracks and addressed the Rpock, "Where's Petty Officer Sievers?"

"I'm right here, sir," Alex said from the back of the room.

"May I speak to you in your office," Commander Hendrick said.

"Yes sir," Alex said and allowed the commander to go first. "As you were gentlemen." The recruits relaxed and resumed what they had been doing.

The commander took a seat behind the desk and Alex sat in front him. Commander Hendrick laid a manila file folder on the desk and opened it. "These are the final results regarding the *Double Salute*."

Alex shifted in his chair and swallowed hard.

"You and Peach tied."

"Tied?" Alex said surprised. He jumped out of his chair. "How is that possible? We won the Captain's Cup and the 500 extra points."

"The final report from the MTD states you and Peach are in a dead heat. This will be decided when the companies pass in review who will get the *Double Salute*, by the captain."

"No disrespect sir, but our captain is not playing by the rules and I think this whole thing is unsat. The deck has been stacked against me from the beginning. I've not complained through any of this sir. I've been a good sailor doing my duty, but this is just not right."

"Look Petty Officer Sievers I know what you've been through. You did a heckuva job whipping these guys into shape. You used ingenuity and outsmarted Peach every way you could. Things have a way of working out. Don't worry about it. Show up tomorrow for the graduation and just see how things go. You never know what might happen."

"Thank you sir. I appreciate your kind words."

LCDR Hendricks rose from the desk and so did Alex. "Oh there's one more thing. The old man changed the uniform of the day for the graduation. He moved up the change over of uniform. Whites are in, blues are out. Salt and peppers will be the uniform of the day for all company commanders. Formal notification will be sent, but I also wanted to let you know verbally too."

"I really hate those uniforms. Those white shirts are hard to keep clean."

The commander chuckled, "I know what you mean. Don't complain at least you get to where black trousers. We've got to where choker white with white shoes. People ask me all the time if I'm the ice cream man. See you tomorrow."

"Yes sir," Alex said and smiled as he opened the door for the commander.

"Attention on deck," The Rpock shouted.

When the door closed to the barracks Alex said, "As you were gents." He retreated to his office and plopped down in his chair.

Graduation Class Division 12 companies took their place in the designated areas. The mustering Petty Officer accounted for each company as they arrived. The Petty Officer checked off each company as the Rpock halted his company and barked their company number and, "All present and accounted for." He scanned his clip board, looked up and pursed his lips and scanned the formation. He shouted, "Where's 195?" and quick stepped to the empty space where 195 should be. "Where's 195? We go in ten minutes."

Alex stood in front of his company and did a quick visual inspection. "Guys. One final thing. This is a long ceremony, don't lock your knees so you don't pass out. Do you remember what I always said?"

The company repeated it verbatim, "If you pass out, you'd better bounce twice or nobody's coming to pick you up."

The company chuckled. "I'm proud of you guys and believe you'll win the *Double Salute*."

Instead of taking their places like the other companies did Company 195 marched in front of the rest of the graduation class. "Column right. March," The company marched into the gap between 194 and 196 then past the other recruits while the Rpock stood in front. "Column right," the Rpock barked. When the entire company cleared the Rpock barked, "Column left," and then another left and then another left. As they approached him he barked, "Company halt."

The Rpock did an about face and barked at the mustering Petty Officer, "Company 195. All present and accounted for."

Ceremonies carry an aura of stuffiness and boredom. However they are markers to draw attention to the accomplishments of the participants. Naval ceremonies provide the cement of discipline, which is the foundation of tradition in which the pride and courage of the sea going warrior is built. The pinnacle of basic training is the graduation ceremony where relatives and friends come to witness the rite of passage from recruit to full fledged members of the United States Navy.

Under the command of fellow recruits, the graduates display their newly acquired abilities in military drill and bearing with traditional Navy pomp and circumstance before reviewing officials.

The gate guard snapped his right hand to his chest and pointed to the visitor's parking lot as each car paraded into the base for the graduation. A steady stream of people slowly proceeded past the navy blue and gold sign which read, RECRUIT TRAINING COMMAND Welcomes You To Recruit Graduation and Review. Semaphore signals flags flapped in the wind stating, "Review Commences at 1330 hours." The hall decorated with maritime regalia. State flags proudly displayed, ringed the perimeter walls just below the ceiling line. The people were directed to two sets of bleachers which flanked the reviewing stand.

LCDR Chris Hendricks approached the podium of the reviewing area. "Ladies and gentlemen, good afternoon. I am Lieutenant Commander Christopher Hendrick, Recruit Training Command Drill Division Officer. I would like to welcome you to the Drill Hall 1600 graduation ceremony. Today you will see 10 companies comprised of 750 sailors who are participating in their graduation ceremony who will be joining the most powerful Navy in the history of our world. Here in the position of center deck will be a review captain and his staff. The review captain is responsible for conducting the graduation ceremony. I will now turn it back over to the announcer to bring the companies in."

The announcer came back to the microphone, "Ladies and gentlemen we would like to now present the recruits of Division 12 Graduation Class." The big door at the far end of the drill hall quickly opened and Company 191 marched in carrying M1 Carbides. The crowd erupted in cheers. Each company paraded past the bleachers and took their place in the back of the drill hall.

LCDR Hendrick came back to the microphone, "Ladies and gentlemen it is my pleasure to introduce the companies, their company commanders and their Recruit Chief Petty Officer. As I introduce the company they will raise their competitive flags they earned during their training. As I introduce the Recruit Chief Petty Officer the flag from their home state will be raised. Please hold your applause until all introductions have been completed."

Company commanders parade in and took their places in front of their companies.

"On behalf of the Commanding Officer and staff of *Recruit Training Command* we congratulate these company commanders and Recruit Chief Petty Officers on a job well done."

"Ladies and gentlemen in a moment you will see the ceremonial side boys, the boatswain and honor guard take their place for the arrival of the reviewing officers. This time honored tradition is our way of honoring the reviewing officer. When requested by the announcer please stand for arriving honors, the marching under colors, the national anthem and the invocation. Military veterans shall remain covered during the entire ceremony. Ladies and gentlemen, one final note, as befitting the importance of this occasion our ceremony is conducted in a formal manner. However, we do encourage you to participate today in this graduation ceremony by letting your applause show your feeling of just how proud of the men you are. Once again, Welcome Aboard!"

Company commanders leave their companies. The side boys entered carrying rifles with white bayonets, their white uniforms are augmented with black ascots, duty belt, leggings, white gloves and black ropes. A bell rang in two pairs announcing the arrival of the Commanding Officer. The announcer says, *"Recruit Training Command* arriving." The companies present arms. *Snick. Snack. Snick.* The flags are snapped parallel to the deck, while the Rpock's thrust out their cutlasses. After Captain Callaghan arrived the side boys commander shouted in the distance, "Order arms." The flags are snapped back into position and cutlasses are along the body of the Rpock's.

Three pairs of bells, *"Naval Training Center,* arriving." Admiral Perkins entered the hall and marched to the reviewing platform.

Today's reviewing party is from left to right, "Captain William T. Callaghan, Commanding Officer *Recruit Training Command,* Our guest of honor is the distinguished John F. Freemen, Secretary of the Navy, Admiral Hugh Perkins, Commanding Officer *Naval Training Center*

Great Lakes, Illinois, Rear Admiral Terrence Breaux, Commander *Naval Educational Center*.

A 13 shot volley is fired as a salute to the two-star admiral present as reviewing officer. During the salute Admiral Perkins left the reviewing platform and inspected the side boys.

"Our reviewing officer is Rear Admiral Hugh Perkins, United States Navy. A native of Connecticut, attended Stanford University, then was appointed to the *United States Naval Academy*. Admiral Perkins also attended *George Washington University*, the *United States Naval Post Graduate School* and the *Industrial College of the Armed Forces*. Admiral Perkins early duty included the Destroyer *Brown*, Guided Missile Destroyer *King* and the Destroyer *Edison*, On staff of Commander Cruiser Division 5, Cruiser Destroyer Group 1 and Chief of Naval Operations. He also served as Commanding Officer Guided Missile Destroyer *Buchanan* and the Commanding officer of the Guided Missile Cruiser *Jouett*. Upon selection to flag rank, Admiral Perkins returned to the staff of the Chief of Naval Operations and was also Commander of the Cinc Pac Fleet. Now serves as Commander *Naval Training Center*, Great Lakes."

The honor guard, consisted of three sailors carrying the flag of the United States, the Navy flag and the Vietnam POW/MIA flag. The three flag bearers are flanked by two other sailors carrying M1 Carbides. After the honor guard, all the guests and officers rose to the playing of the national anthem and the recitation of the invocation.

"Here at *Recruit Training Command* it is important to honor the past with tradition so that we can forge a path to the future. Today we are reinstating a tradition long forgotten, the *Double Salute*," LCDR Hendricks said and paused for the sporadic applause. "For the past eight weeks these 10 companies have trained by competing against each other. Performance was graded in athletics, classroom work, drill and military bearing. The company who accumulated the most points will be given the *Double Salute*. The competition ended in a dead heat between Company 195 and 197. Captain Callaghan will break the tie when the companies pass in review."

LCDR Hendrick stepped away from the microphone, bent over and pointed to a clipboard the announcer was holding. The announcer nodded to Hendrick. "At this time I would like to introduce you to a man who was a member of a *Double Salute* company over 40 years ago. Winner of the Bronze Star and Purple Heart for service during the Vietnam War. Former Chief of Naval Operations and now serving as the Secretary of the Navy, the honorable John F. Freeman."

The auditorium erupted in applause as LCDR Hendrick backed away from the microphone and applauded. The secretary shook Commander Hendrick's hand and approached the podium. He raised his hands to silence the crowd. "Thank you for that warm welcome ladies and gentlemen," Secretary Freemen said and cleared his throat. "Admiral Perkins, Admiral Breaux, Captain Callaghan I am honored to be here with you today and to be a part of the reinstatement of this time honored tradition. It seems like yesterday I wore a younger face and stood proudly in ranks before a reviewing stand much like this. As my heart raced in my chest then, so it does now as we wait to see who will receive the *Double Salute*."

The crowd applauded.

"I would like to say a few words to the recruits standing before me. Wear the uniform proudly and serve this great country honorably. The road you are embarking on today is sure to bring great rewards. It can bring you to exotic places and dizzying heights. Always remember you are Americans protecting your country. Serve and defend her faithfully. In doing so, you will take your place amongst the great men that have gone before you. Men who lived and died to preserve and defend the beacon of freedom that our enemies would love to snuff out. Let the light of liberty shine through you and let it banish the darkness through out this world. Thank you for your service, God bless you and God bless the United States."

The audience stood and responded with a thunderous applause. LCDR Hendrick walked to the podium clapping. "Thank you Mister Secretary. At this time the companies will do a short demonstration of military drill."

The Rpock for the State Flag Company snapped to attention and did an about face. "Atten-hut," he barked. Like one man the ten companies snapped to attention pulling their rifles alongside their right leg.

"Shoulder arms," the Rpock shouted. The companies raised their rifles to port arms across their bodies, paused, then placed their right hand on the butt of the rifle. After another short pause the sailors guided the rifle to the right shoulder. They paused one more time and swept the left hand back to their side.

"Present arms," the Rpock ordered. The companies snapped the rifles to port arms along the chest and paused then twisted the rifles so the magazine well is to the front and about four inches from the body, the left arm is parallel to the deck and the elbows are tucked in.

"Order arms," the Rpock said. The rifles snapped to port arms along the chest, followed by a pause. Each of the recruits right hand across the body snapped up to grab the barrel firmly, followed by another pause. The left hand is removed from hand guard, the rifle is snapped to one inch from the marching surface guided by the left hand on the flash suppressor. On the last count, the left hand is sharply returned to the left side as the rifle is gently lowered to the surface.

"Sixteen Count Manual, Hup!" the Rpock barked.

Each of the recruits right hand yanked the rifle across their body while the left hand came up and slapped it from underneath. The left hand grabbed the butt of the rifle, in conjunction with the right hand twisting the M1 and resting it on the right shoulder. The left hand is snapped back to the left side of the body. The rifle is then brought back to port arms along the body. The right slid up along the stock and the left hand under the butt at it is guided to the left shoulder. The right hand snapped back to the right side of the body and then brought back to the upper part of the stock brought back to port arms. The rifle is then twisted to present arms with the magazine well forward back to port arms, thrust to the deck to order arms. The left hand resumed its position along the body. The rifle is pushed forward, left leg stepped to the left with the right foot planted and left hand to the small of the back.

When the companies thrust their fire arms forward the audience erupted in sustained applause and cheering.

"The companies will now pass in review," LCDR Hendrick ordered.

The Rpock from each company made an about face. The muddle of voices ordering their companies to attention echoed off the walls. The companies snapped to attention, shouldered arms. The roll of snare drums echoed through the auditorium and the band belted out 'Anchors Away."

The first company marched to the cacophony of cheering and applause. When each company paraded past the reviewing stand the Rpock bellowed, "Eyes right." The entire company turned their heads towards the reviewing stand except for the column to the far right which kept their eyes forward. Admiral Perkins, Admiral Breaux and Captain Callaghan snapped a crisp salute to the company. Once clear of the reviewing stand the Rpock shouted, "Ready, Front."

Company 195's Rpock barked at the company, "Column left." The company turned to head toward the reviewing stand. "Eyes right," the Rpock yelled. The guide on snapped the flag parallel to the deck so their company number could be seen. The reviewing officers gave a crisp salute to the company and then dropped their salutes. Captain Callaghan started to raise his hand for another salute, but is stopped as Admiral Perkins placed his left hand over Captain Callaghan's right hand.

Peach's face watched in stunned disbelief when his company passed the reviewing stand and did not receive the second salute. Deflated with disappointment, he shook his head and peered at the deck for a moment. Company 195 approached where he stood and he could not compel himself to join them as they marched by. He turned just as Admiral Perkins dropped his salute and snapped another one to Company 197. Anger and hatred rose with such a violence he took one step toward Alex and ran into a brick wall of humanity wearing a white uniform and a shore patrol arm band.

"Petty Officer Peach?"

His knees weakened and he offered a weak, "Yes."

Company 196 passed by the reviewing stand and 197 came into view of the officers. "Eyes right," the Rpock bellowed. The officers gave the salute, lowered their arms and Admiral Perkins snapped another crisp salute marking 197 as the *Double Salute* company. After passing the reviewing stand Alex rejoined the company and marched to the exit of the drill hall. Once the company had cleared the bleachers, Alex eyed his tearful smiling Cathreen with Lexi's arm around her. John stood with Mary Lou and nodded his approval then snapped a crisp salute.

The company took their place next to Company 196. The Rpock shouted, "*Double Salute* company, halt." The company halted with a stomp. "Order arms." When the rifle butts hit the asphalt, the Rpock growled, "Parade rest." The rifles and the flags shot forward with one movement. The Rpock did an about face and stood at parade rest.

Crowds of people flooded out of the drill hall and fluttered around the companies, pointing and gawking at their loved ones. "Guys, I'm going to make this quick. You did great and deserve this I'm really happy for you. Enjoy your weekend and we'll see you Sunday night." Admiral Perkins and the Secretary of the Navy stood behind Alex. "The admiral and secretary would like to say a few words to you." Alex did an about face and saluted Admiral Perkins and Secretary Freeman.

"Congratulations Petty Officer Sievers," The Secretary of the Navy said, extending his hand and smiled.

Alex took his hand and said, "Thank you sir."

The secretary turned to Company 197. "Congratulations men. Don't forget this day and the honor that you've earned. Pursue the rest of your naval careers with the same enthusiasm and you won't be disappointed. I guarantee it."

Admiral Perkins piped up, "I know you have some loved one who want to see you so I won't be long. Congratulations on a job well done. With the *Double Salute* you have been given an extra day of liberty. Enjoy it and have fun." The admiral turned toward Alex. "Congratulations son. I am proud of you."

"Thank you sir. But what about Petty Officer Peach?"

"I know about everything. Commander Hendrick filled me in.

Captain Callaghan has been relieved of his command and Petty Officer Peach has been placed under arrest." The admiral pointed to the drill hall door as Peach was escorted by two Shore Patrol.

When Peach saw Alex staring at him he ripped free from the shore patrolmen and ran toward him screaming, "You should've been dead, not Mattingly." The shore patrolmen tackled him and the pile of humanity came to rest at Alex's feet. The two shore patrolmen wrestled Rod to his feet. His face bloodied by the take down twisted toward Alex. He hissed, "It should've been you." The two patrolmen yanked him away. He yelled over his shoulder, "It should've been you Scarecrow. It should've been you."

He watched and shook his head in bewilderment at the site of Peach handcuffed and being led away by the Shore Patrolmen. "What?"

The admiral placed his hand on Alex's shoulder and said, "Petty Officer Sievers, It'll all be explained to you. I've got to go. I'd like to talk to you some time next week."

Alex snapped a salute to the admiral, "Yes sir. Thank you sir for everything."

Admiral Perkins returned the salute, "Your welcome. Commander Hendrick will explain it all to you."

The state flag company snapped to attention and the Rpock saluted as Admiral Perkins retreated with the Secretary of the Navy.

"Petty Officer Sievers," LCDR Hendrick said. "After the posting please wait for me in the drill hall."

Alex snapped to attention and saluted, "Yes sir."

The Rpock shouted above the din of voices. "Company Rpocks front and center." The Rpocks marched to the front and received orders from the State Flag Company Rpock and then returned to the companies.

The crowd quieted and the Rpock shouted, "Division 12 guide-ons post." Each guide-on carrying the company flag took one step forward and handed their flags to the company commanders. "Company commanders left face." Each of the commanders snapped 90 degrees. "Company commanders post." The commanders marched inside of the drill hall with their company flag. After the last commander disappeared into the drill hall the shrill twitter of the boatswain pipe sounded and when it fell silent the Rpock barked, "Liberty Call!"

The recruits unloaded an earth shattering shout and broke ranks. The white uniformed sailors became speckled spots in the sea of colorful civilians.

"After we talked the other day," LCDR Hendrick began. "I interviewed Shuster and he was able to identify a member of Peach's company. He confessed and told me Peach ordered him to do it. I spoke to the XO who brought it to Admiral Perkins."

"I'm puzzled Commander, what did he mean it should've been me? And why was the captain here for the ceremony?"

"The admiral wanted to spare the captain the embarrassment in front of the secretary. As for Peach we'll get to that in a minute."

"Ok."

"Alex. Alex," a familiar voice yelled from behind him. He whirled around and Cat jumped into his arms. He twirled her around and kissed her.

"I'm really sorry about everything." Alex squeezed her tightly. "Lexi explained everything to me." Alex released her and looked over at Lexi who flashed him a big smile. Cat released him so that he could give her a hug. Lexi rocked him back and forth and squeezed her eyes tightly shut.

"Thanks Alex, for everything," she shouted into his ear. "I am so sorry."

Alex loosened his hug and looked her in the eyes. "Thanks for making things right. I really appreciate that." She hugged him tightly one more time and then let him go.

Cat slipped her arms around him and he squeezed her tight. "I didn't think you would be coming," Alex said.

"Are you kidding I wouldn't have missed it for the world. I wanted to surprise you and make you sweat a little. But I am so proud of you." She kissed him again.

"Whew, whoo. Shucka, shucka," John said as he clomped his big paw on his shoulder, pulling him away from his wife and bear hugging him with his good arm. "Congrats man. You did it. You really did it."

"No. We did it. This is just as much yours as it is mine."

"Petty Officer Sievers," LCDR Hendrick said. "There is someone else who would like to congratulate you."

With a look of awe and a crisp salute John and Alex greeted his former commanding officer. "Commander."

Captain Austin returned the salute. "Captain now. I received promotion to full Captain after leaving *Ingersoll*. I owe it to you."

Shaking his head in stunned amazement he answered, "Com . . . I mean Captain. How could I? I don't understand."

"You were unconscious when you were airlifted off the ship and didn't know what happened. If you hadn't gotten that cable undone like you did, we wouldn't have been able to break away when we did. There was inbound F1 Mirage's, Phalanx came on line and blew the two Exocet missiles they fired at us out of the sky. The details of the fire were not found out until much later and was not addressed by the board of inquiry. Cigar residue was found, but had been a mystery until now. We were unsure who caused it."

"Peach started the fire?"

"I'm afraid so."

"It wasn't your fault. The record will be changed to reflect this fact."

Cat's heart was bursting with pride and love for her hero.

Puzzled, Alex asked, "How come I was never told about any of this?"

"It's been classified to keep from starting a war. Some rogue officers in the Iraqi Air Force sent those planes out there to start something with us. Well we finished it before it got started. If those missiles had hit us, my career would've gone up in smoke. Who knows if I would even be alive today? You saved the life of a lot of people. Thanks Alex." The captain shook his hand and started to walk away.

Unable to contain himself, emotion welled up in him and tears streamed down his face.

"Oh. Alex there is one more thing I forgot to mention. Admiral Perkins asked me to come and present this to you today." He took a step closer and LCDR Hendrick handed the captain a black velvet bag. He removed a white combination cap with the fouled anchor officer emblem at the crest.

Cat gasped and slapped her hands to her face. Alex's jaw dropped.

"Congratulations Ensign Sievers, you've been accepted into the LDO program. You are now a commissioned officer."

Alex took the cap as if someone was handing him a Stradivarius violin. He turned it over in his hands admiring it.

"Put it on," John said.

Removing his enlisted cap he handed it to Cat to hold. He turned his back and took a deep breath. He slowly placed the cap on his head, and then turned to the admiring gazes of his superiors, friends and wife.

"Let me be the first to offer you your first salute," Captain Austin said as he stepped in to face Alex.

"No sir, you are a senior officer I can't accept that from you."

"Do me this honor."

"Yes sir."

Captain Austin snapped his hand to the corner of his right eye and Alex quickly returned the salute. "Congratulations."

Company 197 had quietly stood in the doorway observing the ceremony. The Rpock barked, "Present Arms." The company snapped their rifles and the Rpock rendered a hand salute to their company commander. Alex returned the salute.

The Rpock brought them back to order arms and all those present applauded.

Buddy had snuck into the crowd surrounding Alex and pulled his ear to his mouth. "You found your way."

Alex smiled and took his hand into both of his and pumped it furiously. "Thanks Buddy. You're the best."

Cathreen hugged Alex and whispered in his ear, "Your son is going to be just like his daddy."

Alex wiped his eyes and stared at the salty tear for a moment then fixed his gaze on his wife. "A son?"

She nodded and smiled.